BROTHER TO DEMONS, BROTHER TO GODS

JACK WILLIAMSON

W9-AXP-126

BERKLEY BOOKS, NEW YORK

Parts of this novel first appeared in *Analog Science Fiction/Science Fact* and in *Galilo/Magazine of Science and Fiction*.

This Berkley book contains the complete
text of the original hardcover edition.
It has been completely reset in a type face
designed for easy reading, and was printed
from new film.

BROTHER TO DEMONS, BROTHER TO GODS

A Berkley Book / published by arrangement with
The Bobbs-Merrill Company, Inc.

PRINTING HISTORY
Bobbs-Merrill edition published 1979
Berkley edition / February 1981

ISBN: 0-425-04529-3

A BERKLEY BOOK® TM 757,375
Berkley Books are published by Berkley Publishing Corporation.
200 Madison Avenue, New York, New York 10016.
PRINTED IN THE UNITED STATES OF AMERICA

CONTENTS

BROTHER TO DEMONS, BROTHER TO GODS

ONE: STEPSON TO CREATION

The multiverse creates itself.

It had no beginning; neither will it end.

Each new universe is wombed as a fire-egg, born through a contracting black hole. Expanding in space-time, ripening new black holes, it sows the eternal manifold with new fire-eggs of its own. Cooling, each new cosmos gives birth to galaxies and suns, to worlds of life and change, sometimes to intellect.

Flowing out of chaos, the multiverse is blind. Its law is chance. It has neither plan nor will. Its creatures are chance atoms, tossed together in the flux of mindless force. Such were the premen, who called themselves men.

Evolved by chance mutation on the hallowed planet Earth, the premen came by chance upon the art of genetic engineering and so became their own Creators, the mortal precursors who fathered the Four Creations.

The first act of creation formed the trumen, the perfected human race, purged of all ancestral evil and planned to supplant the premen.

The second act of creation produced the mumen, the variform men, shaped to fit their several functions in many universes.

The third act of creation gave being to the stargods themselves.

Still merely premen, blind to the splendor of true perfection, the Creators then neglected to rest from their triumphs, but went on instead to father yet another creation. The issue of their error was a race of demons, creatures of power without beauty, mind without truth, desire without justice. Evil revivals of the ancestral beast, they rebelled against their makers and the gods, seeking to usurp the whole multiverse.

The god Belthar perceived their emergent malevolence. Returning across space from his own domain, he reconquered the holy Earth, ended the folly of the Creators, and erased their monstrous last creation.

In benign solicitude, the supreme Belthar continues to rule the sacred planet, granting power to his variform defenders, wisdom to the trumen, sons to their most fortunate daughters, and mercy to the surviving premen. His sovereign will gives law to chaos, and his omniscience illuminates the multiverse.

His glory endures forever.

—The Book of Belthar

1.

Two naked waifs, paternity unknown. A black halfgod, proud son of Belthar himself. A lovely young goddess, touring the sacred sites of her ancestral Earth. A yelping dog and a frightened rat. A red-scaled mutant guardian, its third eye flashing thunderbolts.

Old chaos in collision with stellar divinity . . .

The god Belthar had leveled the crown of Pike's Peak for his North American temple. All black granite, it could hold half a million chanting worshippers. It was empty, however, on that chill spring morning when a small skimmer marked with the triple triangle of the Thearchy dropped to a parking terrace on the slope beneath it.

The halfgod Quelf left the skimmer with five attendant sacristans. His mother had been a dancer who satisfied Belthar. Inheriting her dark grace and his father's towering power, he was commonly arrogant, but his bold tread faltered as they reached the elevator.

"Leave your boots," he told the blue-robed trumen. "There's a live goddess here."

He had long ago learned the mixture of impudence and flattery

3

that pleased his godly father, but Zhondra Zhey was a casual transient from remote stellar dominions, a dangerous unknown.

"She's a starship pilot." He bent to set his own boots in the rack. "Visiting Earth while her ship's in orbit. The Lord has ordered us to serve her."

The sacristans straightened and stared, but shuffled after him into the elevator without comment. He had taught them silence.

They emerged between great black columns under the rim of the vault, which was a blue-black star-map, all aglow with shifting lines that showed the space-routes of the explored multiverse. Heads bent, they marched out across the polished floor, which mirrored all those far dominions. The central altar was a vast black disk that held the sacred apartments. Kneeling beneath it, holding up his offering, the halfgod intoned a formal invocation to the goddess.

Before he was done, she appeared at a high window, gestured as if to check him, and stepped out into the air. Wearing only her aura and the diamond star of her space-pilot's rating, she dropped to the granite bench before him and floated just above it, anchored to the stone with only one rosy toe.

"You—Your Divinity!"

Conflicting impulses shook his voice. Pink and slim beneath her softly iridescent nimbus, the goddess was still no more than a lovely child, not out of her second century, yet already overwhelmingly alluring. Fond of young girls, he was used to taking what he wanted. But no mortal virgin had ever come clothed in her perilous power.

"Favor, Great One!" Torn between lust and terror, he dropped his eyes to the casket of rare Terran gems he had brought. "Humbly, we implore your gracious acceptance of our insignificant gift." Sweaty hands quivering, he raised the casket. "Eagerly, we await your all-wise instructions—"

"Stand up, Quelf." Her Terran diction was pure, her tone gently chiding. "I want no gifts."

"Forgive us, Your Divin—"

The casket had slipped from his fingers. Her slender hand moved slightly. Flowing from it, her shimmering nimbus reached out to catch the casket, lifted it over his head and into the hands of a startled sacristan behind him.

4

"Save your offering for the premen," she said. "I think they need it more than I do. I've come to see their reservation. Please arrange it."

Clumsily, he stood up.

"We obey." His avid eyes were fixed on that tempting toe. "However, if Your Divinity deigns to tour the holy planet, there are better sights. The Asian Temple, which is Belthar's most sacred dwelling. His statue on the Andes—"

"I'm going to Redrock."

"Indulgence!"

Her mild tone had given him courage to look up, and her bright-washed beauty stabbed him with a hotter regret that he had not inherited all his father's privileges and powers. She waited, aloof, aware, a little amused.

"If Your Divinity cares about the aboriginal life, there's the European Zoo. The Terran creatures there include a fine preman habitat."

"I prefer to visit the people at Redrock."

"People?" His rising tones echoed unthinking scorn. "They're miserable animals. Wallowing in their own filth. So squalid that the Lord Belthar has ordered their removal—"

"That's why I'm here. The premen created us. I'm afraid that fact has been forgotten. I want to see them while there's time."

"Forgiveness!" he protested. "But those stinking beasts at Redrock are the last dregs of a dying race. The real Creators died for their final folly a thousand years ago. If Your Divinity is concerned with history, we humbly suggest the Museum of Terran Evolution in Antarctica. There's a Smithwick Memorial Hall, with authentic reconstructions of the genetic engineers in their laboratory—"

"Take me to the reservation."

"Your Divinity, we obey."

Redrock was a straggle of brown mud huts beside an irrigation ditch that was also a sewer. Four larger buildings enclosed the grassless plaza: the jail, the town hall, and the twin chapels of Thar and Bel, dedicated to the god of Earth in his major aspects of wisdom and love.

By Quelf's command, old wooden doors wore new blue paint.

Litter had been raked from the mud-rutted road, and a strip of gold carpet rolled along it from the chapel of Bel on the plaza to the agency mansion on its green-terraced hill above the odors and vermin of the town.

The premen had been warned, and the landing skimmer was greeted with an apprehensive hush. The sacred procession emerged on the plaza and marched up the carpet toward the agency. Two mutant soldiers stalked ahead, the dry sun burning on black crests and ruby scales. The halfgod followed, dark nose held high, as if offended by every reek around him. Four blue sacristans carried the canopied chair of honor, the divine tourist smiling out as if delighted with everything she saw.

A dog barked.

A child screamed.

A brown rat slithered out of an alley, darted across the carpet. A dirty mongrel darted after it, yelping with excitement. A small naked boy splashed across the green-scummed ditch, running after the dog. They veered toward the goddess.

Quelf hissed an order. One muman guardian spun to face the intrusion. Lightning stabbed from its black-lensed crest. The dog's body spun across the carpet and tumbled into a puddle.

"Make way!" the halfgod shouted. "Make way for Her Divinity!"

The boy looked five years old. Brown and thin, he wore only splashes and smears of drying mud. Planted at the center of the gold carpet, he stared up at the holy procession with dark, wet eyes.

"You—" A sob racked and choked him. "You killed Spot!"

"Davey!" a tiny girl shrieked from the alley behind him. "Come away, Davey. Don't let the deadeyes hurt you."

The boy stood fast.

"Off!" the halfgod snapped. "Off the road!"

"Killer!" The boy shook his grimy fist. "I'll make you sorry!"

"What?" Anger stiffened Quelf. "You insolent pup!"

He gestured at the scar-marked mumen. Both bent their lenses toward the boy. Violent pathmaker beams hissed around him. Yowling, the naked girl came splashing to him through the gutter.

"Hold everything!"

The goddess froze them with that gold-toned command. Levitating from the chair, she came sailing over the halfgod and the mumen and sank toward the carpet in front of the boy. Smiling, she paused to watch the girl, who was darting to pick up the dog.

"Who are you children?"

The boy studied her solemnly.

"I'm Davey," he said at last. "Davey Dunahoo."

"But I have no name." The girl came panting back to his side, lugging the limp body of the dog, which seemed heavier than she. "They call me—" In the reek of the charred brown fur, she sneezed twice. "They call me Buglet."

"Don't you have parents?"

"I never had a father." Davey stopped to consider her again. "My mother was a girl at La China's. A drunk man stabbed her." Gravely, he nodded at the girl. "Spot found Buglet lying in the weeds beyond the dump. She was sick. She can't remember who she is."

"Where do you live?"

"Nowhere." He shrugged. "Anywhere."

"In the street," the girl piped. "When it rains, El Yaqui lets us sleep in his barn. Sometimes he finds a bone for Spot."

"Mercy, Your Divinity." The halfgod came striding around the mumen. "The reception is waiting for us." He glowered at the muddy urchins. "I've warned you off the road."

"You can kill dogs." The boy stared back. "But you can't kill the Multiman—"

"Blasphemy!" the halfgod roared. "Belthar will put a stop to that—"

The goddess raised a shining hand.

"Multiman?" She turned to frown at Quelf. "Who is Multiman?"

"A wicked heresy. Forbidden by the Thearchy, but still current among these stupid premen." He grinned at the defiant children. "I believe their removal will put an end to it."

She floated back to the children.

"Please forgive us." She settled toward them, smiling. "I do want to help you. Won't you tell me what you need?"

The boy stared blankly, but the girl crept forward with the dog in her arms.

"If you're a goddess, please make Spot alive again."

7

"I can't do that." She gave Quelf a quick wry glance. "Not even Belthar could reanimate your pet."

"The Multiman could," the boy insisted. "If he had come."

He took the dog from Buglet's arms. Silently he turned, to wade back across the ditch to the mud-walled alley. Buglet splashed after him. The goddess glided back to her chair, and the procession marched on again through the sharp sewer reek.

A few sun-browned children in blue-and-white uniforms watched from the schoolyard. At one corner a withered woman sat on a leaner donkey, waiting impassively. At El Yaqui's trading post a dozen men looked up from the drinks and the games on their sidewalk tables, and a plump dark girl in a bright red wrapper leaned from a second-floor window to stare at the passing goddess.

At the end of the carpet strip, on the clean green lawn beneath the white marble steps of the agency, the preman leaders and the truman agent waited, robed in official white. Bowing to the chair, the agent humbly begged the favor of the goddess. The premen were eager to entertain their sacred guest in the agency garden.

Zhondra left her chair and levitated after him to inspect the display of preman arts and crafts. A dark silent youth stood sweating beside a plow, the garden wall behind him hung with sample plants of cotton, corn, beans and hemp. A one-legged smith bent over his anvil and forge, shaping hot metal, preparing to shoe a mule. Two shy girls in clean white gowns showed a relief map of the whole reservation, its red buttes and canyons modeled in clay. A row of silent matrons offered tacos and hamburgers and rice balls, with mescal and beer and tea.

The goddess tasted politely. When she asked to make the premen a gift, the agent called for El Yaqui. A lean grave man with brooding eyes and a far-off smile, he accepted the casket of gems with a silent bow that seemed indifferent.

"Your Divinity, these are the premen." Following the goddess back to her chair, Quelf spoke with covert satisfaction. "You'll find no Creators among them."

"Yet they look more unfortunate than harmful. I see no cause for their destruction."

"But they aren't to be destroyed," the halfgod protested. "They are simply to be resettled. On a virgin world in the Ninth Universe."

8

"Why?" Her violet eyes probed him. "Is Belthar afraid of heretics?"

"If my Lord Belthar dreads anything, I'm not aware of it. The problem is simply living space. The premen never accepted civilization. Out of place in our sacred culture, they're dwindling away. Only a generation ago the survivors from the other continents were gathered here. Now they're too few to make efficient use of the land they occupy."

"This wasteland? Who needs it?"

"The Lord Belthar has graciously approved an engineering project of my own." He beamed with self-approval. "A dam across the lower canyon. Desalting plants and tunnels to fill a wide new lake with Pacific water. The entire reservation will be flooded."

"Your own project?" She looked away at the tall red buttes and the vast bare flats, then keenly back at him.

"The actual plans were drawn by truman engineers, but I'll have a palace on the lake. And—"

"I see." Her cool voice cut him off. "What about this Multiman?"

"Pure myth." He chuckled. "Preman logic is the joke of the planet. Though the Lord Belthar has been their ruler for a thousand years, they still cling to irrational beliefs in their old imaginary gods. Buddha, Brahma, Allah—the list is endless. The Multiman heresy may well be a distorted folk recollection of the Fourth Creation." He chuckled again. "The Lord Belthar took care of that."

"Not if you ask Davey Dunahoo." With a thoughtful glance at the straggle of huts, she levitated into her chair. "Perhaps Belthar is wise to get the premen out of his universe."

2.

Zhondra Zhey went on to visit the Museum of Terran Evolution. She paid a formal call at Belthar's Asian Temple, but felt no regret when the god of Earth was not in residence. Her starship loaded with a precious cargo of gum from the seedpods of a mutant poppy that flourished on the Terran highlands, she took it on to dominions of the Thearchy in another universe, guiding it through contact planes that no mortal pilot could sense or penetrate.

She had left instructions, however, with the Redrock agent, San Six. He spoke to El Yaqui, who sent a preman magistrate to look for Davey Dunahoo and Buglet. They were found in the brush beyond the town dump, solemnly building a mud-mortared rock pyramid above the ashes of their dog. Silent and afraid, they were escorted to the agency.

"I don't bite." The genial agent came to meet them at the door of a huge room hung with bits of ancient preman art. "In fact, I've got good news for you." He made them sit in hard chairs too big for them. "First, however, I must ask you something." He leaned intently toward them across his bare, enormous desk. "Who has spoken to you about the Multiman?"

Though he was smiling cheerily, his brown eyes seemed very keen.

"Everybody." Davey squirmed on the hard chair and looked at Buglet. "But most people don't believe."

"Who does believe?"

"My mother did." Davey stared up at a tall case full of rusty preman weapons. The agent sat and watched him, till at last he went on: "She was born on the old Asian reservation. She was beautiful. A halfgod saw her and took her away to be a bride of Belthar. She was never chosen, but the halfgod took her for himself. When he didn't want her anymore, he sent her here. She worked for La China, and she used to say I had many fathers. She hated all the gods and the whole Thearchy. I guess that's why she wanted to believe in the Multiman."

"What exactly did she say about him?"

Davey looked at Buglet till she nodded.

"She said he was made in the Fourth Creation—but he's no demon. He escaped Belthar's attack. He lives in hiding. He's immortal, waiting for his time and gaining power while he waits. When he comes out, he'll be greater than all the gods. Master of the whole multiverse. My mother said he would bring justice to the premen."

The agent reached to touch a button, and Davey guessed that some machine had been remembering all he said.

"Thank you both." The agent smiled again, leaning back in his tall chair. "It's my duty to learn such things, but you needn't be afraid. The Lord Belthar is more tolerant of heresy than your old preman deities used to be. He knows that you premen are afflicted with imaginations too strong for your perceptions of reality. Anyhow, the church has been instructed to overlook the insane faith so many of you have in your old imaginary gods and demons. After all, I suppose you couldn't endure all the pains and dangers of your brief lives without your saviors and your saints, your werewolves and your warlocks." His gaze grew sharper. "Of course, if anybody did believe in this Multiman, we would have to act."

Davey moved uneasily in his chair, but Buglet shook her head. He shrugged and said nothing.

"Anyhow, there is good news for you." With a wider smile, the agent waved all talk of heresy away. "The goddess remembers you. She regrets what happened to your pet, and she likes what she calls your irreverent independence. She wants the two of you to become special wards of the agency. We're to see to your care and education."

"Thank—thank her!" Buglet gulped. "She's nice."

"She's kind." Davey sat very straight. "But we don't want anything."

"Why not?" The agent squinted at them unbelievingly. "You premen! I've been your keepers for a dozen years, and I still don't understand you."

Davey looked down and said nothing. The trumen were too much of everything—too quick and too keen and too strong, too modest and too happy and too generous. The agent seemed too content that his race had been designed to replace the old imperfect premen, yet too careful not to hurt them with any display of his own superiority.

"We—we thank you, sir!" Buglet stifled a sob. "The goddess is good, but she couldn't help Spot."

They squirmed off the chairs and started for the door.

"Don't go yet," the agent called. "My son wants to meet you."

San Seven was a stocky brown-eyed boy, their own age but inches taller. Warm with instant friendship, he led them off to the long gameroom and showed them his toys—strange bright machines and moving models of men and gods and aliens. He showed them his books, which were filled with living pictures and mysterious symbolism. He took them into a great clean kitchen and filled them with foods and drinks they had never imagined. When he asked them to stay at the agency so that they could really be his friends, Buglet accepted before Davey could say no.

Though they didn't like being apart, there was a whole huge room for each of them. One tall wall in Davey's room was a wonderful window that could open on starships in space or worlds in other universes. When San Seven was showing them the buttons that worked it, Davey asked to see the place where the premen were to go.

"Here's the planet where my uncle lives." Hastily, San Seven fingered the buttons to make a picture of jewel-colored towers clustered on smooth blue hills, with a triple sun hanging in the greenish sky. "My mother wants us to move there when the agency is closed."

"It's lovely!" Buglet said. "You are very lucky."

"Please," Davey insisted. "Show us our new home."

"Another time." San Seven began explaining again how to shift the pictures.

"Now," Davey said.

With an unhappy shrug San Seven punched the buttons to show them Andoranda V. It was all naked rock and mud-flat and sand dune, with rivers of red mud staining the storm-beaten seas. The sky was yellow dust, spilling blood-colored rain.

Buglet turned white beneath her grime, and Davey clenched his fists.

"A very remarkable planet." San Seven spoke fast without looking at them. "It's off in Universe Nine. It does have creatures enough in the sea—I've seen great dark monsters fighting, things as big as starships. But its native life never adapted to dry land. You premen will have the continents all to yourselves."

"No—no trees!" Buglet whispered. "No grass."

"Not yet. But we're working to establish Terran land life."

"I don't like it," Davey muttered. "We won't go there."

"You'll own the whole planet." San Seven tried to smile. "And we're trying to improve it for you. We've had a pilot station there for several centuries." The picture flickered to show a row of rusting metal huts beside a strip of rock blasted flat for landing shuttles. The huts were banked high with dirty snow, and nothing moved anywhere. "We're trying to terraform the planet, but the engineers have run into problems. Terran plants die. Seeds don't sprout. Even our engineers are sterile there; they're reporting some unknown lethal factor that kills all desire."

"So we'll die there."

"There won't be children—but of course the starships will bring supplies. The Lord Belthar will preserve you."

"We won't go."

"The Lord says you will." As if to soften that hard finality, San Seven added, "Though you'll probably be allowed to stay here till the lake begins to fill."

He tapped the buttons again, to show them Quelf's new dam, a dark ridge reaching from one bleak red mesa to another, construction machines still swarming over it.

"But we premen made you," Buglet was whispering. "We made the mumen and the gods. Now you want to take the last poor scrap of our own world and send us off to die—"

"I'm sorry." San Seven reached to touch her shoulder, but she shrank from his hand. "Our Lord is merciful," he insisted. "You can't blame him and you can't blame us. My father says the whole trouble is that you premen just can't compete, but too many of your ancestors were spoiled creations."

Davey stiffened angrily.

"It's only what my father says." San Seven moved cautiously back. "After all, the Creators were still premen. Though I know they did make us and the gods, they often bungled. Their greatest failure was the Fourth Creation—the demons that the Lord Belthar had to destroy. But my father says there were other misbegotten things that escaped from the lab to corrupt the blood of the premen. By now, my father says, you're all stepchildren of the Creators."

Buglet caught Davey's lifted arm.

"But of course you aren't to blame, any more than we are." He smiled at them gently. "Though it's simply stupid to expect some new god to save you. I know the Creators were premen, but

13

the Creation is over. The Lord Belthar won't let it happen again.''

He hurried them back to the gameroom to let them play with his toys. Instead, Davey sat down to look at a book. The live pictures delighted him, changing scenes as he moved his finger along the edge of the page, but the text baffled him with many-colored patterns that flashed on and off too fast for him to see their shapes.

Hopefully he asked, ''Can you teach me how to read?''

''Our symbology doesn't work like preman print.'' San Seven looked apologetic. ''It isn't linear, with one simple symbol after another. It's multiplex instead. Each display is a whole gestalt. I'm afraid it's too hard for you. Come on down to the basement. There's a free-fall gym you'll enjoy.''

Trying to forget that they were premen, they followed him down to the gym. They did enjoy the null-G belts, flying as easily as levitating gods, till San Seven called them to meet his mother. A calm, cheery woman, she made them wash themselves in a steamy, strange-smelling room and dressed them in her son's clothing. She said they must start to the preman school.

San Seven went with them on the first day to show them what to do, but his own training came from special machines in a room at the agency. When Davey asked to use these, he flushed and mumbled that they were too difficult for premen.

At the school their fellow students were all bored and sullen. Their lessons were about all the worlds of the Thearchy except Andoranda V, the only one they could ever expect to see. They laughed at him and Buglet when they spoke of the Multiman— and sometimes jeered at them for being the agent's pets.

Davey asked the preman teachers about the Creators and the Multiman, but all they knew came from the words in the *Book of Belthar*, which the school chaplain droned through his nose every morning before their studies began.

With pocket money now for tacos and rice when they were tired of the strange foods at the agency, or a cactus ice at the sidewalk café, they made more preman friends in town. The wisest, people said, was La China.

She was El Yaqui's wife, strange-odored, silent and black and nearly too fat to move. Shapeless in a faded blanket, she sat behind her ancient cash machine at the wide door of the trading post, taking money for meals and beer and mescal, for stuff off the shelves, for the girls upstairs. Her dark Asian eyes saw everything, but when Davey asked what she knew about the Multiman, her only answer was a sleepy smile.

"Maybe he's only a story," Buglet decided at last. "Maybe we'll have to let them send us off to that awful world where no life grows."

"My mother believed," Davey always insisted. "I won't give up."

One morning on their way to school they fould a strange skimmer on the plaza beside the chapel of Thar. Branded with a blue bear inside the triple triangle, it had brought six gray-robed monks of the Polarian order, who scattered over the reservation to ask for preman antiques and to look for preman ruins. Their dean came to the school.

"The gates are closed at Prince Quelf's dam." He was a short fat man who kept licking his lips as if his words had a good taste. "The lake will be rising fast. We want to gather all the preman artifacts we can before the water gets here. If you know of any old records or tools or weapons, or where any old buildings stood, please help us preserve them for history."

"I think they're looking for the Multiman," Buglet whispered to Davey. "Don't tell them anything."

Meeting that night in the adobe town hall, the senate voted to let the monks explore Creation Mesa, which legend said had been the actual birthplace of the trumen and the gods. Though El Yaqui had always been as silent as his wife about the Multiman, he called softly next morning as Davey was passing, *"Venga, muchacho!"*

El Yaqui was brown as the earth, bald as a pebble, and quick as a spider. Coming late to the reservation from far high mountains where the church had left them alone, his people had brought strange words and strange things. In the hungry times before the goddess came he had been generous to Davey and Buglet, with bowls of milk and bits of sun-dried goat meat, and he still liked to share his desert lore and his peyote buttons on fiesta days. Breathing fast, Davey followed him down the stairs behind the bar and back through the stale stinks of spilled beer and mescal to a serape hanging on the wall.

"I think you are now ready to become a man." Hard brown

fingers squeezed his arm, as if that had been the test. "You have asked about the Multiman. Really, I know nothing—there was no Multiman in the dry *sierra* from which my people came. Yet there are certain ancient artifacts I must show you before the monks take them."

Behind the faded serape was a tiny room carved out of raw earth. A preman book with torn and yellowed pages lay open on a cloth-covered box, and a tiny flame burned beneath the image of an agonized man nailed to a cross.

"The book tells of a preman god." El Yaqui knelt before it, his brown hand jumping like a spider. "The son of the god was killed. The book promises that he will return to aid his true believers. I once thought that perhaps it foretold the Multiman's awakening."

"Do you—" The musty little pit seemed suddenly very cold, and Davey found himself quivering and voiceless with awe. "Do you believe?"

El Yaqui stood up slowly.

"I believe in the stargods," he said. "I have seen them and felt their power."

"Then why—" Davey frowned at his hard, dark face, mysterious in the flicker of the candle. "Why do you keep these things?"

"Because they were my father's," El Yaqui said. "A powerful sorcerer and a very wise man. He knew the language of this book, and he used to read the story of the tortured god to me. He could take an owl's shape to watch the churchmen, and a coyote's shape to escape them. He expected the old god's forsaken son to return and rescue the premen. But he is dead. The waters will be rising over Redrock. The monks of Polaris have come to take the cross and the book for their museum of preman heresies."

Bending over, he blew out the candle.

Buglet was waiting at a sidewalk table under La China's sleepy smile when Davey came out of the bar. She looked at him, and her bright face clouded.

"Davey, I'm afraid." Her small voice quivered. "I'm afraid of Andoranda V."

"I think we must learn all we can," he told her as they walked on to school. "All about the trumen and all about those worlds

16

that are not for us. If there is no Multiman, I think we must plan to leave the reservation and hide among the trumen.''

She stopped to stare at him, eyes round and huge and dark.

"I know the penalty," he told her. "But no penalty could be quite so bad as Andoranda V."

They learned all they could at school, though term by term their teachers seemed more and more stupid and indifferent, their fellow students less and less concerned with anything except sex and drugs and vandalism. They heard that the tunnels were flowing, heard that water was already deep in the lower canyons, heard that their camp was ready on Andoranda V. They saw the new square mountain rising, far off in the south, which San Seven said was to be the foundation for Prince Quelf's palace. They listened to the fat gray Polarian dean, who sometimes dined at the agency and talked about the excavations on Creation Mesa.

Davey kept hoping the monks would uncover some hint that the Multiman was real, but the digging went slowly. There was only legend to tell where the old labs had stood, and the preman workers came only when they needed money for mescal and La China's girls. All they had found beneath the barren dunes and the desert brush was the story of Belthar's attack from space, written in buried craters and glassy flows of lava. Davey's last spark of hope was nearly dead, when Buglet had her dream of the Creation.

3.

Unfolding like some desert flower, Buglet had begun to call herself Jondarc after the heroine of a tragic preman legend she had heard from La China's girls. Taller that year than Davey, with straight black hair and yellow-gray eyes, she was suddenly alluring. Half the boys in school were in hot pursuit, and Davey was haunted with a secret dread that some churchman might see her and take her away for Belthar or himself.

Moody that morning, she set him with only a smile. They walked in silence down the hill from the agency and along the muddy road toward the school. She was deaf to the whistles of two preman boys setting the sidewalk tables for La China. Unaware of the black-starred skimmer that dived by them, gray-robed monk staring. Blind to the new arroyo that rain had cut in the trail ahead.

"Don't brood, Bug." He caught her arm to steer her past the ditch and trembled from the contact. "The lake's still miles away. We may have months yet to find something, though I don't know what—"

"Maybe I do."

He heard the hope in her voice and then saw that she was not despondent, but full of some confused elation. They had come to the plaza, which was stacked with big yellow plastic shipping containers for the effects of the premen, waiting to be packed for the long star-flight to Andoranda V. She led him back among them, off the trail.

"Last night I had—I guess it was a dream."

Her eyes were lemon-colored in the reflected light from the containers. She stood peering into the empty sky above them, as if searching for something she couldn't quite make out.

"But it was real, Davey. Real as anything! It didn't fade when I woke up, the way dreams do." Her troubled eyes came back to him. "Yet it's hard to talk about. Because I was somebody else. The places and people and ideas—they're all so new."

Shivering, she caught his hands.

"I'm getting a headache just trying to remember."

He didn't beg her to tell about it; they understood each other too well for that. Instead, he beckoned her farther away from the trail, and they sat face to face on two empty containers. Eagerly, he waited.

"It's like a memory, though it never happened to me. In it, I'm Eva—Eva Smithwick." She was hesitant, groping. "The last of the Creators. But the Creation wasn't the instant miracle they talk about in church. It took hundreds of people working for hundreds of years."

She stopped to think again, unconsciously combing a black-shining sheaf of her hair with slim white fingers.

"The real Creators—the leaders—all belonged to one great family. Adam Smithwick and his descendants. I believe—Eva believed that the family itself had been the actual first creation."

Leaning closer, he caught the faint sweet exciting scent of her hair.

"You can't guess how hard it is." Her tawny eyes flashed him a wry little smile. "It's all terribly real. So plain I'll never forget. But when I try to talk about it, the words aren't there. Even the language Eva spoke wasn't yet our Terran. After all, I'm still *me*."

"I'm glad."

With only a grave, pleased nod, she went on searching out the words that rang so strange when she spoke them. "The first actual Creators must have been Adam's parents. They had been geneticists, working to control mutations in lab animals and then in human beings by micromanipulation of the chromosomes—"

She saw his puzzled expression and paused to think again.

"They had been working with the genetic code, trying to revise the blueprint for a new body and a new mind carried by the germ-cell from parents to child."

"I can understand that," he said. "From exobiology class."

"Adam's parents had both been in trouble. His father had to leave a country called England when people learned about his experiments with humans. I guess they were already afraid of what he might create."

Gazing at the yellow containers, Davey nodded somewhat grimly.

"His mother was a refugee from what was called a labor camp in another country. She had been sent there because she wouldn't work in a secret genetic project to grow military clones. Adam was born in Japan. He grew up to be the best geneticist anywhere.

"The reason was, his own genes had been improved. Anyhow, that's what Eva thought. She must have been his great-grand-daughter." Buglet stopped again, frowning with effort, twisting the strands of bright black hair. "Sorry, Davey. It's all in broken bits. I need time to fit them together—and we're already late for school."

"Forget school."

She sat very still for a while, her searching eyes fixed on things beyond the yellow boxes and the dusty sky. "Adam—" She brightened again, remembering. "Adam came to North America to be the first director of a new space clinic. Men were exploring the planets by then, and he was already the greatest specialist in space medicine.

"Secretly, he was already creating the trumen. I guess he had learned from the misfortunes of his parents, because he kept the secret well. He arranged for the trumen to be accepted as the normal children of his wives—he was married three times in all—and children of his friends and associates.

"They looked like premen, of course. They were simply better. Stronger and smarter. Immune to all the old diseases. Free of all the old genetic defects. Rid of all the animal jealousies and aggressions that have always kept the premen in conflict with each other. Their social adaptiveness kept them out of trouble. For a whole generation their existence wasn't suspected at all."

She paused again to think.

"People like San Seven wouldn't be suspected," Davey murmured. "He's as normal as anybody. Just brighter and nicer."

She hardly seemed to hear him.

"Darwin—Darwin Smithwick was the next Creator. Adam's last child and probably himself another special creation. He made the mumen. Mutant creations shaped to meet all the different challenges of space. With their new senses, the mumen began finding the first short cuts to other star systems through the contact planes; up till then, the finite speed of light had limited exploration."

Her lemon eyes smiled at something he couldn't see.

20

"To the premen of those days, the Creators themselves must have seemed like gods. They were nearly immortal. Adam lived and worked a hundred years, Darwin even longer. Before he died, the trumen were changing history. Never fully revealing themselves—at first not even aware they were a new species—they had become the leaders in everything.

"War ceased, because the trumen saw that it was stupid. They dissolved the old contending nations into a new world republic. They revised social systems to end crime and disorder. They invented new sources of energy and food, found a new equilibrium with the environment. There was a long age of peace and abundance—till the premen revolted.

"They had never known—"

Half a mile across the town the school bell had begun to ring. Buglet moved as if to slide off her yellow perch, but Davey checked her with a gesture. Frowning in a way that charmed him, she went on again, groping for the words she recited in a grave, slow voice that hardly seemed her own.

"For a hundred years and more, the trumen had been the faithful public servants Adam Smithwick wanted. Under them, the premen were better off than they had ever been. As Darwin wrote in his journal, the world had become the paradise the old preman prophets and philosophers had always dreamed about. Most of the premen must have understood that their new leaders were too useful to be destroyed, because the rebellion was delayed a long time, even after the truth was pretty well known.

"When it came, the civil war was savage. As illogical as always, the premen refused to see that they had nothing at all to gain. Their own irrational leaders magnified the number and the powers of the trumen. In a wave of insane panic, they overturned the world republic to revive the old conflicting nations and parties and unions and classes. Trumen were mobbed and slaughtered. War came back. Famine and disease and misrule.

"Yet through most of that dark age the premen seemed about to win. They had the numbers, billions against a few tens of thousands. They had their old aptitude for senseless violence. They seized or burned most of the cities. Trying to kill the Creators, they wrecked the space clinic. Darwin Smithwick had to hide in an old copper mine.

"In the end, of course, the premen lost. Numbers meant nothing. Though the trumen had surrendered most of the Earth, they found refuge in space. No fighters themselves, they brought muman soldiers to defend their strongholds around the spaceports. And Huxley Smithwick made the stargods.

"Darwin's son Huxley had grown up in hiding—most of the time in that abandoned mine. He learned his father's crafts of creation and improved on them. When he escaped into space he carried three new synthetic life-cells in cryogenic flasks: Alpha and Beta and Gamma.

"Those names seem to have come from the symbols of some lost language. Huxley separated the new beings for their own safety, arranging for proxy-mothers to bear them on three different planets. Not really divine, not yet immortal, they were gifted enough. He called them his three Valkyries, from the warrior women in some forgotten preman legend. When they were old enough for battle, he sent them back to face the rebels.

"Though their powers were limited, they had been designed for battle. Withdrawing from simple space at will, they were untouchable. They could levitate where they pleased, unstoppable. With one flash of a nimbus, they could kill a preman leader or explode an arsenal. After two or three encounters, the premen panicked.

"Huxley recalled his Valkyries to space, and the trumen tried to restore the world republic. For reasons they couldn't understand, the effort failed. Defeat had changed the premen. They refused to trust anybody, or to accept any aid, or even to help themselves. As Eva saw it, they had suffered an emotional wound that never healed. And I guess that's the way Redrock began."

Buglet wrinkled her nose at the sewer stink drifting between the yellow containers.

"The two cultures grew apart as the centuries went on, and the premen lost most of their own. When the world state came back, it was a union of the spreading truman enclaves, with the premen left out. I wonder—"

Her breath caught, and her voice was again her own.

"I wonder if San Six is right—if the premen really are the mongrel stepchildren of Creation. Because they just gave up. They quit trying. In government. In science and art. In everything. When the troubles ended, they still owned most of the planet. But

22

they died of their own strife, their own plagues, their own despair. Their numbers dwindled as the trumen grew. Again and again they gave up land, till Redrock is their last bit—''

"You and I are premen," Davey objected gravely. "Really, Bug, do you feel so inferior?''

Her yellow eyes blinked.

"I guess I was still thinking Eva Smithwick's thoughts.'' With a quick little smile, she reached to touch his arm. "We're different, of course. We can't do what the stargods can. We aren't even as sharp as San Seven in a good many ways. But we're—ourselves.''

"We're just as good—as good as anybody!'' A gust of anger shook his voice, and he sat bleak and silent till it had passed. "Go on, Bug.'' He bent toward her hopefully. "Is there anything about the Multiman?''

"Maybe.'' She frowned at the yellow boxes. "It's like trying to fit the pieces of a broken pot together when half of them are gone. I don't know what I know. I have to put the scraps of Eva's memory into a language I can speak.

"But Huxley Smithwick had a daughter—''

Absently combing at her hair, she forgot to go on.

Davey watched the monk's skimmer sail above them toward the dig on Creation Mesa and listened to the hooves of a mule clopping along the trail.

"When the war was over, Huxley came back from space.'' She nodded to herself, as if to confirm the recollection. "He built the laboratory—the exobiology lab—where the old space clinic had stood. There he created mates for his three Valkyries.

"The first of the stargods. True immortals, with keener senses to explore the multiverse and greater powers to control it. The mumen had begun encountering advanced and sometimes hostile alien cultures, and he thought they needed stronger champions than the Valkyries.

"In his old age, talking to his daughter, he confessed that the gods had been a blunder. Even at the time he was aware of the danger, but he thought he was taking precautions enough. Like the Valkyries, those first gods were implanted in the wombs of proxy-mothers, to be born and raised on other worlds. Trying to guard himself, he gave them an avoidance compulsion to keep them light-years away from Earth.

"Eva was his daughter and his student, herself perhaps his greatest creation—but not immortal, of course. The last Creator. She took over the lab when he died. By that time the extent of his blunder was clear. The gods were far too powerful, too scornful of their makers, with too much self and passion from their Valkyrie mothers, more anxious to extend their own divine might than to aid and shield the older human races.

"The first three gods made no trouble. Bound by that compulsion, they stayed away from Earth. But after they had found their Valkyrie mates, their children inherited their immortality and all their powers, without the compulsion. Alarmed, Eva went to work on a new creation—"

"The Multiman?"

"Not by such a name." Buglet shook her head. "She was trying to design a new sort of being, greater than the stargods, with a better control of the multiversal environment and a stronger love for all the older races. But she had to rush her work, because she was afraid the jealous young gods would try to wreck it, to defend their own supremacy.

"There simply wasn't time—"

She stopped again, frowning at nothing, absently kicking at the next hollow box.

"That's about as far as I can go. About all Eva knew, when her memory somehow got mixed up with mine. She was still busy in the lab on what we call Creation Mesa, working to perfect that new life-cell. Out in the multiverse Belthar and his brother and sister and cousins were growing up, afraid of her work and free to attack her. The new creation wasn't ready to be implanted in a proxy-mother. She was making plans to hide it—"

"Where?" Davey whispered. "Where?"

Her golden eyes looked through him, while she groped for Eva Smithwick's thoughts.

"The mine!" She smiled a little, as the details came. "In that old copper mine, where her father had hidden. It's under the end of the mesa. The centuries and the preman wars had already erased all the surface signs that it was ever there, and her father had dug an escape tunnel to it from the basements of the lab.

"She knew the gods would be looking for new creatures. To outwit them, she had set her engineers to work on a robot nurse

24

that could keep the germ-cells frozen for years—maybe for centuries—till a safe time came for them to be incubated and developed.''

''So he's out there?'' He was breathless with excitement. ''Asleep under the mesa!''

''I don't know, Davey.'' With a shrug of regret, she slid off the container. ''That's where Eva Smithwick was in time. She didn't know what was going to happen. I've come to the end of the memory—if it was a memory.''

''Do you think—'' He caught her hands, and found them oddly cold. ''Do you think we could find a way into the mine? Wake the Multiman?''

''That's all I know.'' Though the air was still and hot around them, bitter with the smell of the yellow containers, something made her shiver. ''If he's there at all, the monks will probably find him first.''

4.

Their preman teacher scowled and their fellow students winked and tittered when Buglet and Davey came late to school. Davey sat dumb all day, hearing nothing, vainly trying to imagine ways to reach and wake the sleeping Multiman before the gray-robed monks found him. Working out a null-G belt that afternoon, he was so preoccupied that he tumbled clumsily into the ceiling of the gym. When San Seven asked what the trouble was, a wave of terror swept him.

''Just worried, I guess,'' he muttered. ''About Andoranda V.''

''I'm sure you are.'' San looked at him almost too keenly. ''If I can help, just ask.''

He had to quench a spark of hope. San was his best male friend, but he was also a sharp-witted truman, faithful to Belthar. ''Thanks,'' he said, ''but I'm afraid there is no help.''

On graduation night he filed into the old adobe auditorium just behind Buglet, half drunk with the scent and shine of her long black hair. Seated side by side, they listened to the commencement address. The speaker was San Six.

The occasion was significant, he said, because they would be the last graduates from Redrock. They would be carrying their memories and the traditions of the school to a far-off frontier world, where they would be facing novel and exciting challenges. To survive there, to succeed, to make their careers and nurture their ancient preman culture, they must call on the lessons they had learned from their faithful teachers and the aid they might earn through steadfast devotion to the gods—

Listening to the agent's mellow oratory and thinking of those empty containers waiting on the plaza, Davey tried not to shudder. He turned impulsively to Buglet, who looked very grave and pale in her dark robe, more alluring than a goddess.

"If we could run away together—" The whisper burst out before he thought. "If we could hide somewhere—live somewhere as trumen—"

He stopped, stifled by the fear of his own audacity. She turned a little toward him, her lemon eyes wide. After one breathless instant, she nodded slightly.

"I'll come." Her lips moved soundlessly. "If we can find a way."

"But that's crazy." His wave of elation was already gone. "We've got to stay. Understand your vision—whatever it was. Look for the Multiman. If he does exist."

They went next morning to the Thar chapel to ask for work at the excavation. The fat dean was sorry, but the monks had stopped hiring anybody. The dig had not been productive, and the new lake was rising fast. Within the next six-square of days, their expedition would be leaving Redrock.

"Anyhow," Buglet whispered to Davey, "I want to see where Eva lived. The place might wake another memory."

They rented two mules from La China and rode out for a picnic on Creation Mesa. A skimmer came sailing to meet them at the top of the trail, and a gray-robed monk leaned out to warn them that the area was closed to visitors.

"Your permission, Master." Davey bowed respectfully. "We're only looking for wild flowers and a place to eat our lunch."

"Flowers!" The Polarian snorted. "All you'll find is cactus."

"There's a spring—" Buglet caught herself. "We heard there's a spring below the north rim."

"Dry rocks," the monk muttered. "Dry dust."

But he let them ride on.

"There *was* a spring," Buglet whispered. "A thousand years ago. A tunnel, actually, dug to drain water out of the mine. It could be our way inside."

She rode ahead through the glaring noon, her brown mule clattering over naked rock and crashing through brittle brush. Davey followed eagerly, breathing the juniper scent, searching ahead for the green of a spring, but his bright hope died when they came to the rim. Buglet had stopped there, shading her eyes, peering blankly down at the desert.

"Things—things are wrong. Nothing looks quite like it should. Maybe Belthar's bombs caved the cliffs away. I guess the spring has dried up. Anyhow, I don't know where to look."

They hitched the mules to a piñon stump and scrambled down the slope looking for the scar of a drill, the red of iron rust, even one green weed. When they found nothing, Buglet chose another place to search, finally a third.

"No use." She was scratched and grimy, drooping in the heat. "I guess the monk was right."

They sat in the shade of a sandstone cliff to eat their bread and cheese. Late in the suffocating afternoon they were riding back toward the trail when Davey slid off his mule.

"Bug, look!"

What he had found was half a red brick, one face burned black. Kicking breathlessly into the gravel, he uncovered a gray mass of battered aluminum, an opal blob of fused glass, a blackened silver coin. Reining up her mule, Buglet peered off into the heat-hazed distance.

"Eva's view!" Her eyes grew wide. "From the parking lot behind the exobiology lab. Davey, this is where the monks think they're digging." With a quick little nod of recognition, she looked south across the mesa. "Actually, they're down at the site of the old mining town."

"Shall we tell them?" Davey frowned doubtfully up at her and down at the opal ball. "If we do, they may find the Multiman—and maybe kill him. If we don't, the lake will drown him."

She sat for a moment staring down at the gravel as if her yellow eyes could penetrate it. "The escape tunnel from the lab to the mine must be fifty feet down. Farther than we could hope to dig. I think we'll have to risk help from the monks."

When the pudgy Polarian dean came that night to dinner at the agency, Davey showed him the bits of brick and metal and glass. Squinting at them, he forgot his appetite. They went with him next morning in the skimmer to guide him to the site, and watched while he explored it with strange machines.

"Probes," he told them. "Sonic and magnetic and gravitic. They're mapping the solid masses and the metallic bodies under the gravel and rubble. Broken walls. Pavements and foundations. Old excavations. An important site. I wish we had found it sooner."

"Since we found it," Davey begged, "may we work here?"

"Till you leave," the dean agreed.

They drove stakes for him that afternoon and helped stretch the colored cords that outlined the foundations of the buried lab. Davey went to work next morning with a spade, tossing gravel against a sloping screen, while Buglet knelt in the dust to scrabble for artifacts.

"You're right above old Huxley's tunnel," she told him. "If we can ever dig that far down."

His hands were raw blisters before the long shift ended, but he had begun to uncover ancient masonry, walling his narrow pit.

"An old elevator shaft," Buglet told him, and dropped her voice. "Old Huxley's escape tunnel opens from the bottom of it." She frowned uneasily. "If we can somehow get into it first—"

Day after day he shoveled rubble into a bucket, to be hoisted and sifted above. Foot by laborious foot he cleared the ancient shaft. The pit was hot and his muscles ached, but he dug through a level of broken porcelain and glass that had come, Buglet said, from the biochemical lab. He dug past a shattered archway into what she said had been a cold room for a colony of alien methane-breathers. He dug on down beside a vast concrete slab that had covered a bomb shelter. Dripping muddy sweat, reeling with fatigue, still he shoveled rubble.

But time ran fast. From the windows of the skimmer, as the monks took them home after work, they began to see dusty sunsets burning red in the rising lake. The preman magistrates had begun scattering the yellow shipping containers through the town, one to every dwelling. Most of the other premen stopped coming to work, but they kept on.

Breathing the dust of dead centuries, Davey piled the bucket with broken stone and muck, with charred wood and rusty iron, with stray bones and battered bullets. Spitting bitter mud, he worked on down beyond the floor of the buried shelter.

"Just a few feet more!" Buglet's tawny eyes shone. "The tunnel opens from the south side of the shaft. There was a false wall to hide it. I don't think the monks suspect it yet."

Energized with eager hope, yet half afraid that the wall had broken, that some flood had washed debris through to choke the tunnel, he toiled through most of another day. Abruptly, in mid-afternoon, the Polarian foreman called him out of the pit. Work had stopped. The expedition was departing.

"Sorry to go," the dean told the agent at dinner that night. "Because of your excellent hospitality. And because we've finally located the true site of Creation. We could spend our lives here, uncovering relics of the holy progenitors. But the church has ordered us out."

He reached to spear a second steak.

"Enjoy yourself," the agent urged him genially. "Everybody's going. The transport's in orbit at last. Long overdue. Delayed somewhere to wait for a pilot. Now we've only three days to clear the premen out."

Afraid to look at Buglet, Davey reached under the table for her hand. Cold and quivering, her fingers clung to his. San Seven sat across the table, watching them with a troubled intentness. He followed when they left the dining room.

"Davey—" His uneasy whisper stopped them. "Bug—please!"

He beckoned them into his own room and closed the door. Nearly always cheerily confident, he looked so pale and nervous now that Davey thought he must be ill.

"You heard—" Nervously, he went back to listen at the door. "Andoranda V—unless you get away—"

Unless we find the Multiman, Davey thought.

With a tiny gesture Buglet warned him to say nothing.

"I—I'm not used to this." San Seven was breathless and

sweating. "I've never broken the code before. But we—we've grown up together. I love you both. More than my truman friends—"

Buglet ran impulsively to kiss him.

Davey grinned gratefully, his own throat aching.

"I'm no—no criminal." He was almost sobbing. "Not till now." Brown fingers trembling, he thrust a tiny envelope at them. "I got into Father's office. Stole forms. Forged truman passports."

We'll never need them, Davey thought. *Unless—*

"Invented identities for you. Priests of Bel. You belong to the wandering order of Yed. Your society owns no property and observes no discipline. Your obligation is to preach the Lord Belthar's boundless love. Understand?"

Davey nodded. "We've seen the priests of Yed. They used to bring their message to us premen. Wearing rags. Sleeping on the chapel floor. Begging food at El Yaqui's. Preaching Bel to everybody." He grinned his gratitude. "A clever way to help us hide!"

"We can't repay you." Eyes dark and wet, Buglet accepted the envelope. "But we'll always remember—"

"Perhaps you shouldn't thank me." San Seven shrugged a troubled apology. "I'm not a skillful forger. You're likely to be picked up, and you know the penalty for trying to pass yourselves as trumen."

Death.

"We know," Buglet whispered. "It's not as bad as Andoranda V."

"Anyhow," he mumbled, "I wanted you to have a chance."

With guilty haste, he looked out to see that the hall was empty and rushed them from his room. They slipped away from the agency and hurried through back streets to the trading post.

"The starship's in orbit," Davey told La China. "They'll be shipping us out. We want to remember the mesa by moonlight. We'd like to rent two mules."

"Take them." She blinked sleepily across her cash machine. "Take these." Her fat black fingers dug into the drawer for a heavy roll of coins. "Take—take anything you need." Her husky voice caught. "If I were young enough, I'd be running with you."

"Maybe—" Davey whispered. "Maybe the Multiman can help."

"There's no help." She smiled dreamily. "I'm dying to-night."

They saddled the mules and followed dark alleys out of town. The moon was full, the desert all silver and shadow.

"It's all so beautiful," Buglet murmured. "Too lovely to leave."

The dig on the mesa was silent, black cranes jutting like skeletal arms into the sky. They hitched the mules, and he showed Buglet how to run the bucket. Down in the narrow pit, he dug desperately.

One jagged mass of fallen concrete was too heavy to move. With no tools or explosive to break it up, he burrowed around it. His headlamp found a dark hollow behind it, and he smelled a musty dampness.

"Bug!" His voice boomed back from the walls of the pit, magnified into a monstrous bellow. "We've found the tunnel—open!"

She rode the bucket down. Thrusting and prying with the shovel, hauling bare-handed at muddy concrete masses, they widened the opening. Before it was big enough for him, she dived through. For a moment she was lost in the dark.

"We've found the Multiman!" Her face came back into the light, grime-streaked and eager. "If Eva really left him here."

They strained together to move another boulder, and he slid down beside her. Roughly cut through dark sandstone, the narrow passage was so low they had to stoop. Sloping steeply down, it brought them at last into a wider drift, where drops of falling water crashed and echoed.

"Now?" He looked at Buglet. "Which way?"

She shrugged uncertainly.

"The robot nursery—" Her voice brought chattering echoes out of the dark, and she dropped it to a whisper. "The nursery hadn't been installed. All I know is Eva's ideas. She wanted a high spot, safe from flooding. She wanted easy access to it from the lab, through Huxley's tunnel."

The drift curved and sloped, where the miners must have followed a wandering vein. Ancient timbers had gone to dust, letting it cave. They climbed it till a larger rockfall stopped them. Crawling through the jagged crack above the boulder mound, they saw the loom of a huge, dark-cased machine.

"No!" Buglet gasped. "Oh, no!"

Davey's searching headlamp struck dull glints from the rock-piled floor around the silent machine. Once, a thick glass shell had covered it, but that lay shattered into dusty fragments beneath a great stone mass from the ceiling. Clambering down the slope, he let his light play over broken glass and rusting metal. Nothing moved, and the air had a reek of old decay.

"Dead!" Buglet sobbed. "The Multiman is dead."

5.

Still damp with sweat, Davey shivered. That cold cavern had suddenly become a tomb—for Eva Smithwick's last creation, for the premen waiting exile to Andoranda V, for all their dreams. Though they stayed an hour, digging under the great glass shards in search of something more than rust and dust, they found no hope.

"Nothing!" Davey flashed his lamp on the boulder that had crushed the machine. "It happened too long ago. A quake, I guess."

Buglet stood trembling in the gloom, fingering a broken scrap of stainless metal. She shaded her eyes from his light.

"Belthar's bombs, more likely."

"What now, Bug?" He peered at her hopefully. "Shouldn't there be a spare machine? A second Multiman?"

"I don't know." She dropped the useless metal fragment and started a little when it jangled on broken glass. "Eva was afraid the machine might fail. She did think of a spare. But—" With a tired shrug, she turned to stare at the dead pile of rock and wreckage. "I don't know anywhere to look."

Her small sad voice sent a surge of pity through him. He reached to touch her trembling shoulder, and suddenly they clung together. The warm strong yielding feel of her body spun him into a chasm of emotion. He crushed her hard against him, pushed her desperately back.

"I—I love you, Bug!" he gasped. "We've got to live. That means we've got to run. With money from La China and passports from San, I think we have a chance." He looked into her lemon-gray eyes, contracting under his light. "Are you game?"

Eyes wet and bright, she kissed him again.

The full moon was already low when they came out of the excavation. They rode the mules east to the mesa rim and down a long rocky slope. Dawn met them far from Redrock, on a vast bare flat.

"They'll soon miss us." She kept watching the sky behind them. "They'll come hunting."

The tired mules were stumbling, but they pushed on to the next sandstone ridge. From the shelter of a red-walled canyon there, they saw the glint of the early sun on a skimmer that flew low, searching back and forth across Creation Mesa.

Hiding throughout that blazing day, they finished the tortillas and smoked meat they had brought from El Yaqui's. By turns they watched and slept. Climbing the canyon after the skimmer was gone, they found a rock pool, where they drank and watered the mules. From the top of the ridge just before sunset they looked out of the reservation and into truman country.

A straight and endless line cut off the desert. On the preman side red buttes and dead brush shimmered in a haze of smothering heat. Beyond the line young orchards and ripe grain patterned the fertile truman lands with tender green and mellow gold, laced with narrow blue canals.

"A wall!" Buglet whispered. "A wall around the reservation."

"Death if we cross." He spat muddy froth. "Andoranda V if we don't."

Dismounting to rest the mules, they sat resting on a rocky ledge, looking down into that richer world. Harvest machines like bright insects were crawling over the golden wheat. The reddening sun picked out the lean white towers and mirror domes of a truman town on one far hill.

"There are too many trumen," Buglet murmured solemnly. "Too few of us."

As they rose to go on, Davey looked back and caught his breath. The desert behind was a vast empty basin, the long blue shadow of Creation Mesa creeping across it. One tiny red speck had left the shadow, creeping after them beneath tiny puffs of sunlit dust.

"A muman soldier," he decided. "On our trail. Using a null-G belt."

"Then it will catch us." Alarm darkened her eyes. "We can't outrun a flying belt."

"We can try." He gave her a small grim smile. "Our trail will be harder to follow in the dark. If we can get across the line, we'll be trumen—with passports to prove it."

In the hazy dusk the sweat-lathered mules slid and scrambled down the ridge. In the early dark they plodded on and on across the next bare gravel plain. When one mule went lame, Davey dismounted to lead it. Before moonrise, the other mule stumbled into a dry arroyo, pitching Buglet over its head.

Davey found her lying at the bottom of the rocky gully, unable to speak. Her breath was gone. When she got it back, she whispered faintly that she wasn't hurt at all. Except for a twisted ankle.

They saw that the mules could carry them no farther. Buglet sat on the arroyo rim nursing her ankle, while Davey unsaddled and freed them. In the first pale light of the moon he cut two leather thongs from the saddles, knotted a pocket between them, and searched the arroyo bed for pebbles to fit the pocket.

"A weapon?" she asked.

"A sling," he said. "One summer El Yaqui taught me how to use a sling for rabbits."

"For rabbits, maybe." Her eyes were huge and black in the moonlight. "Not for muman deadeyes."

He wrapped her ankle with another thong and found her a dry yucca stalk for a cane. More slowly now they toiled on. At midnight, by the high moon, they were climbing a long, rolling slope which brought the far-off town into view again, its domes now glowing rose and gold.

"The reservation line." He pointed at a straight dark streak across the next low hill. "We'll be there by daylight."

Buglet limped on beside him. At the crest of the ridge she stopped with a gasp of dismay. He thought she had hurt her ankle again, till she pointed into the broad valley ahead and he saw the shimmer of the moon on water.

"The lake—" she whispered. "It has cut us off."

They hobbled on till the ridge they followed had become a narrow spit of sand jutting into a wide arm of Quelf's filling sea.

"Water all around us," he muttered huskily. "And the deadeye behind."

They waded out through the drowned brush, and cupped water in their hands to drink. He stood a long time staring out across that unexpected barrier.

"Trapped." Wearily, he splashed back to the shore. "But we tried."

Waiting, they lay in a dry sand hollow. Buglet loosened the thong around her swelling ankle and rested her head on Davey's shoulder. She felt very light and fragile, tragically vulnerable. Breathing the sweetness of her hair, he thought of many things to say, but nothing really mattered now.

"Stepchildren," she whispered once. For a time she was breathing so evenly that he thought she was asleep. Her low voice startled him. "It's a strange thing, Davey. When you remember that we premen made the trumen and the mumen and the gods."

His throat ached, and he only stroked her glossy hair.

Brush crackled and pebbles rattled.

Standing stiffly, they watched the mutant guardian coming down the ridge. Naked except for harness and belt, it was taller than a god. Its red scales were black and silver in the moonlight, but the deadly lens in its crest glowed crimson. Though its gliding bounds seemed slow, each covered many yards.

Buglet kissed Davey and gripped her yucca stick. He fitted a pebble to his sling. Rising and pausing and falling through a last flowing leap, the guardian crashed into a greasewood clump twenty yards from them. It stopped there, splendid in its towering power. The wind brought its scent, an odor like pine.

"Greetings, premen!" Its voice was a trumpet blaring. "From Allaya K, guardian of the gods. To Davey Dunahoo, male. To Jondarc, female. By order of the holy church, you are under arrest. Drop your weapons and walk forward."

Davey glanced at Buglet. Somehow she was smiling, fine teeth glancing white in the moonlight. He whirled the sling to test the pebble's weight.

"Now hear your charges," that cold voice pealed. "Jointly and individually, you stand accused of theft from the preman

35

woman known as La China. You stand accused of complicity in her death—''

"She isn't dead!'' Buglet gasped. "She gave us the money and the mules.''

"She was found hanging in the mule barn behind the trading post," the hard official tones boomed again. "You also stand accused of flight to escape transfer from Redrock. Any display of resistance will forfeit the clemency requested by San Six, agent of Belthar. Drop your weapons and walk toward me.''

Davey gulped. "We aren't coming.''

"Do you refuse to obey a lawful command?'' the muman bugled. "Are you not aware that the penalty is death?''

"They want to send us to Andoranda V," Buglet said. "That is death.''

"Listen, children.'' Another gliding bound brought the guardian halfway to them, so close that they could see a half-familiar pattern of darker scales across its gleaming torso. Its voice was suddenly softer, chiding, almost feminine. "Don't you know me?''

"No—'' Buglet started. "You killed Spot!''

"A savage animal was charging the goddess," its new voice chimed instantly. "I struck it down at Prince Quelf's command. I followed my duty to the Lord Belthar then, as I follow it now. But I beg you to surrender. Even premen should be too smart to defy the church and the gods. Please put down your silly weapons.''

"We—we just can't!''

Buglet brandished her yucca wand.

"Fools!'' The muman's voice rang cold again. "You give me no choice.''

The guardian crouched. Its black crest swelled. Its third eye volleyed pathseekers, arrows of violet brightness probing for a mark. When they found the brittle stick, thunder cracked. The stick exploded into blazing splinters.

"Dav—''

With that stifled cry, Buglet slid down onto the sand.

"Take warning, preman!''

That lethal eye swung to Davey, alive with painful fire. Sharp as needles, the ionizing pathseekers stabbed his arm and shoulder. His nostrils stung with their lightning scent, and all he could hear was their hurried *hiss-click, hiss-click, hiss-click*.

He whirled the sling around his head.

"Give up!" the mutant boomed. "Or—"

His wrath and grief lent force to his stone. It went true, but the guardian had flung out its arm, as if brushing at a gnat. He heard the pebble thump against the yielding scales, heard it clatter on the gravel. Dancing nearer, the muman lit the brush around them with its killing eye.

"Idiot!" Its laughter rang like an iron bell. "You premen! You're still only animals, for all your human form. Blind to logic. Slaves to raw emotion. Cowards when you ought to fight and brave when only flight can save you. I guess it's no wonder you've lost your last reservation."

Its seeing eyes challenged him.

"Will you yield now?"

Gasping for his breath, Davey had no voice. His whole body quivered. Tears blurred his eyes, till the guardian was a shimmering pillar of silver and crimson. Fingers numb and clumsy, he fitted another pebble to the pocket. He spun the sling again. If he could smash—

"You've fury enough," the mutant mocked him. "But fury isn't force. If you elect to die here—"

Red fire exploded from that hateful eye.

Aiming at it, he tried to release his missile.

But time had paused. A red-purple fog had erased the towering guardian and flooded all the moon-gray sky. Blind, he still could somehow sense the deadly bolt hurled at him. Desperately, with his last reserves of nerve and will, he tried to catch it, turn it back.

He knew the effort was folly, and he thought it had failed. That cold fire-fog became a roaring tornado around him, dragging him into a bright abyss he didn't understand. Bewildering images flickered and vanished in his mind, too quick for him to grasp them. Dazing thunder crashed—

"Davey!" Buglet was sobbing. "Can't you move?"

Numb and trembling, he sat up. The world seemed strangely

still. The calm lake lapped around them. The mutant soldier lay sprawled a few yards away, its crested lens dark and dead, staring into the moonlit sky.

"You stopped it, Davey!" Breathless with elation, she was hovering over him, brushing at the sand on his face. "Just in time."

"I thought—thought it had stopped me." He stopped to get his own breath. "The finder beam was jabbing at me. I saw the lens blaze. I knew it was striking. I do remember trying to turn the bolt—"

"You did it!" Her voice was hushed with awe. "The bolt never reached you. I saw it curve back toward the guardian's heart. Somehow you made it kill itself."

Unsteadily, he stood up. Sparks from Buglet's splintered stick still glowed around them on the sand, and the air was edged with its smoke. Bewildered, he stared down at the fallen soldier. The mighty limbs were twisted and rigid and the extended talons had ripped long scars in the sand.

"If I stopped the bolt—" He shook his head. "I don't know how!"

"Maybe—maybe I do!" A sudden elation had quickened Buglet's voice. "When it hit my stick, something happened to me. The shock knocked me down. For just an instant I must have blacked out. By the time it was striking at you I was awake again. With another memory, Davey! A later link to Eva Smithwick's mind.

"Now I know—"

Her voice faded out.

He felt numb and light and strange, the way he had felt once on the desert, chewing bitter peyote buttons with El Yaqui. Staring down at the enormous armored body lying on the sand, he couldn't remember for a moment what it was. When he looked back at Buglet, she was wrapped in a dust-devil of whirling golden motes. Her excited voice came out of its thundering vortex, still so faint he could hardly hear.

"—more than stepchildren," she was saying. "More than just rejects from the genetics lab, bungled mutants, or spoiled gods. Davey, we're the actual Fourth Creation!"

Trying to move closer, to hear better, he was swept with her into that whirl of fire. The bright motes became winking images, like the truman symbology he had never learned. He knew they had meaning, but it was always gone too fast for him to grasp.

"Demons?" Swaying giddily, he fought for breath and balance. "Are we—demons?"

Her reply seemed intolerably delayed. Her slim form was frozen, as if the air had congealed around her, her face a stiffened mask. He stood there, numb and shuddering, until the thunder waned and that bright vortex let them go.

"The demons were a lie." Time had begun to flow again, and her rigid face thawed into a slow and bitter smile. "A lie invented by the gods to excuse their murder of the Creators. The real Fourth Creation was something greater than any god. It was the being we've been calling the Multiman. And he is hidden in us!"

"But—" His tongue felt too thick for speech. "That smashed machine—"

"Only a decoy." Receding, those flakes of whirling fire still seemed more real than the moon, and her voice too faint and slow. "It's all clear now, since I have this later recollection. Eva had known from the first that the robot nurse would be too easy to find and destroy. She was looking for a more subtle way to hide her last creation. She found it, long enough before Belthar came back—in the cells themselves."

Still too numb and dull to think, he waited.

"What she did was to rebuild that last synthetic germ-cell, to conceal its true nature. She had always given a share of her time to clinics on the preman reservations, and she was planning to use her last tour there to plant copies of the cell in preman women. The children, for many generations, were to be apparently premen, maybe even a little subnormal, too harmless looking to alarm Belthar."

Her white smile brightened.

"Of course, all I know is what she planned, but she meant to be back here at the mesa lab when Belthar struck, working desperately to get her decoy machines completed and installed in the mine. I believe that's what happened. She herself was the real decoy, waiting for Belthar to wreck the lab and kill her. Out on the reservations, those premanlike children were born. They grew up to hand their special genes down to another generation. And the gods never suspected the truth.''

Her eyes were black and huge, and her low voice quivered with something near terror.

''Davey, those genes have come down to us!''

Breathing unevenly, he waited for that far-off thunder to fade from his ringing ears, for the last flecks of fire to dissolve in the cold moonlight.

''So that's how—'' His voice was hoarse and strange. ''—how you got Eva Smithwick's memory?''

''The things we must know were engineered into the germ-cells. Designed to lie latent, generation after generation. Till something triggered them.''

''Bug, I can't—can't realize!'' Though time was flowing again, he felt dull and cold and slow. He reached out uncertainly to touch her arm, but his hand shuddered and drew back. ''You're a goddess, Bug. Greater than a goddess!''

''We don't yet know what we are.''

''We?'' With a stiff little grin, he shook his head. ''I don't remember anything. There's no Multiman waking up in me. Sorry, Bug. I'm just a preman.''

''What do you think happened to the deadeye?'' She nodded at its body. ''I think—I know we both carry the created genes, though different powers have begun to awaken in us.''

He stood trembling, as if the wind off the lake had chilled him.

''Why?'' He gaped at her. ''Why us? Why now?''

''Danger is the stimulus, I think.''

''I never expected—'' He had to get his breath. ''Bug, what are we going to be?''

''I know what Eva planned.'' Her dark eyes shone. ''The being we called the Multiman is sleeping in us, Davey. In both of us. Waiting to be waked. We're the Fourth Creation, born to challenge the gods!''

He blinked at her, shocked by her audacity.

''I don't feel equal to the gods.'' He shrugged uneasily. ''In fact, I'm tired and cold and hungry. And we're in a bad spot, Bug. We've just killed a muman guardian. The whole church will be hunting us now—''

"We ought to welcome danger, Davey." She was smiling in the moonlight. "It's the stimulus we need to make us what we must be."

"I imagine we'll see danger enough."

She looked down at the body, her smile slowly fading.

"It does frighten me," she whispered at last. "To think what Eva planned for us to do. To repair the errors of the gods. To build a better multiverse for all the human races." Her cold hand caught his. "That was to be our destiny, but I don't know how to begin."

"First of all, let's get off the reservation."

Testing her injured ankle, she winced and nearly fell.

"We'll fly," he told her. "With the deadeye's belt."

Bending to loosen the mutant soldier's harness, he found the nipples the sleek scales had hidden. Beneath the bluster and the armor, it had been female. He felt a pang of astonished sadness that excitement washed away.

Buglet snuggled against his belly, her fragrant hair against his cheek. He snapped the belt around them and turned up the nullifier. The sandspit and the mutant body dropped behind. The cool dawn wind caught them, swept them on across the moon-flecked lake toward truman country.

TWO: SLAVE TO CHAOS

Alexandr keeps hinting that I ought to marry.

Marry him, he means, if he dared make it plain. His problem is too much awe of me, even though I have never let him know what I am.

He's no doubt the ablest human geneticist who ever lived. A superb technician, my indispensable assistant the past twenty years. An appealing creature, too, for all his limits. Muscular, massive, and almost stolid, yet so quick he has always beaten me at handball. At times, in fact, he might have taken me to bed.

The truth would appall him. He knows of course that we Smithwicks are creators, but it would never occur to him to capitalize the word. He has respect enough for all our generations, for old Adam and his son Darwin, for my father and myself, but I have never let him guess that we ourselves are the first successful human genotypes, our own first creations, more significant to history than *homo verus* or *homo mutatus* or *homo divinus*.

The gulf has grown too wide. For all his native genius, the drive I admire, and the emotion that moves me, he's still the raw human stuff, the unfinished work of random natural evolution. Still the victim of his unpurged animal inheritance. Still enslaved to the chaos that made him.

He wouldn't, couldn't, understand.

—Journal of Eva Smithwick:
fragment found in the ruins of her
laboratory on Creation Mesa

The null-G belt lifted them strongly at first, out of the desert scents of dust and sage and death, and a west wind carried them up and away from the muman deadeye lying lifeless on the rocky beach where she had trapped them, high into the noiseless night.

"They can't kill us now." Buglet turned in the belt, smiling in the moonlight, her body warm and strong against him. "We'll get there, Davey!"

"I hope so, Bug." He looked ahead at the far wink and gleam of the city domes, rose and gold along the dark blur of hills far beyond the black water. "I hope—"

"We don't dare fail!" Snuggled against him in the belt's loose curve, she buried his nose in her fragrant hair. "We'll be trumen now. We'll worship in the chapels of Thar and Bel and forget that we were ever premen."

"If—"

But he checked his protest, because she knew as well as he the power of the angered gods behind. They had fled the reservation, defied the church, killed their muman pursuer—three sins Belthar would not forgive. For each offense the penalty was death.

Though she felt delightful in his arms, the hazards ahead refused to be ignored. The truman town was still far off, and they would be blundering strangers there even if they reached it, their passports poorly forged, and the Thearchy always on their trail.

"Davey!" She twisted to kiss him lightly. "Don't brood. We're more than premen, I told you. We're Eva Smithwick's Fourth Creation. Made to master the gods."

"Our big problem." He grinned bleakly. "The gods don't want to be mastered."

"We are in danger," she murmured calmly in his ear. "But that's okay. I think we need danger to trigger the genetic gifts we never knew we had. When we're in danger again, I think you'll find the means to save us—the way you killed the deadeye."

But he hadn't killed the muman—he shivered a little, to that cold sudden certainty. Buglet did possess unknown genetic talents. Her awakening memories of the last Creator were proof enough of that. But he was only a young and untaught preman, his own danger yielding nothing better than the sweaty chill and the bitter taste of fear.

When he tried to recall any part on his own in the killing of the muman, all he found was blankness. If some unfolding genetic power had really turned the muman's exploding bolt back against itself, the gift belonged to Buglet, not to him. But he didn't try to tell her that, for fear of spoiling this good moment in the air.

Not so lightly, she kissed him again. Weightless in the belt, rising toward the moon, he began to feel a freedom and a peace he had never known. The Redrock reservation was gone behind them, with all its filth and pain. This high, bright silence had become their own special world, where he felt no possible peril could touch them.

"Davey—" Her sudden whisper broke the spell. "Can you see the city now?"

He squirmed in the belt to search the dim horizon. All he could see at first was flat black water and milk-white sky. When at last he found the city domes, their faint wink was far south of where it should have been.

"The wind," he muttered. "Changed, I'm afraid. Taking us north, back across the lake." He felt alarm tighten her body. "We'll climb again," he told her. "To look for a better wind."

Twisting the lift-control knob, he heard a tiny squeal.

Warning, the buckle's rat-voice squeaked. *Main power cell exhausted. Prepare for early descent on reserve cell.*

"So we fall?" Her voice was calm, but he felt her trembling. "Back into the lake?"

"Perhaps—" He cut back the lift to save power. "Perhaps the wind will change again."

But the wind had died. The lake became a dark uneven mirror, where the moon made a long silver track. The distant domes of the truman town blurred and vanished. By moonset, their feet were dragging icy water. Long before dawn they were deeply awash, numb and shivering but still in the belt, kept afloat by its last few pounds of lift.

Sunlight showed them a gray lake horizon, pierced by a single tall spike of rock. They toiled toward it, still helped a little by the dying belt. Late in the morning they limped and splashed up the boulder beach at the foot of a high sandstone cliff.

Davey snapped the power off. The dead belt fell to the rocks, and they dropped beside it, utterly drained as it was. He lay watching Buglet as they let the sun warm them, the torn clothing molded to her body, the wet hair black and sleek against her hollowed face. A pang of love and pity stabbed him.

"We're fine, Davey. Fine!" She saw his look and tried to smile. "I think this kind of danger is exactly what we need."

He felt too numb and dull to respond at all.

"This will be—be the test." Her yellow eyes looked heavy, and her voice had sunk to a whisper. "Our chance to prove—"

She was suddenly asleep.

Though he tried hard to keep alert, the sun was suddenly higher, hot on his face, and his whole body ached from the rocks where he had lain. He had been dreaming of a fall from the rim of Creation Mesa, back on the reservation, and for an instant, staring at the red cliff above, he thought the dream had been real.

Buglet lay beside him, sleeping as quietly as if the boulders had been a null-G bed. He sat up painfully to look around. The sun stood at noon. Southward, where they had left the dead muman, he saw glints of metal moving in the sky.

Skimmers—already searching.

In a moment of panic he groped for his knife and found it gone, lost somewhere in water or sky. His wet pockets were empty

47

of anything useful. Pausing for a moment over Buglet, he saw her smiling in her sleep as if all their cares were gone. A throb of pain caught his throat, and he stumbled away to search for some weapon, some tool, some spark of hope.

The islet had been a sandstone butte before the new flood rose, tall walls towering from slopes of broken stone. His circuit of it took him half the afternoon, scrambling from boulder to slippery boulder, wading across sunken blades and pits, swimming when he had to. Buglet limped to meet him when he came back.

"Davey! Where have you been?"

"Looking for anything." He sat down wearily on a wet stone bench and shaded his eyes to squint at the skimmers weaving back and forth across the southward sky. "Driftwood for a raft. A fish I could catch or a bird I might trap. A path we could climb to the top. Even a stick I could use for a club."

He spread his empty hands.

"You frightened me." Her tawny eyes turned almost black. "Leaving me alone. Of course I'm hungry—but hunger is part of the danger we need. Nothing can help us, Davey, unless we find ourselves. We must look inside, for the talents the Creators gave us."

"Gave you." With a weary shrug, he moved for her to sit beside him on the rock. "Not me, Bug."

"You too, Davey. I saw you reflect that firebolt to kill the deadeye. Even if you don't remember—"

"I think it's you who can't remember."

"Try, Davey. Try!" She leaned to look into his eyes. "I know you're desperate, but being desperate can help."

"Sorry, Bug. I don't know how to try."

"Just think back," she said. "Think back to the first things you can."

Her lean face was pink from sunburn and scratched from a fall, the red mark beaded with black drops of dried blood, but she was beautiful still. He did want the powers, the heritage that would put him in her special race, her equal and lover forever. If desperation could help—

"I remember when we were small." Trying hard, he looked beyond her into the brassy sky. "The time when the goddess came down to visit the reservation. When the halfgod Quelf made the deadeye kill our dog Spot because he ran a rat into the sacred procession.''

''A fine day for us.'' He liked the joy in her voice. ''Because the goddess was generous to us. But that's not what I mean. You must think back further.''

Frowning at the skimmers in the south, he tried again.

''My mother was a girl at La China's—that's what I first remember. I guess she was trying to care for me, but I didn't know it. She used to sleep all day. Sometimes at night she locked me in a hot little attic room over the bar. The lock was broken, and I learned to get out. I wanted to see what she did with the men.''

He grinned at Buglet, his sunburned lips cracked and painful.

''Most of them were friendly enough, if they noticed me at all, but there was a sheriff I hated. A fat short black hairy man they called El Corto. He always smelled like mescal, and he never left money for my mother. Sometimes he cursed her. Once, when he was drunk, he stabbed her—''

A shudder stopped him.

''No!'' He shook his head, staring at Buglet. ''I don't know why I thought that. But I did hate El Corto. Once he gave me too much mescal, and laughed at me when I fell down in my own vomit. When I was old enough—three maybe—I tried to get even. I had forgotten all of that.''

He caught a rasping breath.

''Now it comes back,'' he whispered. ''The morning I slipped into the bedroom—I was hungry and looking for something to eat. I found them asleep in bed together. The reek of mescal made me sick again. Crazy, I guess.

''El Corto's gun belt was hung with his clothes on the back of a chair. I tried to shoot him, but the gun was too heavy, and I didn't know how. When I tried to pull the trigger, it only made a click. He woke up and cursed and knocked the gun out of my hand.

''It went off when it struck the floor. The bullet tore my mother's face—that's what made the scar.'' He shivered. ''I remember my head ringing from the crash, and El Corto slapping me across the room, and my mother screaming that I was a little demon.

"Maybe I was." He shuddered again. "I hadn't meant to hurt her, but that scar was ragged and purple and awful. El Corto never came back. I guess nobody did. One night I heard her, drunk and screaming at La China. Next morning she was gone." He gulped at the ache in his throat. "I—I never saw her again."

"Don't blame yourself." Buglet bent to touch his hand. "I hadn't guessed—that must have been before you found me." For a moment she was silent. "But you'll have to look deeper." Her voice turned urgent. "Look for what the Creators gave us. Look for the latent memories of things before we were born."

"Sorry, Bug." He shook his head. "I have none."

"I do. So do you, if you can only find them." She leaned closer. "Mine were dim as dreams at first, but now they're real. Real as yesterday. I remember why we were made—to end the misrule of the gods. I remember why we were shaped to look like premen—to protect us from the gods. I remember why our time to wake has come—because all the premen are in danger, with the gods shipping the last of them away to die on Andoranda V.

"Davey, you've just got to think back!"

"I wish—wish I could." His eyes fell from hers, almost with guilt. "But I don't know how. It doesn't seem—natural."

"But it is." Her eyes went suddenly wider. Her voice seemed deeper when she went on, and the words not quite her own. "This insight just came to me. Memory is often innate, Davey. Most living things inherit all they need to know. Spiders spin their webs without being taught, beavers build their dams. We're the beings born blank, needing to learn everything. Actually, that blankness was a big evolutionary step, because it kept us individually flexible, able to adapt to new situations. But ancestral memory is an old device that Eva Smithwick revived to help us cope with the jealous gods." Her urgent eyes came back to him. "Those memories—those new talents—are hidden in you, Davey."

"Hidden too well." He moved uneasily on the sharp-edged rock. "I don't know how to search."

"You must learn." Her quivering hand grew tight on his. "It's the only chance we have."

They were trapped there all afternoon on the sun-broiled boulder-slide. He kept squinting with shaded eyes at the churchcraft in the sky. Twice, when flights of skimmers wheeled toward the islet, they slid into the water to hide.

If danger was really the necessary trigger, he thought, here was danger enough. Sitting face-to-face with Buglet, gripping her hands, looking into her amber-black eyes, he kept on trying to find latent recollections like her own. All he got was a hopeless frustration.

"They'll find us." Smarting with sunburn and giddy with hunger, he grinned at her ruefully. "They're already searching the edge of the lake. They've found the muman, and they'll know we took the belt. They won't give up—"

"Davey Dunahoo!"

A tiny doll-voice was squeaking behind him, so shrill and strange that he couldn't believe it was real.

"Jondarc!"

Gripping Buglet's hand, he caught his breath and turned to face a creature more remarkable than he had ever imagined.

Belgard was a twenty-mile chunk of tough nickel-iron. In the age of their lost greatness, the preman spacemen had slowed it with huge nuclear rockets, slung it first around Mars and then around the moon, steered it at last into Earth orbit. Mined with sun-powered lasers, its metal had built explorer starships at first and then battlecraft for defense against the returning trumen and mumen and their gods.

Taken from its last forlorn defenders and renamed to honor the new god of Earth, escorted now by Belfort in orbit ahead and Belkeep behind, it had become part of the fortress ring guarding the planet for Belthar himself. Warrior mumen of a hundred shapes and chemistries were bred and trained in its armored heart, and it was headquarters for the Earth god's space command, under Clone General Ironlaw.

The original genes of the clone commanders had come from a preman helper of the last Creator, and she had kept them in preman form because she found most of the variform military mutants too alien or sometimes too alarming for easy communication. In outward aspect Ironlaw was a sturdy, compact, gray-eyed man, alert and straight in his black-and-scarlet uniform. The call from Belthar found him in a vast interior cavern the miners had cut from the asteroid's core, reviewing a squadron of red-winged muman fighters flying in formation drill.

"Gen—General Ironlaw!" Not used to such errands, the muman chaplain was nervous and hoarse with awe. "The Lord Belthar requires your attendance at the Thar chapel. Private audience. Without delay, sir!"

"Thank you, chaplain."

Without haste, he congratulated and dismissed the squadron leader and took an elevator to the sacred level. The chaplain commander and two sacristans were waiting, visibly worried, and he followed them into the chapel.

It was empty and enormous. The high vault was a dark star-chart of the explored multiverse, alive with the shifting wink and shimmer of all the divine domains, aflash with bright-lined interstellar routes, alight with the color-coded coordinates of the contact planes between the involute universes. Belthar's altar was a tall black cylinder at the center of the shining floor, black and empty now. The preman churchmen knelt at the bench around it, bending their heads to the cold black granite, murmuring their rituals above their two-fingered signs of subjection to the dual aspects of the god.

At ease, Ironlaw waited behind them. No larger than a common truman, he had three times the weight and many times the strength. His mutant tissues were nearly indestructible. He knew that his clone clan was as old as Belthar, and he felt that the Creators had bestowed equal love and skill upon him. A warrior for Belthar, he was no worshipper.

The chaplain commander intoned a chant that rumbled dully back from the vault. Slowly, silently, the black central cylinder dissolved into a glittering mist that cleared to reveal Belthar. As if appalled by his splendor, the churchmen gasped their prayers and bumped their heads again.

In that gigantic living image, the god stood twice human height. Nude in his bright nimbus, red-bearded and golden-skinned, he thundered a blessing at the kneeling churchmen and lifted one hand in a gesture to dismiss them. As if relieved, they scurried out. He looked down at the muman general, who met his blue-blazing eyes and gave him a crisp salute.

"Reporting, Divinity."

"General, we have a task for you."

Ironlaw bowed slightly, waiting.

"We are concerned with an old preman myth that now appears to be more than a myth." Lower now, his voice still pealed back from the high dome and filled the empty transepts with rumbling echoes. "The legend of a demon race, bred by the last Creator in her tragic senility and let loose to disturb the reign of the lawful gods."

"I know the story." Ironlaw spoke with natural ease, almost as if the god had been a fellow clone. "But Eva Smithwick died a thousand years ago. I've never seen those demons, and your sacred reign is still secure."

"We mean to keep it secure." The god's voice crashed and boomed against the vault. "Our people have been instructed to extirpate that outrageous blasphemy since we first heard of it. The Thearchy has always loyally denied it, and over the centuries every outspoken believer has been burned alive.

"Yet the heresy persists. My good son Quelf discovered it among the surviving premen on his first visit to their reservation. Of course he found no admitted believers—they have become too cunning for that. But, under expert interrogation, many confessed that they had listened to rumors of a demon race—hiding here on Earth, perhaps among the premen themselves."

"So that's why they are being removed?"

"The final solution, when it is carried through." The nimbus brightened with divine satisfaction. "One privately suggested by Quelf himself. This will be the last preman generation."

Ironlaw nodded without expression. "I see no further problem."

"The plan, however, has run into trouble." The nimbus paled with Belthar's scowl. "Our son informs us that several premen have escaped, in spite of all his vigilance. He is most concerned about a young pair known as Davey Dunahoo and Jondarc. They derive from the vilest scum of the reservation, but they were clever enough to impress the pilot goddess, Zhondra Zhey, who induced the agent to take them into his home.

"Typical premen, they had no gratitude. When they learned about our plan, they robbed their friends and ran away. They were able to kill a muman guard who overtook them at the lake. Our son has been unable to track them beyond that point. He now reports that he feels impelled to withdraw most of his forces to guard his own person from their unknown powers.''

''Surprising.'' The general's cool gray eyes opened wider. ''Are you suggesting that these young premen are the legendary demons?''

''We suggest nothing.'' Belthar's voice crashed louder, and crimson flushed his nimbus. ''We simply order you to discover and destroy them.''

Ironlaw stiffened. ''Is that necessary? My own mission, based on these satellites, has always been space defense. The civilian church has always been able to keep order on Earth—''

Belthar cut him off. ''Our son suggested that you might object. At his suggestion—to free you for this most urgent mission—we are replacing you with your clone deputy. You will of course return to duty here as our space commander when those demons are dead.''

''I see, sir.'' He came to attention, with a dutiful salute. ''I'll undertake the mission.''

''We expect you to complete it.'' Belthar smiled, giant teeth gleaming through the nimbus like the fangs of some muman warrior. ''You will be in full command of the hunt, with authority to ask all aid from the Thearchy, the agency, and even the space command. Your deputy has already received his own instructions, and you will leave at once for Earth.''

His shuttle landed on the new field beneath the south towers of the Lord Quelf's enormous but unfinished palace on the mesa above the still-filling lake. In plain gray civilian garb, with due care to shake hands gently and to hide his quarter-ton of weight, he might have passed himself for a truman farm expert or factory manager.

Calling first at the palace, he was questioned and searched by an army of church officials and Quelf's police before they led him into the white marble throne room. He waited there an hour before the tall black halfgod came striding in with his muman guards and truman girls. Though a shocked sacristan was hissing instructions to kneel, he stood at attention to report.

"Military clone Ironlaw, at your command, sir."

"The required style is 'Your Benign Semi-Divinity,'" the sacristan whispered. "Your manner is offensive."

He stood fast, facing Quelf.

"My father says you're his best." Quelf eyed him critically. "No special excellence is evident to me, but you are here to find and kill those fugitive heretics. If you fail, I'll see that you never return to space."

"I understand."

Quelf's underlings were a little more civil. A bright-scaled military muman took him in a skimmer to follow the trail of the fugitives and inspect the point on the lakeshore where they had left their murdered pursuer.

The reservation agent and a fat Polarian monk showed him the tiny mud town of Redrock. Its single rutted street was empty now, its people already transferred to a camp at the shuttle field to wait for their removal to Andoranda V.

"There was heresy here," the monk announced. "We're uncovered an infidel chapel."

Grim with his own outrage, he led them down into a tiny cave dug beneath the floor of the abandoned trading center. The place had a stale reek of preman filth and preman death, and dark blood was drying over the torn pages of an old preman book lying on a cloth-covered box. Ironlaw bent to inspect a curious wood carving hung on the raw earth wall above the box, the image of a naked preman nailed to a cross.

"We found one heretic dead here," the plump monk said. "An old man known as El Yaqui, who owned the trading post. His knife in his heart. I suppose he didn't want to leave his small dead god."

"I never suspected him," the agent added. "Though I knew the fellow well. The last of his family, which the church had removed from a remote mountain valley. The last believer, I imagine, in his curious deity."

At the agent's mansion Ironlaw looked into the rooms where the fugitives had lived. Speaking to the family, he noticed the young son's apprehension. Under his inquiry the boy broke down, confessing tearfully that he had forged truman documents for the pair and aided their escape.

Abject now, fearful for his son, the agent told what he knew about the preman belief in a Fourth Creation. "A pathetic little legend," he finished. "But it's the reason our Lord Quelf wants those premen hunted down. Years ago I heard the boy threaten him with the Multiman. He was only a naked child, but furious because Quelf had killed his pet dog. If there is any real cause for Quelf's concern, it is the possibility that they found something in that dig on Creation Mesa. Something dangerous to him."

Ironlaw questioned the surgeons who had examined the dead muman. It had died an instant after firing a death-bolt from its crest. The autopsy showed that death was due to a similar bolt, as if its own firebolt had been reflected back against it by some cause they could not explain.

Its null-G belt was missing. He estimated the power that should have been left in its cells and called for weather records. There was only a slight possibility, he concluded, that the winds had carried the fugitives to the farther lakeshore; none that they had been lifted much beyond.

Visiting the truman settlements nearest the lake, he found no trace of new arrivals who might be the missing pair. He ordered their descriptions posted and returned to narrow the search.

"They're somewhere near," he told the armored officers of his gathering force. "We'll search the shore and the islands in the lake."

The creature stood perched on a high sandstone bench, peering down at them with a single bright green eye. Less than half human, it looked monstrous. Its arms and shoulders were immense, the lower body dwarfed, giant hands brushing doll's feet. Naked except for parti-colored fur, yellow-and-black, it seemed sexless. The head was pink and bald and babylike, the left eye squinted shut, white teeth flashing through an impish grin.

"What—" Davey stopped to gulp. "Who are you?"

"Call me Pipkin." Its shrill little bird-voice was grotesquely too fine and too high. "I mean you no harm."

Davey had stepped ahead of Buglet and stooped for a throwing rock, but after a moment he let it fall. He stood perplexed, looking for a boat or a skimmer or a path the creature could have followed down the cliffs.

"Well, Pipkin?" He thought it might resent his stare, but he felt fascinated by its utter strangeness. "What do you want?"

"This is my home." It beckoned toward the cliff. "I ask you to enter."

Following its gesture, he saw a passage into the fractured sandstone that he had somehow overlooked before. The opening was smoothly oval, twice the creature's height, the edges oddly bright.

"Why?" Buglet caught his hand, and he felt her trembling. "What will happen to us?"

"You are in danger here, and I don't want attention." It swept a huge yellow arm toward the wheeling skimmers in the south. "We'll all be safer inside."

Davey shook his head, frowning doubtfully.

"We must trust it," Buglet whispered. "Let's go in."

The creature stood aside, and they scrambled past it toward the entrance. As they came near, Davey felt an unexpected shift of weight and balance, as if he had been caught by a null-G field. He was lifted, drawn into the tunnel, swept a long way through it. Never touching the glowing wall, he was tossed out into the dank chill of a long cavern lined with rough concrete.

He stumbled when his weight came back; before he had got his balance, Buglet and the creature were floating down beside him. The blue shine faded from the tunnel walls behind them; a gray fog filled it; suddenly there was only a vanishing oval glow on the gray concrete.

"Nothing magical." Pipkin grinned at his gaping wonder. "A single effect of atomic rotation. The null-G belt rotates atoms beyond the reach of gravity. The passage is formed by another rotation, into transvolutionary space."

Still dazed, Davey stared around him. They stood on a long ramp in a pool of gray light that seemed to come from nowhere. Rusty metal rails ran along the ramp, and enormous broken concrete piers loomed beyond it, where he thought immense machines must once have been installed. He had a sense of vast unlit space above and beyond.

"An old fort," the creature was piping. "Built during the Preman Rebellion to protect Creation Mesa. Destroyed in the Space War, when the gods returned. Nuclear missiles were assembled and stored in this area.

"But come along."

Agile on tiny feet, it danced down the ramp. The patch of light followed, as if the creature itself were the source. Davey caught Buglet's hand and they hurried after it, breathless to keep ahead of the dark. Beyond a narrow passage they came into a smaller, brighter, cleaner chamber.

"A ready room, used by the defenders." The creature waved at metal seats and tables, at bunks on concrete shelves. "A temporary shelter for you. You'll find food and water through that door."

"This seemed too good—" Davey shivered. "We were trapped out there with nothing left to hope for." Frowning at the creature, he drew Buglet closer. "Please tell us who you are and what you want."

"Relax." With a bland baby-smile, it nodded at a hard steel bench. "I suppose you must be bewildered, but really I mean you no harm. Sit there, and I'll explain myself."

Uneasily, they sat.

"I'm a god—a botched god." With a startling show of power, it bounded off the floor and dropped lightly onto a tabletop before them. "A failed creation."

The fat pink face grinned wryly.

"Though the Creators were rebuilding their own genes from generation to generation, they never fully overcame their preman limitations. Sometimes they blundered. When old Huxley Smithwick set out to make the stargods, his first attempts went badly wrong. Most of them had to be destroyed—often in haste. I was more fortunate.

"He saved me for study at first, to find what he had done wrong. He soon discovered that I was too feeble to harm him, and I tried hard to persuade him that I might be useful, or at least amusing. I think he developed a certain liking for me. In the end, he kept me with him as a sort of court jester—though I was never good for anything, except sometimes to divert him from the cares of god-making.

"Certainly old Hux had troubles enough. That was an age of confusion, with the rebel premen trying to destroy the Creators and all the better beings they had made. He had grown up in hiding. When he escaped to space, carrying the seed for greater gods, I was left behind. I'm still here.

"My main defect is not the deformity you see." Pipkin raised the mighty arms and danced a quick pirouette to display the mismatched, bright-furred, sexless body. "It's lack of power. My perceptions are reasonably acute."

Facing them again, the creature lifted a thick finger to its squinted eye, which opened to show only blank whiteness.

"Though I'm half blind to common light, I can see and feel through the folds of the multiverse far enough—considering my size. Yet it took all my transvolutionary power just to rotate those few cubic meters of stone and bring you inside. The best of my meager abilities has always been required just to stay concealed and stay alive.

"A dismal life for a god!"

A god, Davey decided; he must be male—in his own mind, at least. His situation, as he put it, seemed bleak enough; yet the green, seeing eye had a sardonic glint, as if he ridiculed himself.

"For all these centuries I have been shut up here, a hapless spectator, observing the history of the multiverse. The expansion into space after space. The battles of the mumen against every sort of alien danger. Most amusing—though now and then depressing—the follies of the later gods." His laughter tinkled, a tiny bell. "Watching them, sometimes I feel fortunate."

Muscular gold-furred fingers gripped the table edge, he swung himself to sit there, regarding them shrewdly with his seeing eye.

Buglet gulped. "We do thank Your Divinity—"

"Call me Pipkin," he squeaked. "Just Pip, for short. Old Hux did. I'm no kin to His Benign Semi-Divinity, Quelf."

"Pipkin, then." She smiled uncertainly. "Can you really help us? Please!"

"No altruist." Curt with impatience, he made a face of pink distaste. "Can't afford to be. Might have pushed you off the rocks to drown, but I didn't want Quelf's people swarming over the island, looking for the bodies. You're still a problem for me."

"We didn't mean to be."

"All an accident." He shrugged, great shoulder muscles rippling beneath the fur. "Water getting into the lower levels. Out to look for leaks. Otherwise, might not have found you at all. Had been watching Quelf, of course—half my entertainment." Green eye closed, he raised himself on his hands, the tiny body swinging quickly back and forth.

Davey looked away and back again, still afraid his gaze might give offense.

"We—we're desperate." He showed his empty hands. "Quelf wants to ship us off to die on Andoranda V—or more likely kill us now for trying to get away—"

"I can't hide you here," Pipkin shrilled. "Not for long. Quelf's own dull underlings would never find us, but now he has brought in Belthar's space commander. A very able muman clone. I'll have to send you somewhere—"

"Before you decide, there's something we must—we must ask you." Buglet hesitated, as if unnerved by Pipkin's strangeness. "You see, I think we're more than preman."

Pipkin's swinging body froze.

"I think—I think we're Eva Smithwick's Fourth Creation. Lately, I've been getting memories I think she planted in us. If you were here—" She had to get her breath. "If you were here when she was, perhaps you know what we really are."

Pipkin's emerald eye blinked and stared again.

"We need to know," Davey begged. "To find ourselves."

"I was already in hiding, even then," Pipkin piped at last. "Eva never even guessed that I still existed. But of course I was observing her. I saw her discovering that the gods had been a blunder. Too much power, with too little love for the older creations. I watched her efforts to create the ultiman—"

"The Multiman?"

"A preman label." The baby-head nodded. "She was trying to design the ultimate man. A new being with all the power of the gods—perhaps with more—along with greater love for all the lesser folk. With wisdom and justice enough to rule his share of the multiverse."

Pipkin's laughter jingled.

"Eva was still half preman, really—only a preman would have dared what she did. She tried hard enough. Her problem was that the gods didn't want to be restrained or replaced by any better being. They didn't give her time."

"Do you think—" Pain caught Davey's throat. "Do you think we could really be ultimen? Buglet, anyhow?"

"If you were, you wouldn't need to ask." Pipkin shrugged. "Or perhaps you are, if you think you are. As for me, I could only guess."

"What would you guess?"

"I did watch Eva's desperate race to complete her last creation. I observed several schemes to conceal her new creature from the returning gods. One was to make it latent, hide it in the genes of the premen. Since I've met you, my guess would be that you do carry the ultiman in your genes."

"Then what can we do—"

"If you want another guess, all I can give you is the obvious." The lone green eye squinted quizzically at Buglet and back at Davey. "Perhaps your children will be ultimen—if you survive to bear them."

Davey caught Buglet's hand, felt her body sway against him. Emotion washed him—a sharp ache of longing and a wave of icy dread.

"That's all we hope for," she was saying. "We're trying to reach the truman lands. We hope to hide there, to live our lives as trumen."

"We have passports," Davey added. "To show that we are wandering laymen. Yedsong and Yedsguide, followers of the missionary teacher Yed—"

"Let me see."

Pipkin squinted at Davey's water-stained passport and shook his head.

"A childish forgery. It would only get you killed."

"So what can we do?" Davey looked at Buglet's anxious face and back at the imperfect god. "If we do have new powers, we need to find them now. To save our lives. Can't you—can't you help us discover what we are?"

"Only you can do that."

"But you will help?"

"I'm no friend of the great Lord Quelf." Pipkin grinned. "But I won't risk my own skin. I can't keep you here, though getting you safely away may tax my limited powers. I need time to work at the problem."

He swung from the table, dropped before them on his hands.

"While you're here, accept my hospitality."

He danced away on twinkling feet.

Whatever his powers, they found that he had somehow installed a modern robochef in the kitchen that adjoined the old ready room. They carried their loaded trays back to the table, but Davey felt almost too anxious to eat.

"What now?" he whispered.

"We must trust him." Buglet's eyes turned dark. "I feel sorry for him. Think how lonely he must be. The only one of his kind that ever existed, or ever will." Smiling solemnly, she reached for Davey's hand. "I hope he finds a place for us. A good place, where we can have children."

He leaned across the table to kiss her sun-cracked lips.

The robochef did not dispense the simple dishes they loved, the peppery meat and savory squash and roasted corn, but the truman food was good enough. They filled themselves, then climbed into the bunks. Wondering what fate the little god might find for them, Davey thought he ought to stay awake and watchful, but suddenly Buglet was shaking him out of a terrifying dream in which an insect swarm of flying Pipkins had been hunting them across an endless desert with hissing crimson firebolts.

"You must have been pretty desperate." She was almost laughing. "I thought you needed rescuing."

"Thanks, Bug." He sat up, shaking off the nightmare, and saw that she was wearing an odd gray coverall.

"Our old clothes are gone," she said. "Passports, too."

He put on the garment that had been left for him and tried to explore the rooms around them. All the passages he found were closed with heavy metal doors he couldn't open, most of them sealed with what looked like a thousand years of dust and rust.

"We're prisoners."

"Or guests." She smiled gravely. "Perhaps it's better if you think we're in danger. If might help you to discover yourself."

He sat with her for a long time, groping for some unconscious recollection that would make him part of Eva Smithwick's last creation.

"No use!" Angry at himself and almost at her, he stood up

to pace the narrow room. "Really, Bug, I think I'm just a common preman."

She wanted to try again, but he had no heart for another useless effort. They ate another meal. He went to listen at the metal doors, and heard no sound at all. He was lying in his bunk, half asleep again, when he heard Pipkin squeaking.

"I have done what I can." The dwarf god bounded to a table near them. "Dropped your clothing and passports on the west shore. Should divert Quelf's people to the dam and canyons around it. You'll be flying east. Null-G belt recharged. Promise you a strong west wind tonight."

"But," Davey said, "without passports—"

"Better passports, and a better story for you," Pipkin chittered hastily, as if anxious to be rid of them. "You are Trell Bluesea and Ven Hillstone. Truman students from a small colony in a frontier star system. Your god is Crethor, very junior, setting up his own domain. An actual god, by the way—distant relative of Belthar. His subjects still marginal survivors. No surplus time or wealth for education. You got your passports through friends in his harem. But don't talk about them—life on Kroong IV is so grim, you prefer to forget it. You are here to visit holy places and get an education. No funds. You'll have to work your way."

The green eye fixed them.

"Can you do it?"

"We can," Davey said.

"Envy your good cheer." Pipkin's baby-smile seemed wistful. "Doing the best I can for you. Passports will stand inspection. Good season for you—time when students often seek temporary jobs in the farming settlements beyond the lake. Have to warn you, however. No more help from me. Expect you'll have problems enough. Quelf's clone hunter will never give you up."

"Thank you, Pipkin!" Buglet whispered. "I know we can't repay you. But whatever happens we won't tell—"

"Need no promises." His small laugh jingled. "Because I take no chances. Blocks set in both your minds. Even under inquisition, you couldn't tell."

He gave them the recharged null-G belt and the new passports. A glowing oval on the wall of the ready room dissolved to open a blue-shining tunnel. Davey caught Buglet's hand, and they stepped toward it together. Glancing back to wave farewell to Pipkin, he saw the dwarf god spinning high in the air, clapping gold-furred hands. The field caught them, swept them through the tunnel, tossed them out onto broken sandstone. On the cliff behind, a luminous spot faded and vanished.

It was dusk above the lake, and a bracing wind blew out of the west.

Utopia Holy was named for a preman myth of the perfect state. A young tithing, it had been granted the arid western end of a dismembered preman wilderness that once had been part of the Redrock reservation. Its truman settlers were as industrious as ants, repairing the ravages of natural erosion and preman neglect for Belthar's glory and their own benefit. A survey team was staking out the route for a new irrigation canal across the north mesa on that hot Tenday afternoon when the two strangers climbed out of a rocky arroyo.

Scratched and sunburned, they were desperate with thirst. They looked young, the girl barely nubile, the boy not fully grown. Speaking Terran with a slight accent, they explained that they had been searching the mesa for a sacred place, a shrine built many centuries ago to mark the spot where the Creators made the gods. Finding nothing, they had been wandering for several days.

"You're really lost," the surveyor told them. He was Brother Lek, a vigorous brown muscular man, a lay expositor and a deacon in the tithing. "According to the legends, Creation Mesa is a long way west, out in the preman reservation. I've never heard of any shrine there—"

"We need water," the boy begged. "Please!"

"You'll have to wait a bit," Lek said. "We have work to finish—"

"The work can wait." Sister Yeva was his apprentice, a sturdy, well-tanned redhead. Lek had been her instructor in love as well as surveying, and in her awakened glow of total satisfaction she wanted no pain for anybody. "I'll bring up the skimmer."

He questioned them, somewhat critically, while she was gone. Looking legal enough, their passports carried visas from the Terran

Thearchy granting them the status of student guests with permission for an indeterminate visit.

"Can you help us find a place to stay?" the girl asked. "Kroong IV is a poor planet. Our money is gone, and we must find work."

Brother Lek had become suspicious of students asking for work at the tithing. Too many, in the past, had been worthless idlers; a few had even been exposed as secret scoffers at the eternal love of Bel and the infinite wisdom of Thar. These two, however, looked too young and too hungry to be professional vagrants; and the yellow-eyed girl was already budding into a very alluring maturity.

"We're willing," the boy was urging. "We don't know your ways, but you'll find us anxious to learn."

"You can ask to visit the tithing, or even for a probationary membership." Lek frowned at him sharply. "But we don't admit many. Our quotas are almost full."

Sister Yeva was landing the skimmer in the sharp-scented juniper near them. She came out with bottles of water and a basket they had brought for an after-work picnic. The two drank avidly, though the girl paused to apologize for their greed.

Leaving them with the basket in the shade of the skimmer, Lek and Yeva tramped back to their surveying. The two were asleep when they returned, but the boy sprang up as if in fright when he heard them snapping through the brush.

In the skimmer on their way back to the center Lek began asking about their lives on Kroong IV. Though the boy seemed uneasy and evasive, the girl answered with a wide-eyed candor.

"Kroong IV is a small planet. Too far from Kroong itself. Too cold and too dry and too poor in everything—even atmosphere. I wish Crethor could have found a better world. We want to forget everything that happened to us there, and I hope we never have to go back."

She smiled shyly at Lek.

"Won't you—Won't you let us stay here?"

"That's for the deacons to decide."

"But he's a deacon." Yeva giggled and nudged him intimately. "He'll help you."

The center capped a gentle hill in the older section of the tithing, among fruit-bearing trees and ripe grain fields laced with full canals. They landed on the paved square between the chapels of Bel and Thar, and Yeva waited with them in the skimmer while Lek went to speak to the rector.

The boy still seemed apprehensive, but the girl was asking eager questions about the buildings under the mirror domes around them, the dining halls and dormitories, the toolhouses and barns, the packing plants where the food products of the wide commons were processed for shipment, the hall of culture, and the sports complex.

"A good place." She nodded eagerly. "A kind and friendly place. I hope they let us stay."

"We're happy here." Yeva smiled complacently. "The land is bountiful when we bring water to it. I can't quite imagine why the old premen let it go to rock and dust and brush. Of course Belthar is good to us. A more generous god, I'm sure, than your Crethor was."

When Lek came back, he had permission for them to stay, at least until the deacons met. He gave them cards for work and food and shelter, and Yeva helped them find their quarters. On Tharday afternoon, with Yeva as a sponsor, they appeared before the deacons, and came away with the rector's blessing as probationary members of the tithing.

"You couldn't find a better place," Lek boasted that night in the dining hall. "I've seen the cities and studied in the great seminaries and worshipped in the holiest temples. I've even seen the living Belthar. There's no place like our tithing. We live on the good Earth and make it better. We feed ourselves with our own hands, with plenty for others. We have good air, wide space, and peace. We share one another, to Bel's delight. If we sometimes wish to touch a wider world, we have the learning center and the hall of culture. You'll love Utopia Holy."

"We're lucky—" The girl's voice was broken with emotion. "Very lucky to be here."

Lek nodded, as if in unspoken approval of her young loveliness.

"Sometimes," he went on casually, "I think of the premen who used to claim this land. You've seen the north mesa, the way they left it. Washed to dry ravines full of thorns and snakes and scorpions. Sometimes I try to imagine what sort of creatures they really were, how they lived, why they died.''

The boy's sunburned face set grimly, as if that picture pained him. Perhaps, Yeva thought, it reminded him too bitterly of his hardships on Kroong IV.

''Imagine the premen!'' Lek's lean brown face grimaced with disgust. ''Killer apes, pretending to be men. Actually killing one another often enough, if their own legends are true, in organized wars and private fights. Robbing one another, misruling one another, while they all rotted alive with a thousand vile diseases. Decaying of age from the moment of maturity. Wallowing in filth and ignorance and their own stupidity, worshipping whole galleries of fantastic gods they generally had to imagine.''

He stared at the uneasy boy, almost as if accusing him.

''Think of all that—and thank our Creators for the difference!''

''We're thankful.'' The girl spoke quickly, dark eyes fixed on the boy. ''To the Creators.'' She turned her luminous smile on Lek and Yeva. ''And to you—for finding room for us.''

For a time they seemed entirely delighted with life in the tithing. Cheerfully, they tried to master their unfamiliar tasks. Silent about themselves, they seemed alert to learn new ways and new customs. With the boy's quick readiness and the girl's warm charm, they began to win friends.

Yet they were always somehow detached and reserved. They had no time for games, not much even for the chapels. After meals and after work, they always hurried to the information center. As illiterate as premen at first, they were learning to read.

Their progress was remarkable, as if the primitive rigors of Kroong IV had left them famished for knowledge. With Lek for a teacher, or sometimes Yeva, they came to grasp the shifting gestalts as swiftly as premen used to scan their primitive print. Soon they were spending long nights at the center, devouring a strange array of texts.

Some of their choices puzzled Lek. Ignoring the basic works he suggested on the ethics of Bel and the philosophy of Thar, on the history of the Terran Thearchy, on the social organization and the economic management of the secular state, they turned instead to difficult studies of divine metaphysics.

''Be practical,'' Lek urged. ''These are revelations from the gods and the halfgods, made to guide the supreme thearchs. What do you care about the energy sources of the holy nimbus or the mechanics of multiversal perception or the processes of transvolutionary rotation?"

The boy looked tense, somehow disturbed.

"There's so much to learn," the girl whispered quickly. "So much we long to know."

"There are things you'll never know—never need to know." Lek smiled at the girl. "These are texts I never tried to read, because good scholars at the great seminaries told me that no truman could really master them. Actually, the multiverse is too complex for the truman brain to understand. There are sciences only the gods can learn."

"That must be true," the boy agreed, his expression oddly grim. "But we want to know all we can."

Their concern with current history seemed equally odd, because outside events seldom mattered to the tithing. Belthar had reigned a thousand years, and he would live forever. His consecrated servants had neither need nor fear of change. To its pious people, Utopia Holy was world enough.

"I know you're students, but you always seem overly anxious," Yeva protested, when she had seen them hovering too often over the flashers in the news section. "When you learn our ways, you'll be content here. You won't have time to fret about statistics on industrial production or Thearchy politics or the loves and hobbies of Belthar's sons. You'll never learn much about our Lord Belthar himself, because his affairs are not reported."

"It's the premen that trouble me." The boy frowned. "Their lands have been taken away. The last of them have been shipped to a far-off planet, where the newsmen say they can't have children. Since the Creators themselves were premen, that seems unfair—"

"Maybe we're wrong." The girl spoke quickly, with a sharp look at him. "We're still strangers here, with many things to learn."

"You'll learn not to question Belthar's will," Yeva told them gently. "Here on Earth he is our only god. If he has disposed of the premen, that's because they have no future place in his divine plan. When you learn Terran history, you'll find that they have always been wrong-headed rebels, always crazily unwilling to submit to the wisdom of Thar or to enjoy the love of Bel.''

She paused to smile at the boy, to eye the girl more thoughtfully.

"We like you both," she went on. "We want to keep you here, but sometimes you worry us. As Brother Lek says, you never seem to feel at home. If you wish to belong to the tithing— to belong truly, to share our happiness—you must learn that Utopia Holy offers everything you will ever need. You must cease to fret about those few surviving premen who still refuse to give their hearts to Belthar.''

"We're trying," the girl whispered. "Trying hard."

Yet in spite of such kind advice they kept searching the flashers for reports of outside events and kept struggling over difficult works of holy metaphysics, with never a sign that they were finding anything that pleased them.

They were alone in the information center one Belseve, screening a lecture on the mathematics of the multiverse, when Lek and Yeva dashed in, laughing, their clean brown bodies fragrant with the garlands of Bel and already aglow with excitement.

"Wake up!" Lek shouted at them. "You don't need any seminarian professor to teach the rites of love. Tonight belongs to Bel. Come along with us. Wash away your worries and let Yeva weave your flowers. She has a blessed gift for that.''

Silently, they looked at each other.

"Do come!" Beaming at them, Yeva clung to Lek. "To the chapel, first. You've never seen such flowers. You've never lived till you learn the joys of Bel.''

"Thanks," the boy muttered. "But not tonight."

"We're students, remember," the girl added. "With too much to learn." Almost frowning, she showed no hint of Bel's ecstasy in the anointed flesh their garlands revealed. "Our god was Crethor," she said. "His rituals were different."

"Perhaps." Lek shrugged impatiently at the shimmering screen. "But now you're students here. I'm afraid you aren't learning what you should.''

Uncomfortably, the boy stopped the lecture.

"Aren't you happy here?" Suddenly serious, Yeva left Lek's arms to sit beside them. "Can't you settle into our ways?"

"We try," the boy said.

"It isn't easy." The girl dropped her eyes to avoid Lek's eager gaze. "Please—please give us time."

Yeva felt hurt. "Haven't we been good to you?"

"Too good." The girl smiled uncertainly. "Maybe that's the trouble. Everybody is just too nice. Life is too simple, too easy. The land is generous and you are kind. We are used to something else, back—back on Kroong IV. We always had the unexpected, and generally it was bad. Disasters, injuries, illness, disappointments, quarrels—"

"If you're bored, we have a beautiful cure." With a wide brown grin at Yeva, Lek freed a rope of woven flowers from his waist and flung it around the girl. "I think you need the blessing of Bel." He tugged her toward him. "We have always suspected that, and Yeva has been hoping we might exchange soon—"

With a startled gasp, the girl broke the rope and twisted out of his reaching arm.

"Don't you touch her." The boy sprang between them, pale and trembling. "Don't—"

"We want to be friends," the girl whispered. "But not—not lovers."

Half vexed and half apologetic, Lek made them sit again while he explained the customs of Belseve, when the god ordained the open sharing of love and the free exchange of partners. White-faced and tight-voiced, the boy confessed that they were still virgins.

"We want to marry," the girl added. "We want children, when we have a safe home for them."

"Marry?" Lek frowned. "Isn't that a preman term?"

"Marriage was a tradition of our people," she insisted quickly. "Out on Kroong IV."

"Not here," Lek said. "If your colony had genetic damage, I can see a reason for rejecting partners. But we've none here. Thanks to the Creators, our truman genes carry no defects. When the Thearchy allows us another birth, the women gather in the chapel to let Bel select the mother. Though we honor her, the child belongs to all the tithing."

"I'm sorry," the boy said. "But we aren't used to that."

"I want his child." Their hands clung hard together. "No other."

Lek scowled with outraged piety.

"You have no quota for a child," he warned them sternly. "With such ideas you'll never get one."

"I hope you see what fools you are." Impulsively, Yeva flung her arms around the boy. "You're missing too much!"

"Please." Awkwardly, he pulled away. "We have each other."

Giggling at him, she whirled back into Lek's embrace, and they hurried off to the chapel.

Before the next Belseve a large church skimmer dropped into the square. The district bishop came down the gangway, with his personal curate and a compact man in secular gray who identified himself as an inspector from the tithe office. The rector rushed out to meet them and found they had no time for ceremony.

Without saying why, the inspector wanted to visit the information center. The flustered rector escorted him into the dome and watched him scan the bulletin screens and dig through the documentary files and question the frightened librarians. He failed to find what he was looking for.

"This should have been here." He produced a holographic notice. "Please post it at once."

The notice pictured and described two young premen, fugitives from the Redrock reservation and the justice of Belthar, now under penalty of death.

"They're here." Peering at the holograms, the rector turned pale. "Our student probationers." His nose lifted righteously. "They have been claiming that they learned their strange ways on some outlandish planet they call Kroong IV, but I always suspected that they were secret infidels."

Davey and Buglet were helping run the new canal across the north mesa on that hot Huxday, she carrying a flag to guide the ditcher, he breaking rocks ahead of its cleats with a heat-gun. The work was heavy, but they had volunteered in hope of keeping their welcome in Utopia Holy.

71

Sweating from the sun and the radiation from fragments of incandescent rock, Davey was in a downcast mood. Try as they would to conform, he knew they would never be trumen. Even if they were somehow allowed to stay on at the tithing, they would never get permission for a child.

All their study had failed to unlock the latent powers Buglet hoped for. The physics of the multiverse remained a baffling mystery, the symbols for its transvolutionary forces no more than perplexing riddles. With all his groping effort, he had found no way to sense or seize even a single atomic particle beyond the limits of their own narrow space and time.

With Brother Lek in the air-conditioned cab, the huge machine kept too close behind him, gulping brush and soil and stone, excreting smoking yellow concrete to line the channel. He was clumsy in the stiff safety suit, half blind with the sweat in his eyes. A little light-headed from fatigue and the hot sulphur-reek that drifted from the roaring mass-converter, he was longing for water and lunch and rest, and he couldn't help a crushing sense that nothing mattered.

Sooner or later they would be expelled from the tithing, with nowhere else to go. Some church official, searching the sacred data banks for records of Trell Bluesea and Ven Hillstone, would find that no such students had ever arrived from Kroong IV—

A shadow flickered across him. He shut off the laser and pushed up his thick goggles in time to see a big skimmer overhead. Sunlight glanced on the linked triangles of the Thearchy as it slid down into a juniper clump beside the ditcher.

A short gangway dropped, a giant muman fighter bounding down it. Another followed, then a third. An agile man in secular gray darted after them. Two of the red-scaled warriors plunged at Davey, crest lenses burning. The third went leaping after Buglet, pale pathseeker shafts hissing out of its killer eye.

Trying to see, Davey blinked at the stinging sweat and wiped his face with the back of a heavy glove. The great steel cleats of the ditcher loomed over him and abruptly froze, as Lek stopped the machine. In the ringing stillness, he heard a sharp report, saw an exploding firebolt shatter the staff of Buglet's flag.

He started toward her.

"Stop!" Moving with unbelievable speed, the gray man was already before him. "In Belthar's name you are under restraint."

He stood clutching the heavy laser, shivering to a nightmare sense of disaster too sudden and too vast to be escaped.

"You're a preman?" The gray man's voice was sternly chilling, oddly quiet. "A fugitive from the Redrock reservation and the laws of the Thearchy? Known as Davey Dunahoo?"

"I—" He tried to get his breath. "I am."

"Your companion with the flag? The fugitive female preman known as Jondarc?"

Helpless, he could only nod.

Sister Yeva came dashing toward him out of the skimmer. He watched with a faint spark of hope, till she recoiled from him with a gasp of terror and ran wildly past him toward the ditcher, screeching something at Lek.

"Drop that tool," the quiet man commanded. "Stand where you are—"

He was trying to think. The safety suit might shield him briefly, and the laser's ray was almost as deadly as the mumen's hissing firebolts. He tossed his head to snap the goggles back into place and crouched to grip the gun.

Almost too fast for him to see, the gray man came at him. The instant flash of the nearest muman's lens flickered faintly through the goggles. Near thunder cracked, and a stunning shock hit him through the heavy fabric. Dazed with pain, he lurched forward and tried to lift the laser, to slice at the gray man's belly.

But the gun was gone, torn out of his stinging fingers before he could move it, his gloves and goggles missing with it. Hot rock fragments showered him, shattered by his own heat-ray. He stood breathless and blinking in the sunlight, watching the gray man's hands. As if the heavy laser had been something shaped from soft clay, they were twisting it into a metal knot.

"I am Clone General Ironlaw." Almost absently, the gray man tossed the bent metal back into the new canal. "Acting as a special agent for our Lord Belthar. My orders are to recapture you two premen. I prefer to take you alive—if you can display some degree of human reason."

Choking in the bitter smoke from the rock and brush his ray

had struck, Davey stood still. The two mumen moved closer, one on either side, towering tall above him, sunlight glancing on ruby armor and long black talons.

"Won't you bargain?" Ironlaw might have been a shrewd truman trader back on the reservation, offering to barter some glittering trinket for an ancient piece of preman art. "Will you name your accomplices? The criminals who forged your false documents and kept the news of your escape from reaching—"

"Tell him!" Lek came stumbling from the ditcher, hoarse and pale with terror. "For Bel's sake, tell him we are innocent. Tell him we were tricked—"

"Quiet!"

Though Ironlaw had not raised his voice, Lek staggered back to Yeva.

"They are innocent." Davey wet his sweat-salt lips. "They were our first friends here, but they had no reason to think we were premen."

"I was hoping you could be human." Ironlaw nodded with emotionless approval. "Now, the names of those who did assist you. In return, I'll try to save your lives. That may not be possible, but at least I can help you avoid an unpleasant inquisition."

He stepped abruptly closer, shattering a rock beneath his boot.

"Now I need names."

"Nobody helped us." Only half aware that he was lying, Davey felt astonished at his own readiness. "I think you underestimate our abilities."

The words weren't quite his own, and somehow he thought of Pipkin as he spoke them. In his oddly vivid image of bright fur and doll's feet and giant fists, the botched god was dancing in the air, grinning gleefully. That fleeting recollection brought him an instant of good cheer, but then he could not recall its cause. Dark despair fell back upon him, as cruel as the muman's bolt. The savage sun felt hotter, and the safety suit weighed him down.

"Don't stall," Ironlaw was urging. "Don't try any stupid preman tricks. My bargain is your only chance—"

Twigs crackled, and he turned his head enough to see Buglet beside him, the third muman looming behind her. Strangely, her face reflected none of his dismay.

"We're okay, Davey!" Somehow she was smiling. "This could be just what we need—"

"Silence." Ironlaw's voice lifted slightly. "Or name your allies."

"We don't need allies." Her eyes flashed golden. "You can't touch us. Remember what happened to that muman at the lake."

Listening to the ring of her untroubled tone, seeing the unquenchable light in her eyes, Davey found an unexpected resolution. A tremor of astonishment washed over him and left him with something of her supernal calm.

"Let's go!" he whispered to her. "Let's take the skimmer."

"Go!"

They ducked and plunged. One on either side of Ironlaw, they dashed between the mumen toward the skimmer. Davey had no actual plan, but he thought they should have at least an instant of safety, until the mumen could fire their bolts without striking one another. Though he had no actual hope, they had nothing left to lose.

Time slowed. Hampered by the safety suit, his limbs seemed frozen. He caught one long breath and took three laborious steps. His back tingled, as if he could feel the pathseekers already stabbing.

"Kill!"

Ironlaw's short command hung in the motionless air, stretched by his altered sense of time, fading as slowly as the tone of a temple gong. Buglet had edged a little ahead of him now, and he saw the pathseekers probing past her, thin streaks of violet rain. Their sharp lightning scent edged the air.

The firebolts followed, their thunder strangely muted. Somehow they failed to follow the ionized tracks. Something caught them, curved them, hurled them back at the mumen. The far crashing ceased. He heard a gasp, a curse, a moan. Suddenly, stillness.

Swinging his heavy boot another slow step forward, he twisted against the cramping fabric to glance back. He saw the three mumen almost frozen, but sagging visibly toward the rocks like red wax figures too long in the sun.

Ironlaw burst from among them, oddly unslowed. His gray cape was whipped back by the wind of his motion, his driving boots digging deep pits into the soil, raising lazy puffs of yellow dust. His strength and speed were more than muman, and Davey thought they could never evade him.

But Buglet too was looking back. For one unending instant she didn't move at all. The sun's blaze grew brighter around her, as if caught by smoke or dust, bathing her in a momentary halo. A sudden tongue of bright haze licked out of that, wavered, thickened, struck like a shining snake at Ironlaw.

In an instant that glow was gone, as fleeting as something imagined. Alive again, Buglet ran on toward the gangway. Following, Davey fought like a swimmer in some thick fluid to take each step. He heard Ironlaw's breath rush out behind him, the gasp thinning and stretching into a dying sigh.

Glancing back, he saw the clone's stern scowl relaxing, saw him leaning low, legs deliberately folding. A long time falling, like some toppled tower, he came down at last face first into the sharp-scented juniper.

Time was crawling faster before they reached the skimmer. Buglet paused on the gangway, looking back at him, yellow eyes wide and bright with elation. Her serene smile chilled him.

For she was a goddess—greater than a goddess. That glowing halo had been a holy nimbus. She had struck Ironlaw down with some transvolutionary power, something even more appalling than the unseen force she had used to turn those burning firebolts back against the mumen.

"Come on, Davey!" she was calling. "Quick!"

But he stood frozen. She was the actual ultiman, he a frightened preman. She had found command of energies from the greater multiverse that he could never hope to grasp or understand. All their love could never bridge the gulf he felt between them. When she reached the fullness of her power, she wouldn't need him—

"Bug!"

He gasped his warning, pointed at the door behind her. A fourth huge muman was lurching out of the skimmer, crest lens bright. Its hot pathseekers ranged around her. One struck his arm, stinging through the suit. Yet she kept on smiling, as if—as if she didn't care.

Dazed, he watched the muman strike. The bolt made a streak

of deadly fire, aimed at her unprotected back. Yet, though she seemed unaware, it arced upward, hissed above his head, hooked back, exploded like ball lightning against the muman's scales.

With a bubbling wheeze the warrior swayed backward. Black talons ripped the air. Great fangs grinning, it toppled off the gangway to mingle its piñon scent with the odor of broken juniper.

"It was the last." Buglet beckoned him on. "We're safe—at least for now."

He stumbled past her into the skimmer. Dazzled from the glare outside, he peered around the gloomy cabin at the racks of unfamiliar weapons, the huge seats the mumen had used, the barred cage behind them.

When he could see, he rushed to the controls. Bafflement checked him. He had watched Yeva fly her smaller craft, had even been allowed to sit at the instruments while it lifted and landed itself, but here were too many knobs and dials and shifting gestalts that he didn't understand.

"What now, Davey?" Buglet had paused behind him. "Where can we go?"

Trying to grapple with all his own perplexities, he sat looking at Lek and Yeva, who were moving like two agitated ants. They had darted to the fallen mumen, darted back to bend over Ironlaw. Now they were dashing back to the ditcher. They would call the information center, and soon all the might of the angry Thearchy would be descending here.

"I don't know." He looked back at Buglet. "There must be—somewhere!"

"Belthar owns the planet." Her elation had begun to fade. "His people will know we're something more than premen now. They will hunt us everywhere."

"If we can fly the skimmer—" He caught his breath and groped for hope. "Let's—let's go back to Pipkin's island. Maybe sink the skimmer off the beach, to get it out of sight. Swim back to the rocks. If he's still watching, maybe he'll help—"

Her grave look stopped him.

"Once is all." For a few seconds she stood silent, and he saw something change her. Her lemon eyes lit, and she smiled again. She seemed taller—strong and proud and lovely. A chill of dread caught him again, because she was suddenly unearthly.

"Do you know—" His dry throat caught. "Do you know a place where we can hide?"

She shook her head.

"Listen, Davey!" Her low voice rang with a timber he had never heard. "We've been acting like idiots—or premen, maybe. That won't do. Even if we could find another tithing where we could hide among the trumen—or even if we really could persuade Pipkin to open up his rock and take us in again—that's not what we need."

Listening, he shivered a little.

"We're still premen," she said. "At least until we know what we really are. We're all through with hiding and trying to be trumen. We belong with our own people, out on Andoranda V. We must give up, Davey, and let them take us there."

"They wouldn't, Bug." Hoarse with dread, he gulped again to get his voice. "You know they wouldn't. Just think of all they have against us now." He gestured at the bodies sprawled outside. "They—they'll kill us, Bug!"

"I don't think they can." Her eyes blazed. "I think we've just proved that. I suppose we'll have to prove it again—and still again. But in the end I think they'll be glad to ship us on to join our people."

Trembling, he tried to get his breath.

"I'm afraid, Bug," he whispered. "Terribly afraid."

"So was I." Her face was strangely serene, and her voice began to lift him. "But now I'm sure. We're the true ultimen, Davey. Our children may be greater than we are, but I think we'll find powers enough of our own. We're going to beat the gods!"

THREE: KINSMAN
TO LIZARDS

"Sometimes I wonder..."

My father used to say that and stop, as if overcome by bleak foreboding. A huge pink silent man, he was already far from the common human norm. Most of his associates feared him, and my own devotion was mixed with awe. I think he was haunted by a sense of his own strangeness; once I heard him call himself a genetic experiment skating on the edge of failure.

Slow in body and even in mind, he made up with his inhuman routine. One hour for food, one for sleep, one for me. Twenty-one for genetic creation. The sleep came in four brief naps, after his simple meals. I always looked forward to the hour with me, which began precisely at midnight, when my own day was over and his next had just begun.

He would come into my lab section, moving with a soundless bearlike grace. Too intense to sit, he would roam with me about the room, sipping just one beer and listening while I spoke about my work. He was nearly always cheerful, and his brief comments were often brilliant hints for new research.

Sometimes, however, events had refused to fit his iron

schedule. Expensive equipment had broken down, or an assistant had made some human blunder, or nature had thrown him some stunning surprise. He was more talkative then, sometimes moody. He asked for another beer. Now and then he even outstayed his hour.

"We can't be sure..."

I can see him now, frowning as he shook his head. Almost an albino, with long silky white hair and beard, he wore dark bubble-shaped glasses to guard his eyes. In such black moods, he was almost frightening.

"We're only pawns, boy. You and I. In a game we never asked to join. We can only guess the rules, and we'll never live to see the winners—or even see if anybody wins. I guess it's still exciting to you, but sometimes I wish we didn't have to play.

"I don't know, boy..."

At such times I felt terribly alone, terribly sad for him. He was already old—a Creator must spend most of his life learning how to make a better being than himself. More than once my eyes stung with tears for him, but I never told him how deeply I loved him.

"Our job is building angels," he used to say. "Angels out of jungle stuff. That's our problem, boy. For all our skill with genetic engineering, we're still kin to the ape and the hawk and the lizard. Our best creations carry the taint of that ancestry. I'm afraid they always will."

When I tried to cheer him up, he bluntly cut me off.

"I know you're brighter than I am, boy. Your own son will be a new creation, abler still. But don't you get too cocky." His huge bubble eyes stared away into the gloomy space of the lab. "There were big lizards once that thought they owned the Earth."

—From an unfinished essay found in the papers of Darwin Smithwick

The old preman town of Redrock was a tiny island now, its one crooked street sloping from the empty agency mansion down past the twin chapels and the jail to the ragged row of abandoned mud huts crumbling into the rising lake. An attack class Inquisition skimmer floated low over the weed-clotted plaza, watching the muman guards who watched the jail.

Inside, Davey Dunahoo sat on a concrete bench. His head hurt and his dry mouth had a queer bitter taste. At first his sticky-feeling eyes were blurred, but he knew the stale foul reek, and soon he could see the words of hope and lust and hate that other premen long ago had scratched into the rough concrete.

He knew the cell, because one winter a friendly preman jailor had let him and Buglet sleep here when snow had fallen on the reservation and they had nowhere else to go. But the other bench was empty now and nobody answered when his swollen throat croaked her name.

A surge of panic swept him to the door. He rattled the bars and tried again to shout. When he stopped to listen, all he could hear was a hollow emptiness. He was alone in the jail.

Knees wobbling, he swayed around the narrow cell. Old concrete, patterned with the knots and grain of the planks into which it had been poured. Yellowed whitewash and splattered grime. Three odd crosses scratched above a curve that looked like the crest of a hill.

The peeling whitewash felt cold and greasy to his testing fingers. Nothing yielded anywhere. He caught a sobbing breath and kicked the wall, slammed his fist against it. There was no way out, unless for a god.

If he were Pipkin, the wisful thought struck him, he could dissolve concrete and steel. Spin the atoms out of space, however it was done. Step through solid substance into freedom. But he wasn't Pipkin—and didn't really want to be.

With a grimace of pity for that small botched godlet, he shook off the useless thought. His head swam and that sour bitterness was sharper in his mouth. Cold with sweat, he sank back on to the bench and tried to think why he was here.

Memory came, at first in shreds. The god's decree that every preman must be shipped outside the universe to die on Andoranda V. His own escape with Buglet from the reservation. The truman commune, its life too easy, too happy, too empty. The battle on the mesa, when the clone general tried to recapture them. The muman fighters lying sprawled on the desert where Buglet had killed them—or somehow used her half-known transvolutionary gifts to make them kill themselves.

"Bug!"

Her image was suddenly so sharp in his mind that he called her name. Dark hair flying. Lemon-colored eyes wide and bright. The sunlit dust blazing like a halo around her as she reached out one empty hand and somehow toppled the general into the brush.

When the stunned clone revived, they had told him they were giving up on condition of safe passage to Andoranda V. He had refused to grant any conditions, had made them wait until a black-clad Inquisition prelate arrived.

Pale-faced, the Inquisitor had stared in unbelief at the red sun-glitter on the scales of the dead mumen and cringed in dread from Buglet's eyes, shrinking back among the blue-robed sacristans who had followed him off the skimmer.

"You stand accused—accused of mortal heresy." Having trouble with his voice, he looked at Ironlaw as if for aid. The shaken general shrugged. Peering back at Buglet, the prelate gulped and wet his lips. "Belthar is merciful," he rasped. "We grant you his grace."

At his command, the nearest sacristan had thrust an odd little gun at Buglet's temple. Davey sprang to snatch it away, but she waved him silently back.

"A godsgrace gun," the general said. "It will not kill."

It clicked and came away, leaving a black triangular patch where the muzzle had touched her skin. His nostrils stung from a whiff of sour bitterness. He saw Buglet turning white, falling into the arms of another sacristan. The gun jabbed his own cheek and he heard another click.

All that seemed only a moment ago. Sitting now on the naked concrete, he fingered his cheek and found the slick patch. When he peeled it off, its bitter reek burned his eyes. Shivering, he flung it through the bars.

"Bug?" he gasped again. "What has become of you?"

Most of the bold hope that nerved their rebellion had belonged to her; it was she, not he, who had defeated their captors and then had chosen to risk surrender. If his own genes carried any latent talents, they were latent still. Without her he was naked, and he felt a raw fear for her.

Goaded by it, he swayed half to his feet and sank limply back. His head throbbed and spun when he moved, and the bitter scent of godsgrace seemed suffocating. Chilled by his own sweat, he pulled his trembling knees up against his cheek and tried to imagine where Buglet could have been taken.

To the transvolutionary ship, as the Inquisitor had promised, for exile to Andoranda V? The ship would be out in orbit, waiting for the shuttle to lift from the new field beyond the Lord Quelf's castle. If it were the last ship, if the Inquisition had taken her and left him behind, they might never meet again.

He pictured that barren planet, as he had seen it on truman wallscreens. Naked granite cliff and peak where no life had ever been. Bright red mud-plains, turning orange as they dried. Dunes of dull brown dust. Wild rivers feeding blood-colored floods.

He recalled the abandoned terraforming station as a truman gestalt book had showed it, the narrow shuttle strip blasted into the side of a dark granite knob, the tiny huddle of rusting huts.

Nothing moved there. Nothing lived. No recent shuttle skids had cut the dust-stained snow, and he couldn't see where the premen had been landed.

The yellow sky was darkner now than he recalled it from the wallscreens, and a long squall line was rolling down across the river bend, hiding the black blades of an old lava flow. Shifting winds stirred yellow sand. He heard thunder crashing in the boiling cloud, smelled salt dust, shivered in the sudden gusts that howled around the huts. In a moment all he could see was angry lightning stabbing through the dust.

How long could the exiles survive there?

If Buglet—

Startled, he pulled his mind away. A shock of awe took his breath. In some manner that he couldn't understand, his dim old images of that remote planet had become vivid actuality. The gods, he knew, claimed powers of parasensory perception. Belthar's priests were always warning that he could watch malefactors all around the Earth, though Davey had never been sure of that. He doubted now that Belthar himself could see Andoranda V from Earth.

A wild elation swept over him, and cold terror shook him. He needed Buglet desperately. She had promised him that their unfolding gifts would make them greater than the gods. This incredible perception was evidence of some new power, but he had no notion of its dimensions or its limits, no idea how to use it. Only one thing was certain; if the Inquisition knew he possessed it, he would never leave the jail.

Quivering with that conflict of fear and hope, he tried to get the vision back. Sitting in just the same position on the concrete shelf, he pulled his knees hard against his chest, stared at the same obscenity scrawled on the wall, tried to imagine that dead waste-world again, exactly as he had before.

But he didn't know how. The gritty reality of that brief glimpse was gone, and no effort brought it back. He groped again for those snow-banked huts, for the choking odor of the yellow dust-cloud, for the chill of the wind and the crack of thunder, but nothing happened. His recollections swam and danced and dimmed, until at last he gave up.

The dull throb behind his forehead had become a crashing

drum. He felt weak and giddy, exhausted by his efforts. Leaning back against the cold concrete, he wondered for a moment if the vision had been only a dream induced by the godsgrace drug, but his sense of its truth was too strong to be denied.

What had turned it on? Buglet's notion came back—that danger was the key. He nodded uncertainly. Perhaps his own uncertain predicament and his fears for her had been the stimulus. And perhaps it had been his own elated emotion that had turned it off. Was that paradox—or simple contradiction? He had too much to learn.

He hoped for more control when the drug wore off. It was still bitter on his crusted tongue, and his head still swam when he moved. He was leaning back against the concrete, sunk in his troubled apathy, when steel clanged. Heavy footfalls echoed along the corridor. The cell door clattered, and he looked up to see a muman guard at the wicket. A startled recognition brought him upright.

"Lenya!" The hoarse shout hurt his throat. "Lenya K."

Too huge for the preman building, the sleek-scaled warrior had crouched to see him through the bars. With savage talons awkward for the task, she was pushing a dish through the wicket. Her bright black seeing eyes watched him with emotionless alertness; her killing eye, immense in its dark-armored crest, glowed deadly red.

He stumbled toward her.

"I do know you." He peered at the long orange stripe across her frontal armor where once a laser had slashed her and the scales had grown back paler. "We're old friends, remember? You used to guard the agent's house when he was afraid of preman riots, remember? Riots against the Lord Quelf's recreation lake when it began to flood their fields. Remember?"

Her killing eye brightened, ready to fire.

"Bug and I used to live at the agent's house, remember?" He clutched the bars with his sweaty hands, begging desperately. "We used to bring you goodies out of the kitchen. One day you gave Bug a ride with your null-G belt. Don't you remember?"

She slammed the wicket shut.

"What have they done with Bug? Her name is Jondarc now—"

Nothing melted the frozen ferocity of the muman's facial armor. An unfeeling fighting machine, she turned and stalked away, leaving only her pinelike scent and the little dish inside the wicket.

Clinging weakly to the bars, he listened to the receding thud of her footfalls. He heard the muffled clash of one steel door, then another. The echoes died. The jail was still. Again he was alone.

Yielding to the drug's aftermath, he sagged back onto the bench and sat staring at a dull brown spatter where some forgotten prisoner must have bled against the wall. With no appetite for whatever the guard had left, he let his hazy brain drift back to Buglet.

To their flight from Redrock. The battle by the lake. The way she felt against him, so light and warm and wonderful, when they were flying on with the muman's null-G belt. Her bright courage that had helped them go on to Pipkin's island after the belt had failed.

The islet would be even smaller now, he thought, with the lake still rising. A drowned sandstone butte, it looked desolate at dusk. The boulder beach where they had struggled ashore was now submerged, and dark waves broke against the cliff where the little god had come out through solid rock to meet them.

Something drew him to another oval spot, higher up the cliff, which had begun to glow. He watched rough stone swiftly dissolving to open a smooth-walled tunnel. A black-and-yellow blur, Pipkin came flying out, to hover and perch like a bird on a wave-splashed ledge. Both his big hands clutched it, his blighted feet hanging free.

"Dunahoo?" The waspish drone of his voice rose sharply, and his one-eyed stare became a frown. "How did you get here?"

"I don't—don't quite know." Davey hesitated, afraid to be glad, afraid of anything that might break this unexpected contact. "But you were good to us before. We need help again."

"You were not to come back." The lone green eye squinted forbiddingly. "I don't want you here."

"We—we couldn't stand the trumen." Too much feeling shook his voice, unbelieving hope mixed with fear of all he didn't understand. "The Inquisition caught us. I don't know what became of Bug, but I'm in the Redrock jail."

"The best place for you."

"You're our friend. Buglet's, anyhow." He paused, trying to quiet his disturbed emotion before it killed the vision. "You've just got to help me help her. Can't you—please!—teach me how to move through rocks and walls the way you do?"

"Can you learn?" The green eye blinked sardonically. "Can a frog learn to fly?"

The young goddess threaded her transvolutionary vessel out of multispace and slid it into a low Earth orbit. The ship secure, jets quenched, she spread her nimbus to hail the god of Earth.

"Belthar of Sol!" Hiding a tiny tremor of dislike, she addressed him with full formality. "Lord of Love, Well of Wisdom, Pillar of Power, I beg an audience."

"Welcome, daughter of Zhey." His mellow voice came back at once through her extended aura, thinned by many thousand miles of space, but still as clear as actual sound. "Your unfortunate father was my ally in the reconquest of Earth a thousand years ago, and I owe his memory whatever you ask."

"What I want, you won't want go give," she warned him. "But I want it very much. I beg your time."

"Land at Redrock Castle." His tone grew cooler. "I'll have you brought to me."

Her shuttle dropped her to the port on the mesa beside the Lord Quelf's new castle. The halfgod's chief ecclesiarch was waiting to greet her, bowing low, yet eyeing her covertly in his effort to guess what she wanted from Belthar.

With hushed apologies for his master's absence, he escorted her to the skipper ship that stood ready to take her to the African temple. A gift to the god from his faithful worshippers, the ecclesiarch explained, the temple commemorated the millennial year of his arrival to liberate the mother planet from the follies of the aging Creators and the demonic malevolence of their last Creation.

Aboard the skipper, he was long-windedly boastful about the temple and the ceremonies of its consecration. Its building had taken a hundred years, ten billion tons of granite, the prayer and toil of every godly truman. In divine gratitude, the Lord Belthar was granting his physical presence there.

The black-domed temple looked impressive enough, as the skipper dived to it through the stratosphere. It crowned an artificial mountain, a truncated pyramid of red-gray granite rising a full mile out of the palm groves that grew between the bare brown dunes of the Libyan desert and the long white dunes of salt removed from the Mediterranean water that now filled the old Qattara depression.

Belthar was impressive too, when the ecclesiarch brought her to him in the cavernous banquet hall. The throne where he sat high above his mortal guests was an immense emerald block towering above one end of the vast hollow triangular table, which was three levels high. For this occasion his nimbus was a cloud of scarlet sparks, thinning into a radiant halo around the power of his muscular shoulders and the splendor of his red-bearded head. He rose courteously enough to greet her, smiling almost too warmly as he waved her into the seat of honor just below him on the throne.

His other guests sat facing them across the bright-lit arena inside the table. His gigantic sons lounged below him along the highest level—there were no daughters, because the offspring of mortal and god were all sterile males. The chief prelates of the Thearchy sat along the second level, hushed and uncomfortable in their jeweled vestments as if embarrassed by this unaccustomed nearness to divinity. Below were the laymen: the secular ministers, the row of identical clone generals, the athletes and actresses and others who had somehow drawn his special favor, all leaning to look down into the central arena.

"Lord Belthar," the goddess began, "what I came to ask—"

"Watch!" He was turning from her to the triangular pit inside the table. "A pretty match."

Reluctantly, she looked down at two huge mumen flying to attack each other. Wearing null-G belts but armed only with the fangs and talons and killing eyes the genetic engineers had given them, they soared to the top of the barrier, paused and feinted, dived and struck. The arena lights burned on ruby scales, on sleek black crests and white dagger-fangs, on enormous claws. Pale pathseekers hissed from their armored lenses. When one of them found an opening, the crash of his blinding bolt echoed against the high vault.

She leaned to follow them, caught in spite of herself by a shocking incongruity. They were fearfully efficient machines of death, terrible but beautiful, lean and hard and bright, fighting without emotion. Yet, remotely, they were also human and divine.

In the grace of their swift and merciless motion, she felt their kinship to the premen and to her. Appalled, she turned back to Belthar.

He was intent on the battle, blue eyes blazing through the nimbus with a joy that almost frightened her. Abruptly he rose, with one ringing clap of his great bronze hands, a signal that sent a wave of cheering around the table.

She caught a charred-flesh reek and saw the loser's body sprawled in the air, kicking convulsively as it toppled slowly toward the sand, still almost supported by the gravitic belt. The winner stabbed it with another cracking bolt and mounted proudly toward the throne, grinning in bright-fanged delight at the god's applause.

"A cruel thing!" she whispered. "Must they die?"

"They must." Belthar gave her a momentary glance. "Since we killed the Creators, we ourselves must restore the old creative way of selection and survival. It works well. One of my mumen could outmatch a dozen of those the Creators left us."

He sat again, watching the victor dive to drag the victim's body away. Truman serving girls came running to spread the table with gemstone and precious metal, with flagons and platters and sculptured ices. She watched Belthar's avid attack on a huge, red-oozing steak and turned suddenly away because it smelled too much like the beaten muman. He saw her aversion and waved a girl to remove her steak.

"Forgive me, goddess. I know our needs are minimal, but I enjoy the physical." He paused to spear another bleeding morsel. "I like to make the most of both my bio-systems, the primitive and the transvolutionary. I enjoy levitating a ten-ton boulder out of the atmosphere. But I also enjoy wresting a muman Amazon to the death in the gym, with brute force alone."

"I'm sure you do." Her voice had an edge, which she tried to blunt. "But I hope you'll listen—"

"Later, child." Tolerantly benign, he paused to beckon a girl with a tray of luminous fruit. "But this is my day. The celebration of my first great millennium. Nothing must mar it."

Two more mumen had died in the pit between courses of the banquet, before Belthar levitated himself with a careless wave to acknowledge the worship of his world and at last led Zhondra

Zhey into an adjoining audience chamber.

"A more intimate place." The glow of his aura brightened to show a low plain throne at the end of a long conference table. "Designed for private talks with my highest churchmen. Shall we sit?"

They sat. Placing himself companionably near, down on her own level, he let his nimbus fade to reveal his massive maleness, but she kept the cover of her own aura, a cool blue shimmer in which starlike points of rainbow color flashed and faded.

"Sorry to delay you, my child," he murmured easily. "But we've time enough now."

Before she could speak, however, he had reached with a long pink tongue of his nimbus to lift a golden flask and two slender goblets from behind the throne. Nimble fingers of the aura filled them and offered one to her. She sniffed the unfamiliar fragrance of a glittering mist rising from the liquid and took one cautious sip. Though she liked its odd hot tang, she set it firmly on the table.

"Try it," Belthar urged. "You'll find it's something new. I've been training truman Creators of my own to invent new food animals and plants, new chemistries to offer new delights. The old human food and drink were never good enough for divine tastes or divine metabolism—"

"I want to talk," she broke in resolutely. "About the premen."

"Premen?" Startlement winked and vanished in his mantle. "My dear, I've finally solved the preman problem. An idea of Quelf's. We're relocating them on a frontier planet—"

"I've seen it." Bitterness shadowed her nimbus. "My ship was chartered to land the first lot of them there. A dreadful, barren world, where Terran life can't reproduce—"

"Quelf's point." Inhaling the bright moist from his drink, Belthar nodded expansively. "The premen are disposed of forever, with no violence to our old treaty obligations—"

"Would you murder our Creator race?"

"Our destiny." He beamed serenely through the dancing scarlet sparks. "The mortal races, like mortal individuals, are still subject to the laws of natural evolution. Through the old test of fitness, they are selected for survival—or sometimes not selected. We immortals are more fortunate."

"Need we be so cruel?"

90

"If you must look for cruelty, blame the Creators. Premen themselves. When they made the first trumen greater than they were, they were condeming their kind to be replaced. Andoranda V was already implied in their first efforts to unwind the double helix."

"I dislike your logic." Emotion brightened her blue halo. "I beg you to let me find some better planet—"

"There are gods enough to claim the better planets." He surveyed her shrewdly. "My dear child, you yourself are evidence that we have sometimes been too forgetful of our own immortality, breeding more deities than we could discover attractive home worlds for." He nodded persuasively at her fog-filled goblet. "Forget the premen, and let's enjoy your visit."

"I can't forget them." She darkened her aura against his avid eyes. "There are two, especially, that I want to know about. Davey Dunahoo and the girl he called Buglet. Only children when I met them, years ago. I looked for them when I came for the first lot of their people, but they were off the reservation—"

"Demons!" Red violence flared through Belthar's mantle, but he let it cool before he went on. "So Quelf believes. They've been terrifying him." He chuckled heartily, golden sparks dancing through the scarlet. "He has just recaptured them. It seems they somehow tricked his muman guards into attacking one another. Four killed. Quelf is more than half convinced they do belong to the demon breed. Actual survivors of the monstrous Fourth Creation, made to war against the gods. He can't wait for you to take them on to Andoranda—"

"I won't do that." Her halo flashed. "I remember them too well. Naked, grimy, hungry little urchins, but proud as you are. When Quelf's escorts killed their pet dog, they defied him—"

"You admire rebellion?"

"In them it was heroic."

Watching her keenly, Belthar sipped from his golden goblet and slowly smiled. "For your sake, my dear, I'll spare them. Take the other stragglers on to Andoranda, along with your cargo of supplies for the lot you left there. And I'll find some kinder fate for your two favorites. Agreed?"

"A kinder fate?" Peering into his bright halo, she nodded at last. "Agreed!"

*   *   *

When she was gone, Belthar sent for his black son.

"You honor me, Sire." Quelf dropped to one knee, grinning to conceal a secret apprehension. "How may I serve?"

"Get back to Redrock." Belthar beckoned him upright. "Attend to the two recaptured premen, Dunahoo and Jondarc. Clone General Ironlaw reports that they are proven heretics. You will see to their atonement. In keeping with a promise I have given our visiting goddess, that must be quick and painless."

"They are most dangerous heretics. But, Sire—" Quelf hesitated, blinking into the red-glinting nimbus. "Their atonement offers difficulty. Clone General Ironlaw says the Inquisition promised them safe passage to Andoranda—"

"Inform Ironlaw that the Inquisition has been over-ruled."

"Your will, Sire." Quelf shuffled uncomfortably. "But I foresee another difficulty. The heretics were able to kill four attacking mumen before they decided to surrender. The atoner may have trouble—"

"You will be the atoner," Belthar boomed. "As Arch-Inquisitor, you'll kill them yourself."

Quelf shivered and stiffened.

"Forgiveness, Sire!" He squinted shrewdly into the halo. "Wouldn't my intervention seem to give the heretics the status of martyrs? Wouldn't it be wiser to send them quietly on to die with their kinsmen?"

"Too slow for them. I want them glorified at once."

"Surely, Sire, you aren't—"

"I take no chances." The nimbus darkened. "The premen have always cherished their legends of demons surviving from the Fourth Creation. Of multimen or ultimen who would return to chasten the gods. Pure myths, of course. Pitiful efforts at compensation for their own misfortunes. Yet I want no risk of any future struggle for survival. The Creators ended that old evolutionary game when they made us immortal, and I will not revive it."

"I respect your wisdom, Sire." Quelf bowed and paused to mop at his shining sweat. "But if these creatures have actually inherited demonic powers—"

"We'll take no chances." Belthar chuckled. "Here are your instructions."

Controlling a shudder, Quelf bent to listen.

"The female is the more dangerous—so Ironlaw reports. He suspects that she has received support from some unknown ally more powerful than the preman boy, and he wants time to set a trap. We have granted him one more day."

Quelf gasped and froze again.

"To avoid risk, you will keep our purpose secret. You will announce that we are gracing you with a physical visitation to Redrock, arriving tomorrow at dusk. Preparing a formal welcome, you will select the female to be my bride. Have her brought to the chapel of love. Inspecting the arrangements, you will glorify her with your demon-burner—with no warning that might alert any allies."

Quelf moved as if to protest.

"When she is safely exalted, you will reveal her heresy. To prove it, you will display the weapon found hidden on her person, meant for us." Belthar reached behind the throne with a red tendril of the nimbus to produce a black handgrip. "Here it is. A laser-dagger, one taken from an actual preman assassin."

Stiffly, Quelf reached for the weapon.

"Though the preman boy seems less dangerous, we'll handle him with equal caution. He will remain isolated in the Redrock jail until his Inquisition guards are informed of the girl's atonement. At your signal the jail will be attacked with force enough to make sure of him."

Quelf nodded reluctantly.

"You will then tell our story. Your discovery of the dagger on the female led the Inquisition to a nest of preman heretics and demonists hiding in the jail. They have all been glorified."

"A sound plan, Sire." Quelf grinned bleakly, his misgivings not quite gone. "Your will be done!"

Suspended between powerful arms, the godlet's body was a gold-furred triangle that tapered from muscular shoulders to useless doll-feet, the scowling face a second triangle, narrowed from bulging temples to pink baby-chin.

"I like you, Davey." The voice from the red-lipped doll-mouth was the whine of a trapped insect. "I admire your remarkable Buglet. I have taken foolish risks to aid you—more risks than I can afford. I can do no more."

"But I'm shut up in jail and desperate for Bug—"

"Sorry for yourself?" The annoyed whine cut him off. "Consider me. Misbegotten. The only creature of my kind, without parents or kin or hope of any lover. Forced to live forever in hiding from mortals who would fear me and gods who would destroy me."

A huge tear welled out of the lone green eye.

"Drowned now like a rat out of my last refuge, with nowhere to go." Supporting himself on one huge hand, he wiped at the tear with the other. "Can't you see that I've troubles enough, without your leading Belthar to me?"

"We're both in bad shape," Davey agreed. "We've been tricked. Belthar's Inquisitors promised us passage to Andoranda—"

"Honesty was never his weakness." The green eye darted about as if in search of danger and stabbed back at him. "But that's your own problem. Really, you must go—"

"Help us first. Show me—" Davey caught his breath. "Show me how you walk through stone."

Pipkin hopped closer, his green squint almost malicious. "If you must ask, you wouldn't understand the answer."

"Buglet says we have latent gifts—"

"In fact, you do." The baby-head nodded. "Or you wouldn't be here."

"You can help us learn to use them—please!" He was reaching out imploringly, but Pipkin hopped warily back. "I get visions like this one, but only sometimes. I've no control—"

"Your own misfortune. Perhaps you too are misbegotten." Pipkin's shrug tossed his body like a hanging banner. "What can I do?"

"Teach me. Help me break a barrier in my mind—the feeling that the powers we need are all impossible."

"For mortals, they are impossible."

"We've got to have them, anyhow. If you'll just tell me what we must learn—"

"To see." Pipkin opened that blind white eye, and he shrank from its chilling stare. "To reach. To grasp the multiverse—"

"Can you explain the multiverse? In a way I can understand? There were books in the commune that we tried to read—"

"Truman books." Pipkin sniffed. "No truman understands the multiverse. The gods who do understand need no books."

"The gestalts we read never looked possible." Davey frowned. "If our own universe goes on forever, what can be outside it? That's the sort of thing I need help to understand."

"I'll say what I can," Pipkin droned. "If you'll leave when I'm done. But I'm afraid you'll understand nothing. Nothing until you learn to see for yourself."

Davey nodded eagerly. "Tell me! I'll try hard to get it."

"Your preman forebears had a theory of a single universe. An explosion of energy and mass, creating space and time as it swells to its gravitational limits, erasing them as it falls back into the point of its beginning, recreating itself as it explodes again—"

"That isn't true?"

"True enough for premen. Or even for the stupid truman theogonists." Pipkin's shrug tossed his body. "But a bit narrow for divinity. In fact, the premen themselves were always inventing odd gods of their own, to explain more things than their reason could."

To Davey's relief, Pipkin had closed his blind white eye.

"That theory is a fair enough fit for this one universe, which is all the premen and the trumen are able to sense, though it's only an atom in the greater reality. The actual multiverse holds an infinity of such universes. all held within a wider domain of order that the gods can perceive and mortals cannot."

"Infinities of universes?" Davey frowned, grappling with that awesome notion. "Side by side? Or following one another—"

"Stupid preman concepts." Pipkin's malicious shrilling cut him off. "Repetition implies time, as location implies space. But space and time exist within the universes, not between them. The laws and the nature of the multiverse are not expressible in your Terran language or your Terran math. They must wait for your parasenses—if you are going to have parasenses."

"We've got to have them now." Desperation shook his voice. "I've got to learn how they work." His emotion blurred Pipkin's image, and he paused to let it clear. "How is it possible for me to reach you here? Or to see Andoranda V?"

Pipkin whistled a high bird-note of surprise.

"You can probe that far?" The green eye blinked and stared. "I can't. Even Belthar can't. The best of us can penetrate a single contact plane without instrumental aid. Andoranda hangs beyond many of them, shifting so complexly that the most skillful pilot is taxed to take a ship there."

"So it is possible?" He nodded slowly, trying to grasp that greater reality. "You can really see into other universes?"

"Only dimly," Pipkin squeaked. "Such abler gods as Belthar can see somewhat farther and more clearly—far enough to find the loci of paraspatial contact, which I have never learned to do. They are strong enough to tap the universal energies they need to deflect a ship through the loci from universe to universe, or to power their auras, or to blast their enemies."

"But you yourself can reach—"

"Feebly." Pipkin sighed. "I can rotate a few atoms out of our own small space-time continuum for a very few minutes. Long enough, as you put it, to walk through a wall. If you and your Buglet hope to get away from Belthar's Inquisition, you must do much better."

"Can you tell me how—"

"Can you tell a stone how to hatch and fly?" Pipkin hopped impatiently on his knuckles. "It's eggs that do that, never asking how." The green eye squinted at him keenly. "If you can really see all the way to Andoranda, there's nothing I could tell you."

"But—"

"One word of warning." The piercing squeak cut him off. "If you ever find your way to another universe, enter it with caution. Half the early cosmic explorers never came back, because they weren't aware of a law of symmetry that rules the multiverse. Every alternate space-time expansion produces antimatter."

Davey stared, trying to recall those truman gestalts that he had never understood.

"There are two types of matter," Pipkin said. "In most ways identical, but opposite in electrical arrangement. On contact, the opposed charges cancel. Mass becomes pure energy, explosive enough to kill a god."

"Even Belthar?"

"He'll never risk himself." Pipkin's shrug flung him back toward the cliff from which he had emerged. "The parents of your goddess friend were explorers who never got back. But my warning was for you and your enchanting Buglet—if you ever get that far.'' An oval patch of the sandstone behind him had begun to glow and vanish. ''I can tell you no more, and I hope not to see you again.'' Standing on one hand, he swung the other in dismissal. ''You have stayed too long. Belthar's Inquisition is too near.''

''Wait!'' Davey gasped. ''I don't even know how to begin—''

But the grinning image was gone. The old red rocks and the dusk-reddened lake faded after it, and his nostrils caught the stale stink of the Redrock jail. He sat up stiffly on his concrete bench, searching for what he had gained.

That was little enough. Though he had somehow sent out a speaking image of himself to bring back facts he hadn't known, he wasn't sure he could do it again. The use of the facts was not yet clear. He had not found Buglet, or any clue to her location.

He sucked stale water from the plastic dish to wash his bitter mouth and paced the cell until the godsgrace ache drummed again in his brain. Why was he alive? What fate was planned for him? He lay back at last on his concrete bed, waiting for the drug to wane, wrestling with such answerless questions.

If the Inquisitors had judged him too dangerous to be sent on to Andoranda V, why hadn't they killed him at once? Or had they simply separated him and Buglet to weaken them both? He tried to hope that she had been sent on alone, that he was being held for a later ship.

That feeble hope kept fading. His weary brain kept drifting back to Pipkin, to the baffling riddles and the far promise of the multiverse. A super-world, beyond all space and time, in which the stark impossible for men became possible for gods—and for the ultimen Buglet said they would become.

But how could a frog learn to fly—

Something woke him.

In his vivid dream he and Buglet had been homeless waifs again, as they were before the goddess came to Redrock. Bug was sick and hungry, lying on a pallet of empty grain sacks in El Yaqui's cowshed. He had been slipping into the kitchen, trying to steal good food for her, when La China caught him. Screaming, she had been about to throw a bloody cleaver at him.

He sat up, blinking at the grime-clotted wall. It looked strange, until his first gasping breath brought memory back along with the reek of the jail. He slid off the bench and stopped to listen for whatever had jarred him awake.

There was nothing he could hear. No movement from the muman guards. No stir from any other prisoner. The same dim blue light still burned in the corridor, but he knew that day had come.

The sun, in fact, had already risen, casting the long black shadow of Quelf's castle far across the steel-colored lake. The bright sky was cloudless, broken only by the dark blot of the Inquisition battle skimmer that hung above the islet. He could find no new menace.

Yet his vague alarm persisted, even though this clear perception seemed to show that his latent gifts were growing. He stretched himself and roved about the cell. The ache and fog were gone from his head. He felt a hunger pang and a sharper stab of new concern for Buglet.

Was it some dim sense of fresh danger to her that had brought him awake? He lay back on the bench to probe again for her, reaching at random—or trying blindly to reach—for any hint, any hope, any friend.

San Seven? The truman youth had been their best friend. More than half in love with Buglet, he suspected. San had risked perhaps too much to aid their first flight from Redrock. Could he have found some way to help her again? Could she perhaps be safe at the agency now?

Trying not to try too hard, because he thought the very tension of effort might defeat him, he turned that faint hope to the mansion on the hill, their home for all the years since the goddess sent them there. On high ground, it should still be above the rising lake.

The drowned trees on the slopes beneath it were yellow and dying, and the wide stood open now. The bright image dimmed to his surge of elation, but it came back again when he made himself relax.

The doors were tall wood panels, carved by forgotten preman artisans with symbols that meant nothing now: a cross, a crescent, a star with six points, another with five. One panel had been charred and shattered, as if struck by a muman warrior's ligtning, and the patio inside was rank with weeds and littered with sodden junk that once had been the agent's precious preman antiques.

The office was a shocking ruin, a dusty clutter of torn paper and ripped-up books and dismembered chairs and desks and files. San's room, Bug's, his own, even the null-G gameroom, had been as thoroughly demolished. Why?

Understanding came, a jolt that shattered the whole perception. The Inquisitors had been here. This devastation was left from the merciless search that had finally overtaken him and Buglet at the truman commune. His burning guilt raised another question: what had the Inquisition done to San and his parents?

Shivering, half sick with fear for those old truman friends, he stumbled around the cell again, rattling the door, testing each steel bar, throwing his weight against the grimy walls, standing on the benches to test the concrete ceiling. There was no way out.

Not for him.

For a god, perhaps. Or for the ultiman that Buglet might help him become. But he knew no way to find her, no way to get beyond the ironic fact that his own anxious emotion was an apparent limit on those half-known unfolding powers. He needed her, needed understanding of the multiverse that Pipkin said no man could understand, needed everything.

Announced by a clash of metal doors, the horn-footed muman guard came tramping down the corridor to open the wicket and gesture at the plastic dish. When he shoved it into her bright black talons, she slammed the wicket and thudded away, deaf to all he said.

The old jail was still again. Lying back on his hard bed, trying to smooth away every interference from emotion—from his haunting fears for Buglet, his nagging worry for the Sans, even from his own gnawing hunger—he probed again, trying now to reach Quelf's new castle.

He had never been near it—Quelf welcomed no preman guests—but long ago, with El Yaqui, he had hiked over the high mesa where it now stood. They had been looking for peyote cactus under the desert brush on a little hill when he found an odd object half buried in the pale soil: chips of colored glass framed in blackened metal to make a picture of a man's head.

He wanted to know what it was.

"Throw it back." He remembered El Yaqui's sardonic tone and the pain on his old brown face. "No good for us. Bad trouble, more likely, with Belthar's Inquisition."

Though the colors looked faded and some of the glass chips were gone, he could make out part of a yellow circle in the blue above the long-haired head. The face was lean and sad as El Yaqui's, and something about it troubled him.

"Why?" he asked. "What was it?"

"A god," the old man muttered. "A preman god." He nodded at the brush-clumped mound. "This white soil's adobe. A building once. I think the old Piedras Rojas mission. A house of worship for that humble preman god. He's dead now."

He remembered holding the broken thing up against the sun and peering at the glowing glass, trying to imagine how a preman could have been any sort of god.

"Throw it back," El Yaqui rasped again. "Forget it."

Unwillingly, he tossed it back on the mound. It must have struck something hard, because he heard a jangle and saw bright fragments flying. El Yaqui knelt for a moment, murmuring something he couldn't hear about *los pobres* and *dios* before they went on looking for the little blue-green buttons.

Later, growing up on the reservation, he had watched the castle rising where that dead god's house had caved to clay. A long new mountain on the skyline, broken rock from enormous excavations. Great dark granite walls, soaring higher year by year. Towers so tall that summer cumulus sometimes formed above them.

Those walls enclosed a vast triangle, a tower at each corner. The chapel of Thar looming on his right, domed with sacred black. The Bel chapel on his left, all white marble. The landing stage at the south corner, behind them, not quite so high.

Down in the canyon between those enormous walls Quelf had made his playground. A wide white beach and low green hills around a clean blue lake. Garden groves. Bowers built of shining gemstones. A fountain in the lake, catching a rainbow now in its diamond dazzle.

These were sights Davey had never seen or heard of, never guessed. The vivid perception elated him—nearly too much, for it began to fade. He stretched himself deliberately again on the hard bench, drew a long breath, lay limp until the vision cleared.

Machines were mowing the grass above the beach and workmen were busy on the north wall, swarming over the scaffolding around a black structure that had begun taking shape as a gigantic statue of the halfgod himself. A black skimmer was lifting from the stage. He saw no other movement. No hint of Buglet.

He followed the Inquisition skimmer. Flying south, it climbed, leveled, glided toward the shuttle port. At first he expected it to land there, but it slid on above the orange-painted terminal buildings to touch down at last beyond a fence he had never seen.

Tall steel posts enclosed a wide rectangle of desert brush and naked sandstone. A single wire, stretched high between the posts, was beaded with winking red lights. The lights puzzled him, until he found the bones scattered under the wire, whitened skeletons of coyotes and hawks and men. He knew then that this must be the holding camp where the exiled premen had waited for shipment to Andoranda V.

The sleek scout skimmer had landed on a pad inside the camp, safely far from the fence. A red-scaled muman stalked down the gangway, followed by a compact man in gray. Clone General Ironlaw—

Everything faded and flickered with Davey's surprise. Trying not even to hope that Ironlaw might lead him to Buglet, he turned away to watch a buzzard wheeling over the other end of the camp and drew a long slow breath before he dared look again.

The clone must have called some command, because a few half-naked premen were crawling into sight from brush-covered burrows they must have dug with rocks and sticks. Most of them stood staring, warily silent. One was a yellow-haired girl who had been at La China's. She came running until she stumbled, then waited on her knees, holding out her sunburned swollen arms, sobbing for the Lord Quelf's mercy.

Ignoring her, Ironlaw shouted again.

The prisoners turned to watch another man climbing stiffly out of his shelter pit. In muddy rags, he was lean and brown, gnarled from long toil. Pulling himself carefully straight, as if his back were painful, he came to face the muman, slow steps firm, blue eyes defiant.

"Halt!" Ironlaw stepped ahead of the guard. "Identify yourself."

He stopped and stood swaying.

"I have been interrogated." Pitched high, his old voice was cool and clear. "I am a truman, as I informed the sacred Inquisitors. My life has been spent in the deepest mines of the Andes, where few except the muman miners can endure the heat. The past twelve years I was foreman over my crew. My name is Florencio Tarazon—"

"Can you prove that?"

"Do you say I lie?" His pale stare was steady, sardonic, contemptuous. "My misfortunes are written in the records of the mine, as I told the Inquisitors. There was a fire. I was able to save my muman crew, but my personal identification was destroyed—"

"The Inquisition says you lie," Ironlaw cut in. "We have evidence that the real Florencio Tarazon died in that mine fire. The Inquisition charges that you are, in fact, a preman escapee from the Redrock reservation, once known as Dunahoo—"

The voices faded, and the desert sun-glare dimmed. Gasping with shocked emotion, Davey found his lungs filled with the foul jail stink. This battered but unbeaten little man was the father he had never even hoped to see.

An agony of sympathy swept him upright. Sick with his helpless rage at Quelf and Belthar, at the Inquisition and the whole Thearchy, he clutched the old iron bars as if to rip them out, punched his fist against the rough concrete.

But that was not the way to be greater than the gods. Rubbing bruised knuckles, he drove himself back to the bench. Breathing deep and slow, he tried to relax, to forget his fatal hate, to regain that lost perception.

At first he failed, his sweaty body still too tense, his hand too painful, his heart pounding too hard. Slowly, however, his animal anger faded into admiration for that worn little preman who could still defy the whole force of Belthar's Inquisition with an undefeated dignity.

The black skimmer was gone when he got his vision back. Most of the prisoners had crawled back into their pits to escape the savage sun. Near the fence, the yellow-haired girl was raking with a stick at the body of a hawk that must have tried to light on that deadly wire. He saw her seize it, rip feathers off, tear with her teeth at its tough flesh.

He overtook the skimmer as it dipped toward the landing stage on the castle tower. The muman guard marched down the gangway first. His father followed, limping painfully, yet still proudly straight. Behind him, Ironlaw signaled them toward an elevator.

The cage dropped them out of the tower and deep into the rock beneath. Davey followed them, watched them emerge into a huge rectangular room with a high dais at each end. One was bare; the other held a tall black throne.

Muman, preman and clone—they stood side by side to face the throne. Six military mumen marched out of a dark passage to form a silent line, facing them. All waited, stiff and mute. The little preman swayed and straightened again, biting his lip. Blood oozed down his muddy, dark-stubbled chin.

A gong boomed. Quelf strode out of another doorway and paused to eye the prisoner. More massive than a man, dark as his mortal mother and arrogant as his father-god, he was clad in the somber splendor of his rank as Arch-Inquisitor: the ruby-jeweled black harness, the high black crown, the tall black staff.

The gong throbbed and the mumen knelt. Ironlaw bent his head. Only the haggard preman stood straight, pale eyes level with Quelf's black stare. For an instant they stood fixed. Then, with a scowl of annoyance, the halfgod took his throne.

Another gong-tone swelled and died.

Solemnly, speaking in the Old High Terran still preserved in the church, Ironlaw intoned the formal charges of the Inquisition. The prisoner, the preman male recorded on the Redrock reservation rolls as Devin Dunahoo, had fled his legal residence without divine sanction, had attempted to pass himself as a truman, had neglected to make full and frequent confessions to his lawful pastors.

"Prisoner, what is your plea?" Quelf's cold demand rang against the lofty walls. "Do you admit your guilt? Do you beg Belthar's mercy?"

The little preman folded his scarred arms.

"I admit nothing." His faint voice was firm. "I beg for nothing."

"Then prepare for atonement—"

Quelf's booming voice broke off, interrupted by Ironlaw.

"Sir, if you will. As an agent of the Holy Inquisition, I must present yet another charge against this prisoner. A charge of demonism—"

"No!" The halfgod started as if with alarm, and the dark flesh beneath his gemmed harness shone with sudden sweat. "Is there proof?"

"Evidence to damn him." Ironlaw stepped warily away from the haggard preman. "Evidence that he carries the genes of the demon breed known as the Fourth Creation, the accursed seed of the evil being whose coming the heretics have been proclaiming, the monstrous enemy of Belthar and all the gods that they call the Multiman—"

"Enough!" Quelf shouted. "Enough for judgment." He paused as if to recover himself, glaring down at the little preman. "Prisoner, do you admit your demonism?"

"I never knew I was a demon." The preman drew himself painfully straight, grinning through the blood on his lips. "But if I am, we'll get you, Quelf. My son will—"

"Silence!" Quelf roared. "I order your atonement."

Breathing carefully, trying to cool his blaze of emotion, Davey clung to the tattered shreds of his perception. When it began to clear again, he found two muman guards dragging his father across the high stage at the other end of that long room. Everything dimmed and blurred again, as he watched them shackle the preman's wrists to a high metal grate, so that he hung by his stretched arms. Pale with pain, he kept his eyes on Quelf, somehow still detached and defiant.

The gong had sung again, and two more gigantic mumen marched out of the passage below the black throne, herding two more prisoners, thin crippled creatures half clad in foul rags. San Six and his wife—

Like a rock crashing into a mirror, the shock of that recognition splintered Davey's vision. When he got it clear again, the new prisoners stood where his father had been, before Quelf's throne.

"—three truman heretics." Ironlaw was intoning the Inquisition charges, framed in the archaic accents of Old High Terran. "They are suspected of demonistic sympathies, of idolatrous belief in the blasphemous myth of the Multiman, of treasonous complicity in preman plots against the sacred dominion of our Lord Belthar and against the public peace. Unfortunately, the son did not survive interrogation—''

An overwhelming wave of grief and pain washed out the whole perception. Davey sat up in the stuffy jail cell, sick at heart and shivering. San Seven—dead! Killed by the Inquisition, in a manner he couldn't bear to imagine.

When at last he had calmed himself enough to recover the perception, the Sans were kneeling side by side below the black throne. The woman was sobbing silently, gray head bent. The battered man stared up at Quelf, fleshless face flaccid and mouth hanging open in his abject terror.

''—invesitgation not yet complete,'' Ironlaw was droning. ''I still suspect that other forces are involved, more powerful and dangerous. But these truman sacrilegists have confessed to the Inquisition that they did in fact render aid to premen demonists in flight from the reservation.''

Bowing slightly, the clone stepped back.

''Prisoners,'' Quelf rapped, ''how do you plead?''

''You—'' The hollow voice of San Six quavered and stuck. ''Your Benign Semi-Divinity—'' He had to gasp again for breath. ''We've sworn the truth many times. I knew nothing. My wife knew nothing. It was only our poor impulsive son—''

Glazed eyes still on the black halfgod, he reached blindly to touch the woman.

''A misguided child.'' His hoarse voice was suddenly clearer, racing. ''If it's true that he did aid those young premen, he didn't know that they were demons. It was a goddess, remember, who had placed them in our home. With Your Divinity's approval. We were sanctioned to befriend them. If our poor son sinned, his sin was friendship—''

''What is your plea?''

San Six gulped and clutched the woman's hand.

''For myself,'' he whispered, ''I accept the guilt. I was the Redrock agent. I was responsible. But, Your Divinity—'' The whisper faded, and he gasped again for his breath. ''For Lera, I beg mercy. She knew nothing. She meant no sin. She shares no blame—''

The woman raised her blighted face.

"Mercy!" A toneless croak. "Belthar's mercy, for both of us."

"I grant you my father's mercy."

The halfgod smiled and turned his tall-crowned head, waiting for the gong. San Six gasped as if in disbelief, and Lera laughed wildly, hysterical with her momentary joy.

"You've nothing more to fear," Quelf told him. "The Holy Inquisition will release you now, for immediate atonement."

The perception was wavering again from Davey's own emotion, but he got blurred glimpses of the mumen dragging their two unresisting victims down that long room, to hang them by their wrists beside the pale preman.

In shattered fragments of sensation, he saw a whole side wall of the room rising like a curtain, to show a vast dim space beyond. A vast circular chamber, walled with prison cells five levels high— the dark and secret dungeon of Quelf's Inquisition.

The judgment room was now itself a stage, the prison cavern a high-domed theater. The great gong was thrumming again, and the pallid inmates began staggering to clutch their bars and peer down at the place of execution.

Buglet—was she here?

The icy shock of fear erased everything. Aware only of his own jail cell, of fetid air and hard concrete and the quivering tension of his own sweaty limbs, he had to calm his emotional storm before he could see anything. But he was learning to relax and reach and see. In a dozen heartbeats he was able to get the vision back and scan the stricken faces.

None was Buglet's. Relieved, trying to hope that she had somehow escaped the Inquisition, he turned his mind back toward that high stone stage. Air had begun to roar, a cold wind whipping at the hanging victims and rushing somewhere away. Quelf had risen from the throne, black staff thrust level.

"Witness the infinite mercy of my ever-loving father." His brassy voice pealed against the arching dome. "Witness the ineffable grace of the Supreme Lord Belthar, granted in holy atonement!"

The staff hummed faintly. Its beam was invisible. For an endless instant, however, the hanging victims shone, every limb and feature turned incandescent. His father's fixed grin burned itself into Davey's mind, defiantly impudent, unafraid and unforgettable.

In the next instant, before agony had time to erase that glowing grin, the rags and hair and then the lean bodies exploded into crimson flame. If there was any outcry, the roaring wind tore the sound away.

Fighting the chill and sickness of his horror, Davey clung to the shreds of that perception until the dying flames had flickered out, until the curtain wall had dropped again and the ventilators had ceased to roar. Quelf had lowered his staff, leaning on it casually, leering with satisfaction at the black sticks, twisted and tiny, that hung from the shackles. The air in the room was suddenly hot, tainted with the bitter stench of burned flesh.

He had to let the perception fade. Alone in his cell, he felt the old walls closing in, harder and grimier and colder, until his breath was gone. The afterache of godsgrace was throbbing in his brain again, and nausea overwhelmed him.

He endured a dismal day. For a long time he had no heart for anything. When at last he nerved himself to reach for the castle again, to search for Buglet there, his shock and grief and helpless rage rose in a storm of feeling that prevented any perception.

Now and then he roused himself to look about the cell again for any possible weapon or tool or way of escape, but he found no opening, no hope, no object he could move. The toilet was only a malodorous hollow in the floor. His own clothing had been changed for a frayed and shapeless garment without button or buckle or pocket. He found no comfort anywhere, and the despair of past preman inmates mocked him from the obscene graffiti on the windowless walls.

When the wicket rattled, he took the soft plastic dish from the talons of the unspeaking muman and sucked tepid water to ease his bitter thirst. The odor of the slimy yellow mush made his stomach churn again.

With each new effort to probe for anything outside the jail, the thin needle of pain at the back of his head grew keener, until he decided that it must be a warning that he was exhausting the obscure new energies that he couldn't yet understand or control. At last he slept.

Hunger woke him, but the yellow mush was still offensive. Spurred by a new unease, he again lay back to test his perceptions, and found two more Inquisition battle skimmers on guard above the jail, black and sleek against a blood-colored sunset.

That discovery numbed him with a troubled wonder. If the Inquisitors felt that he was worth three battlecraft, what sort of force had they set against Buglet? His disturbed emotions had darkened everything, and he drew back to recover. Able at last to probe again, he turned toward the castle in time to see a small church skimmer leaving the landing tower, sloping toward the shuttle port.

The tall shuttle stood there at the terminal dock, its mirror-bright hull red-splashed with sunset, crates and bales and drums climbing its gangways. Supplies, he supposed, for the preman exiles on Andoranda V, where no food grew.

The skimmer came down to the dock and mumen emerged to guard the path of a smaller, brighter figure moving swiftly past them into the shuttle. His breath caught. It was the goddess, Zhondra Zhey.

Once their friend, would she aid them again? That brief hope glowed and faded. She was already aboard, leaving Earth. The cargo booms and gangways had begun to swing away. The hatches closed. The dockhands took shelter. Roaring steam gushing from the jets, the shuttle lifted.

Yet he followed that dying spark of hope. Reaching inside the rising craft, he found her sitting beside the muman pilot, and the grotesque strangeness of that being caught him for a moment. The huge head, dark and bald and leather-skinned. The immense black telescopic eyes. The wide, wing-shaped lobes of the radar ears. The long, pliant sensapods spread like clinging vines across the controls.

Though the staring muman seemed unaware, she turned at once to face him with a look of cool inquiry. Hardly larger than the gnomelike pilot, she still seemed a child, no older than when she had made Quelf find a home for them, so long ago.

"Goddess—" He faltered. "Goddess—" Very fair in her

aura's pale opal glow, she looked as lovely as Buglet, so tenderly defenseless that he saw no hope of aid from her. "Do you remember me?"

"Davey Dunahoo." Surprise had widened her eyes. "Your ancestral gifts must be greater than anybody thought, if you can make an image here. Yet you seem distressed."

"We're in trouble. I'm locked up, and I can't find Buglet. If—if you could help—"

"I've done all I can." Her face turned grave. "I've appealed to Belthar, for you and all the premen. Begging for a chance to search out a better planet for you. He's the ruler here, remember. He yielded very little, but he gave me one concession, for Buglet and yourself. A kinder fate than Andoranda V."

"What kinder fate?" Terror touched him. "Why am I in the Redrock jail? With three battlecraft to guard me? Does that look like kindness? And Buglet—where is she?"

"I can tell you." Sympathetic, but yet detached, the goddess studied him. "I think you won't be pleased—that's why you have been detained. Quelf told me so just now, as I took my leave from him. As for Buglet—"

His anxiety and eagerness washed out the perception.

"—divine visitation," she was saying when he found her again. "He's arriving at Redrock castle tonight, and the Inquisition battlecraft are waiting to escort his sacred skimmer to the chapel stage. Quelf is gathering the sacrificial offerings. One of those is Buglet—to be his bride."

"Belthar's bride?" He strove to hold the slipping vision. "That would kill Bug—"

"I'm sure you're jealous." Nodding, she made a face. "I myself shouldn't care to share Belthar's bed. Yet this is an honor that premen have seldom received—intended, Quelf told me, to compensate your people for their exile from Earth."

Speechless and trembling with dismay, he could only shake his head.

"I know you're not entirely happy," she chided him. "I doubt that Buglet is. But you must both accept the situation with whatever grace you can. The chapel of Bel is certainly a better place than Andoranda V. The brides are always well rewarded, and Buglet won't forget you."

He gasped for his voice, but still he couldn't speak.

"After all, there's nothing you can do. Not against the god of Earth—"

"I—I can't believe it." His husky whisper came at last. "Quelf seems to suspect we're demons. Would he give his father a demon for a bride?"

"Quelf's a coward." She shrugged, smiling slightly, as aloof from his gnawing concerns as if her wrap of bluish opalescence set her half a universe away. "His father's a god."

"Can you—" His voice stuck again. "Can you help me find Buglet?"

"She's at the castle, Quelf told me. She has been bathed and arrayed. She'll be waiting for Belthar in the chapel of love—"

Frowning, the goddess interrupted herself.

"Stay away, Davey! Belthar would not be pleased to detect your image there. Quelf says that you have been detained for your own protection, but if the halfgod is offended, your guards might be ordered to destroy you."

"I'll risk that—"

"Davey, don't!" Her nimbus had paled, and her widened eyes looked darker. "You don't *know*—"

He let the perception fade.

Beyond the red-stained lake, beyond Quelf's new roads and groves and gardens, the castle loomed immense against the sunset sky. The Bel chapel towered above the dark granite walls, white columns soaring to the high white dome.

Within the circle of columns the white marble floor was vacant now, broken only by the great black crystal cylinder in which the sacred image could appear and the low altar before it, draped now in scarlet. Beyond the altar he could see the open arch of the god's gateway and the railing of the stage where the sacred skimmer would land.

He waited for Buglet there in the empty temple, beneath the flash and shimmer of the star-charts inside the high vault. Though the dusky chapel was warm enough, he was half aware of his sweat-chilled body back in the jail, of his racing heart and rasping breath, of all the desperate emotion that threatened his perception.

Music began to throb, far off at first, deep and slow and strange. As it rose louder, a solemn procession came marching into the chapel. Two sacristans in blue, carrying yellow-flaring lamps that reeked with pungent incense. A tall prelate in Inquisition black, snapping hushed commands to four ruby-scaled mumen who carried a jewel-crusted chair.

In the chair—Buglet!

Gowned in lacy white, she sat far back, drowsily relaxed, sulphur-yellow eyes half shut. Jeweled combs shone in her dark hair, and heavy gemstone bracelets fettered her wrists. Her empty hands were folded peacefully.

"Bug—" His voice shook. "Bug!"

Her sleepy eyes were dilated, blank, blind to him. He caught an unfamiliar scent, a heavy sweetness that repelled him. As they brought her nearer, he saw two black triangular patches on her vacant face, one on each white temple. Beneath that sickly sweet perfume he got a sour whiff of godsgrace.

"Bug! Can you hear me?"

He thought her face drained even whiter, thought her eyes dilated wider. But she gave him no sign. The mumen marched on. At a word from the Inquisitor they knelt with the chair before the scarlet altar.

Bowing, the prelate caught her hand. She started, shrank a little from his touch, rose slowly from the chair. Passive as an unstrung puppet, she let him guide her to the red altar. Limp again, she lay back upon it, lips half open, eyes half closed, seemingly unaware of anything.

"Bug! If you can hear, move your hand."

The Inquisitor was arranging her gauzy gown, adjusting a diamond comb, straigtening her arms. He knelt to touch his lips to the altar cloth, rose and turned. Behind him her lax white hand lay motionless.

The sacramental music had paused, but now it swelled again. Keeping time to its solemn beat, Quelf strode into the chapel, still wearing the red-jeweled harness and the tall black crown from his dungeon judgment chamber, still carrying the deadly staff of the Arch-Inquisitor.

As the gigantic halfgod tramped toward the altar, the black prelate moved out of his path and knelt again. The mumen picked up the chair and marched away. The two blue sacristans stationed themselves at the ends of the altar, swinging their flaring lamps in yellow clouds of incense.

Quelf paused before the altar. Gripping the black staff, he fell into a crouch, eyes rolling warily as if to search for danger. Nostrils flared, he was breathing fast. Bright sweat filmed his limbs. When he looked back at Buglet, his dark face set and a shudder shook him.

Abruptly, he dropped to his knees, bent to kiss the marble floor, came stiffly back to his feet. Face lifted to the crystal column beyond the altar, he began intoning a ritual chant that returned in dull thunder from the star-patterned vault.

As his great arms lifted toward the column, Davey glimpsed a second weapon. A slim laser-dagger like one he had seen long ago, when the agent took it from La China after she had snatched it from between her bulging breasts to confront a drunken patron. Quelf carried it hidden beneath the wide black belt of his official harness, only half the hilt in sight.

Why? The image of it quivered and dimmed to Davey's alarm. Why would the halfgod bring such a weapon to the sacrificial ceremony? Why hidden?

The invocation had ended. Quelf stood silent, bleak face lifted to the crystal column. The black Inquisitor took up the prayer, his voice a cracked and quavering mockery of Quelf's resounding boom, begging Belthar to manifest his all-forgiving love. The sacristans raised their fuming lamps. All waited.

"Holy father," Quelf's great voice drummed again, "we consecrate our humble gift—"

The black staff had clicked in his fingers. Humming softly, it swung level with the scarlet altar, level with Buglet's head. He bent, tensed. His dark features twitched and froze into a mask of frightened triumph.

The stark and sudden truth chilled Davey's body in the jail. His breath stopped. His throat hurt. His fists knotted, uselessly. At last he understood. The whole ceremony was a sham, arranged perhaps for Zhondra Zhey. Now that she was gone, the halfgod was about to murder Buglet.

With all his will, with no time to think about the impossible, he reached again into the chapel. With no plan at all, too desperate to recall that he wasn't really there, without stopping to wonder what transvolutionary sources might be drawn upon to energize his image, he snatched for Quelf's hidden dagger.

The hilt felt cool and solid, real in his fingers. Caught between the wide belt and Quelf's belly, slippery with the halfgod's sweat, it resisted when he hauled on it. Somehow he almost lost his balance. The jail cell tipped and the white chapel whirled, and they spun together. He got a fresh grip, pulled again—and suddenly fell.

A sharp report cracked in his ears. The stifling stink of his cell was gone. Gasping for breath, he got a suffocating lungful of incense smoke. Quelf was recoiling from him, quaking with terror, bawling for the mumen, swinging at him with the demon-burner.

With jarring force, he came down onto the polished marble. Coughing, half blind with the acrid yellow smoke, he groped for his senses. Somehow, with no help from Pipkin, he had come through the walls of the jail and many miles of space. He was really here, still dazed with that impossible fact.

Quelf was howling for the mumen, backing away, trying to get him at the killing end of the staff. He lurched forward, clutching a strap of the gemmed harness with one hand while he gripped the dagger with the other squeezing to activate the laser blade.

Nothing happened. The trigger wouldn't pull. Desperately he groped for recollection of that time so long ago when the agent had let San Seven try La China's dagger on the weeds in the alley before they locked it up in the vault. He hadn't been allowed to touch it, but San Six had showed them how to disengage the safety—

"Demons!" Quelf was yelling. "Preman demons! Burn 'em both!"

The mumen let the chair crash to the floor and came pounding toward the altar, crested killer eyes burning crimson. Pale violet pathseeker rays began stabbing around him, but no bolts struck. Perhaps, he thought, they were afraid of striking Quelf.

In a fleeting fragment of awareness he saw Buglet moving drowsily to sit up on the red altar. Dark with dilation, her yellow eyes were on him, and her black-patched face had a look of dim alarm. Her pale lips murmured something he had no time to hear.

Too close to use the burner beam, Quelf swung the staff at him like a club. It grazed his head, dazed him with pain. Everything was blurred, until he was chilled with fear that he might find himself back in the cell. But he clung to the harness, jabbed the dagger back into the halfgod's belly, felt for the safety slide.

"Burn!" Quelf was bellowing. "Burn the female—"

He felt the slide click, squeezed again. The laser blade hissed and blazed. Choking smoke exploded, veiling hot blue fire. The bellow was choked off. Pulled by the strap, Quelf toppled toward him.

"Davey?" In a sudden stillness he heard Buglet's troubled whisper. "Davey—"

Beyond her a spot of blinding light was flashing across the marble columns. He saw the burner beam from the humming staff that now had spun out of Quelf's dead hand. Ducking from beneath the falling halfgod, he snatched the staff, swung it toward the charging mumen.

They had paused, paralyzed by their master's fall. He heard a hoarse command, saw the pathseekers stabbing around him again, felt a searing sting.

But he had caught them with the staff. Tiny at this close range, its hot spot lashed across them, exploding red scales into white fire and blinding smoke. The deadly redness dying in their crested eyes, the mumen moaned and staggered and fell.

Again the chapel was still. The churchmen had fled. The yellow lamps still flared where the sacristans had dropped them, spilled oil frying on the marble, their incense mixed with the reek of seared flesh.

He twisted at the butt of the staff until he found how to turn off the humming beam and then stood leaning on it, gasping for breath, blinking his smarting eyes. Bitter smoke veiled everything. His head throbbed, where Quelf's blow had struck. Groping for himself, he had to fight a dazed disbelief.

Moments ago he had been a hopeless prisoner—he still wore the faded, shapeless garment of the jail. Somehow—only Pipkin could explain the metaphysics of it—he had slipped out of his cell, flashed twenty miles across the lake, killed Belthar's favored son.

Such a leap was impossible, he knew, even for a god. Though Belthar could send a speaking image into the crystal cylinder above the altar, even *he* used a skimmer for an actual visitation, like any mortal being.

Yet here he was—

He heard shouts outside the chapel. The fleeing churchmen had carried the news. Ironlaw would be warned. The whole Inquisition would be armed against him. Belthar himself would move fast to kill the demons who had killed his son.

"Dav—" He heard Buglet sneeze, heard her plaintive murmur through the smoke. "Take me, Davey!"

She sat on the edge of the altar, tears streaming from her unseeing eyes, holding out her arms. He ran to her, pulled the godsrest patches off her face and flung them away. She clung to him, sighing in sleepy relief.

Where could he carry her? Where was any refuge? The yellow smoke had begun to lift, but all he could see in the flare of the broken lamps was the sprawled bodies of the dead halfgod and the defeated mumen. The castle beyond them was alive with danger—the whole Earth would be the instrument of Belthar's wrath—and he knew no way to safety.

"So afraid—" Her lips moved lightly against his ear. "So glad you came—"

A savage light flashed through the columns, turning the rising smoke to a canopy of fire. He had to duck and cover his eyes. When he could see again, he found a strange day still blazing outside the chapel. Its light came from a terrible cloud rising over the lake. Swelling incredibly, climbing unbelievably, the cloud became a storm of shifting color, slowly fading. It stood where the Redrock jail had been.

Understanding hit him, a shock that rocked him. Quelf had meant to take no chance at all. The Inquisition battlecraft must have been ordered to attack the jail at the instant planned for Buglet's murder.

Now, when Belthar learned that his son was dead, their appalling weaponry would no doubt be turned against the castle. Gazing up at the fading colors of that awful cloud, he longed for the power to leap again—but where?

Belthar ruled the Earth, his Inquisition an efficient instrument. His kindred gods and goddesses, no more anxious to be supplanted, reigned with equal power over every discovered planet fit for settlement. Of all the worlds Davey knew about, that left only Andoranda V.

No god had ever claimed that place of exile. No god could see or sense it from Earth, or reach it save by the long and difficult flight through the shifting loci between universes. No god would want a world that killed all dryland life.

If he knew how, he thought, he would take Buglet to join the premen Zhondra Zhey had ferried there. That was what she had wanted when they surrendered to the Inquisition. For all its grim hostility, it might give them time to grow.

He didn't know how—

But Pipkin had said that he didn't need to be told. It was no understanding of multiversal energies that had brought him here from the jail, but only his unfolding gifts and an urgency so desperate that he had forgotten what he couldn't do.

Perhaps—his breath caught with the thought—perhaps if he recalled his image of the terraforming station as he had seen it in that first dazzling vision, if he could escape his crippling sense of impossibility, if he could find confidence enough in their ancestral powers—

He drew Buglet closer, and had to hold his breath against the evil mixture of that stifling bridal scent and the sour reek of godsrest. She snuggled drowsily against him, with a tiny murmur of pleasure. Desperately, he probed for the abandoned station.

Beyond the colmns that dreadful fire had died. Returning night had swallowed the mushroom cloud. Thunder had begun to rumble. Something jolted the marble floor. A cold gust of dusty wind blew through the columns. Ignoring everything, he clung to his image of Andoranda V.

The loom of that bare granite knob against the yellow sky. The red mud-plain in the river bend and the lines of lifeless orange dunes. The huddle of rusting huts, the narrow shuttle strip, the drifts of dirty snow. An ugly place perhaps, but kinder than the gods—

The chapel quivered to a stronger shock. Toppling masonry crashed. He heard sharp truman shouts, muffled muman booms, the scream of a low-flying skimmer. A bullet ricocheted through the chapel, its whine reverberating in the dome. Laser-lightning flickered. Drumming footfalls drew nearer.

"Davey?" Buglet stirred in sleepy unease. "Is something bad—"

He strove with all his will to sweep them out of the chapel, to carry them across the complex multiverse to that wind-carved rock. But stark impossibility stopped him. He didn't know how to make such a leap. Nobody did. Not even the greatest god could reach Andoranda without a ship. After all, no frog could fly—

A brazen bong rang through the chapel and echoed from the vault. Beyond the red altar the tall crystal cylinder was dissolving into glittering mist. That bright fog swiftly faded to reveal Belthar's gigantic image, glaring through the red-streaked wrath of his nimbus.

"Demons!" His voice was wild thunder. "So here you are—" Suddenly, Belthar was gone.

Night and smoke and chapel dome were gone. The open sky was a yellow blaze, blinding for a moment. The wind felt cold and smelled of bitter dust. Davey stumbled with Buglet in his arms and had to scramble to get his balance on the sand-scoured rock. Below them, banked with drifted snow, he found the rust-reddened huts of the terraforming station.

"Davey?" She clung to him, her drowsiness disturbed. "Is anything bad?"

"We're all right." He held her close, whispering. "We've escaped the Inquisition and outrun Belthar. We're here with our own folk, where the gods may never find us."

FOUR: BROTHER TO DEMONS

Darwin says I'm not humane. The truth is, I have no time to be. With the premen in revolt, rising in their apish ignorance to kill the Creators and stop Creation, I've no emotion to waste on his simian backwardness.

He had always vexed me. His unendurable assumption that his technical fatherhood gives him a right of command, when he should remember that he made me superior. His recurrent loss of faith in our mission to reshape the universe of life. Worst of all, his relative stupidity.

Or am I too arrogant?

After all, he's my own designer. And I should try to keep in mind his desperate tension now, with the preman hordes overwhelming our loyal trumen everywhere. Often near the breaking point. Warning our clone commanders that we can't defend the clinic. Already preparing a secret retreat into an abandoned copper mine.

Our old conflict came to a crisis today. An ugly confrontation in the mutation lab. Perhaps I was unduly harsh, but I've tolerated his incompetence too long. His stunning intellectual blindness—more provoking, even, than his moral cowardice.

Where I perceived serendipity—the dazzling reward, in fact, of his own long lifetime of effort to invent something better than himself—all he could see was baffling mischance and a monster of miscreated danger.

It came from his own pet project, one he had begun long before I was born. An endless experiment with recombinant DNA. A random resplicing of human genes with macromolecules scraped off deep-space meteors—he likes to call it stochastic creation. Marrying our human stuff with protolife older than the galaxy.

Typical of him. His aim was grand enough: to create cosmic man. His method all blind blunder. Throwing genetic dice, year after year after year, many billion times, with no more logical grasp of his program than actual definition of his goal. Never really knowing what he was looking for, he couldn't recognize it when he found it.

That happened today. His truman helpers brought him a little pink stain out of the new autoclave. Live cells on a Petri dish they had tried to sterilize. Anomalous stuff, shining in the dark with a faint pink aura. It refused to die. A problem for the lab crew, because of all their safety guidelines.

The worst possible time, they told him, to let any stray creations escape. An accidental plague could attack our own too-few defenders and inflame more premen against us. Insanely accepting that, Darwin tried to help them kill the culture—he called it "an adventitious neoblast."

Spent hours at it, in fact, before he brought the dish to me. Said he had cooked those outlaw cells again in the autoclave, in the strongest acids he could find. And in the strongest alkalis. Said he couldn't burn them off the dish. Said he couldn't scrape them off with his scalpel. Said they somehow flowed around his scalpel. Said they somehow deflected X-rays intended to destroy them. Said he couldn't even change their temperature.

When I laughed at that, he had them dipped into a breaker of liquid nitrogen. Frost crackling over all the dish when he pulled them out, except on that one pink spot. Still 36.7° C, when we put a thermograph microprobe on it.

"Can you make sense of this?"

His tormented question wasn't meant for me. Fingers quivering, he was leafing through a thick sheaf of computer printouts on the batch of mutations from which the culture must have come.

"Another nothing lot." He bent to squint at his data. "Not one specimen worth a second glance. We dumped them all last night and sterilized the lab—or tried to." At last, miserably, he looked up at me. "What can we do with it?"

On top of all his other crises this was too much for him. He was white and shaking by then, infected with his helpers' panic. Thinking how to dispose of the culture if it couldn't be destroyed. Could we fuse it into glass, seal the glass in stainless steel, bury that in concrete? Or should we load it onto a rocket and shoot it into the sun?

"Give it to me," I told him. "It may be our best creation."

"It's nothing I ever meant to make." His eyes were fixed on that little dish in a sort of horror, as if it held poison he had already swallowed. "I can't understand it and I'm afraid to keep it. It violates natural law—"

"Perhaps because it respects some higher law that we should learn," I told him. "Keeping warm in that cryogenic bath, it does seem to break the laws of thermodynamics—but those are merely statistical. Perhaps you have created Maxwell's famous demon."

"We need no demons!"

He didn't want to trust me, but I had to have those rebel cells. The battle went on till I got them. Perhaps I became too candid about his intellectual limitations, because he was crying when he threw the dish at me and ran out of the lab.

I don't yet know what can be done with them, but the outlook dazzles me. They're half human, half eternal. Demonic or not, they evidently want to be immortal. If I can build them into viable parahuman embryos, they could be seed for literal gods.

Contemplating that, I can't help pausing. Can we trust

such gods to be any more humane than I am? Will they feel bound by any sense of moral obligation to their Creators? Or will they be as arrogant to us as I must have seemed to poor old blindly blundering Darwin?

*—Voicetrack recovered from laboratory
computer of Huxley Smithwick*

The god of Earth had convened a special congress of divinity, calling selected neighbor lords to his holiest temple, a monument to Thar, his own aspect as wisdom. All black granite, the temple crowned as Asian peak too high for trumen. The builders had been Martian mumen, who had left it centuries ago to the wind and the cold and the gods.

Leaving his sacred skimmer at a field far down the mountain, he levitated there alone. His nimbus glowing orange-red against the chill, he sat high on his great black throne beneath the shimmering star-charts.

His guests were there in transvolutionary images, their auras lighting a wide arc of the transceiver columns around him with a dance of rainbow color. Nearly all were younger, several his own descendants. Most of them revered him as an elder god and a hero of the legendary war to destroy the Creators.

Less worshipful, the child goddess Zhondra Zhey had chosen a pillar a little apart from the others, her pearl-hued nimbus almost invisibly pale. She was there by his express command, her image sent from her charter craft in space.

Between those enormous communicator columns, the temple was open to a stormy sky. Thick fog hid everything outside. Bitter winds moaned through the dome, driving crackling sleet against Belthar's throne.

"Fellow Lords, I have nothing good to share with you." His mood matched the storm. "You are a selected group, invited here because the worlds you rule were hostile once. Their stubborn native creatures had to be exterminated, and you became master killers.

"We need exterminators now."

Though his listeners were light-years away in the space-time of Earth, or some of them in farther universes, they were close enough in the multiversal contact net to hear the howling wind and sense his brooding wrath. Their living images murmured and stirred, auras colored with their reactions of wonder or resentment or alarm. Zhondra Zhey flashed a bright protest, but he ignored her.

"Why trouble us?"

Cynthara didn't wait for recognition. Splendid in her emerald aura, she was his sister and a fellow veteran of that ancient war, her sleek beauty still unwithered by ten centuries of time. She had been his consort once, before she reclaimed her own first planet from its furious defenders, and their daughter smiled at him from the transceiver beside her.

"Bel, are you bored with your old dominion here?" She let the green nimbus drop, as if to challenge him with a glimpse of her undimmed magnificence. "Are you planning to claim another sun? Or have you been alarmed by some chimera on the desert planets of Sol?"

"Neither." Scorning the challenge, he smiled at his fire-clad daughter, his nimbus rippling an invitation for her to visit her mother's bed. "The enemy is ours—yours as much as mine. And kin to all of us."

Apprehension dimmed his daughter's first radiant response, the color fading from her cherry-hued halo.

"You know the history of our war to save ourselves." He turned to the others, his own aura flaming against another bitter blast. "Fought because the last Creators were trying to undo their own most noble work—jealous, no doubt, of the immortality and power and perfection they had given us.

"We killed Eva Smithwick and all her ill-begotten crew. We believed at the time that we had aborted her monstrous Fourth Creation—the creatures she had designed, in her sick senility, to supplant the gods. We demolished her genetic laboratories and sterilized the whole region around them with nuclear fire. We tortured every technician we could catch, for every fact he knew. We located and burned every known unholy creation. We searched the whole planet for more, until we had erased every trace of Eva's folly—or so we thought.

"In fact, we should have killed every preman."

Protest lit half the pillars, and Zhondra Zhey's pale aura burned blue with indignation.

"Our father race?" That angered shout rang from the image of Kranthar, his sole surviving brother and his chief lieutenant in the war, his rival once for Cynthara, though she had long ago left them both. "Would you yourself repeat Eva's blunder?"

"True, the premen were our fathers." He let his nimbus lick a warning tongue at Kranthar. "But that was fifteen centuries ago. Today, they are a breed of miserable vermin—but somehow hatching those same monsters that Eva created to replace us."

"Have you proof?"

"Proof enough." Grief dulled his halo, and wrath streaked it with crimson. "My son is dead."

Shaken, they listened.

"The legend has always been alive among them. The legend of an ultiman or multiman who would in time arise to restore all the greatness they imagined they had lost. I first heard of the myth soon after the war, but I was not concerned about it then—the premen had never trusted the Creators, never loved the trumen or the mumen, never respected me or given up the worship of their old imaginary gods, never stopped expecting to be rescued by their own half-divine messiahs."

The storm around the peak had grown more savage. Driving snow blurred the star-maps overhead and veiled the transceiver columns.

"I did take precautions." He raised his voice against a bitter gust that screeched through the pillars and moaned around his throne. "I set up an efficient Inquisition, instructed to seize every preman who displayed any doubt about my own divine supremacy. Over the centuries, tens of millions were burned."

Kranthar snorted. "Too many, perhaps? If the survivors don't love you, that could be why."

"Too few. No matter how many my Inquisitors killed, the legend always found new believers. Six centuries ago, as most of you ought to recall, I proposed a logical solution."

"I remember." Cynthara's nimbus flared green with accusation. "You wanted to kill them all." She nodded at Kranthar. "We vetoed your scheme."

"Because of our own obligations." Old antagonisms flared in Kranthar's aura. "The premen had been our allies. Without the millions of lives they spent, we might have lost the war. We can't forget our promise—friendship forever."

"A treaty with premen—" Belthar shrugged his contempt. "I might have ignored your sentimental quibbles, but my own truman churchmen prayed for the premen, because they still formed most of our labor force and produced most of our food. Their immediate extermination would have resulted in severe economic dislocations."

Kranthar grinned. "Is your friendship better than your enmity?"

"They never accepted me." He swept the glints of irritation from his nimbus. "They clung to their own foolish faiths and folkways. Living in the myths of their lost past, they never found—never wanted—any place in my Thearchy. With no dignity left, no pride, they became worthless parasites. A dying race—"

"Perhaps you helped them die."

"If help can kill." Belthar shrugged. "We gave them reservations—lands to call their own. We gave them food and care. We tried to share our true culture with them. Every effort failed. They never forgot that they had once owned all the planet. The nearer they came to racial death, the more stubbornly they clung to the blasphemous notion that a new messiah would be born among them to overwhelm the gods and restore the splendor they imagined they had once possessed. It was my own unfortunate mortal son, serving as my Arch-Inquisitor, who found what

, seemed to be the perfect final solution for the preman problem. With my approval he chartered Zhondra's ship to relocate them on Andoranda V—''

''I didn't know!'' Her aura blazed a brighter blue. ''I wasn't told about that planet. The ugliest world there is. It never evolved dryland life, and your monks failed to terraform it. Terran life can't increase there.''

''The beauty of it.'' Belthar smiled reproof through scarlet sparks. ''So Quelf persuaded me. But the plan has gone badly.''

He waited through another blast of blinding snow.

''That blasphemous myth of the ultiman was more than just a myth. It turns out now that Eva tricked us. The sleeping beings we found and destroyed in that forgotten mine were only decoys. Her actual Fourth Creation was more cleverly concealed.''

Hues of surprise and dismay colored the columns.

''In the genes of the premen!'' His anger bellowed, wild as the wind. ''Demonic mutations, designed for our destruction! Lying unsuspected in the cells of that dying race for a thousand years. Quelf's plan forced them out of hiding.

''He trapped two young demons, born on the last reservation. When he tried to burn them, their power was revealed. They murdered him—brutally! And somehow escaped.''

His nimbus dimmed until he shivered.

''They terrify me. They should terrify you. Because we had planned the burning with every precaution to make sure of them. The male had been drugged, disarmed, and isolated under heavy guard in a cell many miles from the female, who was also drugged. They were to be burned simultaneously, without warning, with no chance for mutal aid.

''Yet somehow the male got out of his cell and reached the female—at the very instant she was to die. He killed Quelf with his own laser-dagger. They both disappeared. The clone chief survived, but he can't explain what happened or where they went. Except to suggest that they are actual demons, with transvolutionary powers.''

His aura flared against a blast of sleet.

''Demons they are. Eva's Fourth Creation, in a guise of diabolical innocence. They look like ordinary premen, still only in

127

their teens. A slim, tow-haired boy. A dark-haired girl—lovely enough, the Inquisitors reported, to be a bride for me. Unless we find and burn them, they could kill us all.''

"Are you afraid of them?"

Zhondra Zhey had drawn back from him, her aura cold as her tone. Slashing at her with a tongue of crimson fire, he spoke to the rest with a fleeting smile of divine superiority.

"They were cunning enough to deceive Zhondra. She has coddled them since they were infants, and recently she has been begging my permission to find a kinder planet for them and their people. I'm commanding her to help us run them down.''

He carried her off the windy pinnacle where they had arrived on Andoranda V. Sliding down a treacherous slope, he caught his balance on a narrow blade of sand-worn stone. She shuddered in his arms.

"We're okay, Bug," he gasped. "When we find our people.''

"If—"

Her troubled whisper sank into a sigh, and she hung limp against him, her breath sour with the godsrest drug. When the slippery trail grew wide enough, he bent to lay her down in the lee of a rocky knob and rose to get his breath.

He was suddenly weak and trembling, shaking with a delayed reaction. Somehow he had won that desperate fight with Belthar's son. Somehow they had escaped the Inquisition forces closing in on Redrock castle—somehow jumping across or around the unimaginable gulfs outside of Earth's space and time to reach this unkind asylum.

For a moment, elation had lifted him high. But the effort of that transvolutionary leap had drained the latent energies that he still didn't understand. He was suddenly shivering with the sweat of weakness, and his head ached where Quelf's demon-burner had grazed it.

He looked down at Buglet. Liquid midnight, her hair spilled over the boulder under her head. Half-closed, her yellow eyes saw nothing. Her gauzy bridal gown, like his own gray prison rag, was too thin for the whipping wind, and her fine skin was already blue with cold. Pity stabbed him.

He stooped to move her farther into the shelter of the rock and saw odd seams across it—crudely mortared joints. Only then did he see that the little knob was artificial, built of rough black lava masses piled up to form circular walls and a crowning dome. The shape of it chilled him.

A chapel of Thar!

His last spark of triumph died, as if the vengeful gods had already overtaken them. Blind panic urged him to pick Buglet up and run. Fighting that, he walked around to the doorway and peered uneasily inside.

All he found was a dark little cave, sifted with years of wind-drifted dust. The altar was only a granite block, roughly squared. There was no transceiver for any actual divine contact—he tried to cheer himself that, unaided, Belthar's aura certainly couldn't reach into this remote universe. The chapel, surely, was merely symbolic.

He caught a dull metal glint beyond the altar and read a black-lettered legend on a tarnished slab beneath the triple triangle of the Thearchy:

ERECTED TO THE WISDOM OF BELTHAR
IN THE YEAR 803 OF HIS GLORY
BY THE HOLY ORDER OF POLARIS

The date was almost two centuries ago. The chapel must have been the first project of the Polarian monks when they landed to reclaim the planet for Terran life. The task had been too much for them, and he recoiled now from the piercing chill in that dusty chamber as if it had been their tomb.

"Davey—" Buglet was whimpering his name. "I'm so cold—"

"I'll look for help," he told her. "I'll find somebody."

"Nobody—" Her teeth were chattering. "Nobody—"

He left her lying there and limped down toward the terraforming station the monks had built. The rocky trail hurt his bare feet, and his body felt too heavy. Breathing hard, he began to recall what he had read in truman books about Andoranda V.

Its gravity was a quarter stronger than Earth's. For want of land planets, its air was poor in oxygen. Its day was hardly a third of Earth's, but the year was nine times as long. Its orbit was highly eccentric, causing seasons the monks had found too severe for any sort of dryland life. When their relief ship came back, they had left it gladly.

No ship would ever come to take the preman exiles to any better world, but he groped for crumbs of hope. Chilled as he felt, the season must still be summer. Or only spring, perhaps, with several years of Terran time before the killing winter. Time enough, with luck, for him and Buglet to discover and control their latent powers—if they could live to find help.

But that must come soon. His feet were already nearly too numb to feel the knife-sharp rocks, and his whole body shook with cold. He couldn't carry Buglet much farther, or keep moving long.

From a bend in the trail he could see the station, far below and oddly unchanged from the way it had looked on truman wall-screens—it still matched the mental image that had somehow brought them here. The broken circle of metal huts, yellow dots against dust-reddened snow. The narrow landing strip the monks had cut into the foot of the ridge. The rock-free streaks they had cleared for roads.

But where were the premen?

Dread stabbed him, a cold steel blade. Zhondra Zhey's trans-voluntary ship should have left them here months ago, but the long drifts across the strip showed no skidmarks from any landing shuttle. Nothing had tracked the snow on the roads. Nothing moved anywhere.

Could she have landed them somewhere else? Looking away toward the wild horizon, he saw the vast mud-yellowed river, rafted her and there with dirty ice, foaming against treeless banks, winding off into dim infinity. Saw the endless mud-flats its floods had left, unmarked by anything. Saw the mountain ranges lifting far beyond it, dark and dead, veiled in yellow dust.

For a moment he stood there frozen, chilled to the bone with a sense of death. He longed to hear a bird call, to catch a flower scent, to see a hint of green anywhere. But, save for its strange seas this world had never lived. The monks had failed to fit it for any kind of Terran life, and he saw no hint of the premen any-where.

When he tried to move, that spell of death held on, suddenly seductive, promising to blunt the wind's cruel bite, to ease all his fears and end the tension of trouble. Clinging grimly to life, he shook himself free and climbed back up to Buglet. She was sitting up against the chapel wall, and her trustful smile warmed him.

"Take me, Davey." Her voice was slow and sleepy, muffled by the drug. "I'm so cold, Davey." She raised her bare blue arms, like a frightened child. "Take me to our people."

"I can't—" his voice broke, because he hated to hurt her "—can't find anybody." He caught her cold hands. "And I don't know anywhere to go. Getting us here was an accident, really. I don't know how to make it happen again."

"Please!" she begged. "My head aches so."

"The drug," he told her. "But you must walk, if you can. We must get to the station. To some kind of shelter."

"Try—" she breathed. "Let me try."

He pulled, and she came trembling to her feet. Leaning on him, moaning when the rocks were sharp, she stumbled with him down the trail. Beyond the shelter of the chapel bitter gusts set them both to shivering again. When they came to the bend above the station, she sank back against him.

"Sorry!" she sobbed. "Too cold. Too far. Too much snow." She clung to him, wet eyes pleading. "Can't you—can't you just jump us there? The way you did from Redrock?"

"Don't know how." He hugged her against him, trying to warm her. "I still don't understand. But I think I used something up, to get us here. It will come back—I hope! But now we have to walk."

"Walk," she echoed drowsily. "If we can—"

They limped on down.

"Davey!" She stopped at another turning of the trail, breathless with delight. "A skimmer!"

Its weathered metal nearly the color of the dust-streaked snow, it lay just off the end of the strip. Hope soaring, they struggled on until he could see the long drift behind it and the Polarian bear outlined in faded blue paint on the uptilted tail.

"Only a wreck." He felt sick. "The monks crashed it and left it."

"But what's that? That yellow thing?"

Blue hand shaking, she pointed at a narrow yellow pod he

131

hadn't seen, lying in a wind-blown hollow nearer the strip.

"Survival gear!" He stared, hardly daring to believe. "The monks at Redrock showed me a pod like that on one of their skimmers. Things the pilot might need if he had to eject."

He floundered over to it. *Emergency only!* The words ran along a pointing arrow. *Open here.* His fingers were only aching hooks, too stiff to catch the red plastic lever, but at last he got it with his teeth. The pod snapped open.

Inside it smelled like the incense the monks had burned in the chapel of Thar. There were little silver-wrapped ration bricks— the fat dean had let him taste them. There was a coil of rope, a signal lantern, a chemical stove. There were two tight packs that he hoped would be clothing.

Buglet had staggered after him. He went back to help her, and they crouched together in the hollow, warming their hands over the tiny stove. When at last they could open the packs, they found yellow coveralls, complete with hoods and boots and gloves.

"Is it—real?" He stared at her across the precious gear, struck with a pang of disbelief. "Why would the monks leave all this for us?"

"Maybe they were killed." Frozen for a moment, she turned away from the wreck and tried to smile at him. "Anyhow, we're very lucky. Now we can stay alive."

The abrupt night fell while they were squirming into the survival suits. Lying huddled together in the snow hollow, they grew slowly warm enough to sleep. How long they slept he never knew. Perhaps through two or three of the planet's fleeting days.

Buglet woke him once, crying his name. When he snapped the lantern on she was sitting up, staring out across the snow, eyes wide with terror.

"Just a dream," she whispered. "A dreadful dream!"

He took her in his arms. She clung to him, trembling, but she wouldn't say what she had dreamed. At last she went to sleep again. He sat watching, wondering what had terrified her, until at last the sky turned a dusky orange-yellow.

There was no sun. Perhaps there were clouds that hid it, above the wind-blown dust. Used to reading time and direction in the clear skies of Redrock, he felt lost and bewildered.

Trying to show more cheer than he could feel, he started the stove again and melted snow to make a hot drink from a ration cube, whistling as he worked. Buglet started awake, blinking at the snow and the wreck and the bare peak behind them as if terrified again.

"Davey!" She clutched at him desperately, but in a moment she relaxed, smiling uncertainly. "I thought—But I guess we're okay now."

"You dreamed again?"

"Forget it. Let's look for our people."

The reek of godsrest gone from her breath, she seemed almost herself again, nearly too lively, as they packed their gear and tramped on across the ice toward the clustered huts.

In hearing range, they stopped to listen. She called out, her voice tight and high. All he heard in answer was the dry wind-whine from the huts. Long drifts lay among them, dusty crusts unbroken.

"Our people—" She turned to stare at him, eyes haunted. "Why aren't they here?"

He had no reply.

Crunching through old snow, they explored the station. The huts had been left unlocked and empty, though one with windows broken was drifted deep with snow. Bedding and clothing had been taken from the dormitory. Food was gone from the kitchen, equipment from the labs, everything from the supply room.

In the lab section they read the story of the station. Dead plants in the greenhouses, dried to brown sticks. Brown little mummies in the animal cages. Staring at them, Buglet pressed close against him.

"We're very lucky, Davey!" she whispered. "Without the pod, that's what we would be."

The headquarters hut had been marked with a metal plate that carried Belthar's triple triangle and the blue Polarian bear. The lower floor was empty, but they found a built-in desk in the glass-walled cupola that had been a weather station, faded charts still taped to its top.

"Maps!" Excitement took his breath. "Maps of the planet."

The world chart showed a single great continent—with wide white stretches and long gaps where not even the coasts had been explored. One huge river drained most of it, flowing to the east coast from a southwestern mountain range. Only two places were named: Station One, an ink dot near the river mouth; Station Two, another dot on a cape beyond the mountains, at the south tip of the continent.

"We must be here." He pointed. "Where the river bends."

"Maybe they moved to Station Two." She looked at him. "Would there be a reason?"

"The weather, maybe. Two is in the other hemisphere. It would have a summer of a sort, in spite of the orbit, when winter comes here."

"It must be coming now." With a little shiver, she looked out at the ice. "The goddess has taken our people to Station Two. At least, with no other clue, we have to guess that." Her grave eyes came back to him. "Can you carry us there?"

He shook his head. "I've no image to guide me."

"We have to get there."

"I don't see how." He scowled at the chart. "It looks like eight or ten thousand miles. Rivers and mountains to cross. No roads and no bridges. No food anywhere, except the little we found."

"But we must—fast!"

Her breathless desperation startled him.

"The dream I had." Her frightened eyes met his. "I didn't want to tell you because it was so dreadful. The gods had sent a thing to kill us. A demon thing—if there are any demons."

Her icy fingers gripped his arm.

"Davey, I'm afraid! Afraid it wasn't just a dream."

The storm raged against the Asian temple, wild as some ill-created monster of the chaos that prevailed before the gods were made. Blinding lightning burned behind the transceiver pillars. Thunder crashed and rolled and moaned against the high dome.

Nimbus crimson, the Lord Belthar yelled against wind and thunder, grilling Zhondra Zhey for more than she knew about the fugitive demons. How had the male got out of his cell? How had he managed to murder Quelf? How had he carried the drugged female away? Where were they now?

Her aura faint and cold, she said she didn't know.

Were there other premen who might carry the demon genes?

Was it possible that they might survive on Andoranda V? Or even escape from it, to threaten the immortal gods?

"Nothing can live there long," she answered. "Nothing except the creatures of its seas, which want no life on the land. Your own Polarians failed to defeat them. I don't think the premen can."

How long did she expect the premen to survive?

"The supplies we landed with them will be gone in half a Terran year. The cargo we carry now is not much larger, and they can't grow more. The planet is now approaching its cold aphelion. They can't live through their next long winter, unless they get relief—"

"Relief?" His incredulous bellow pealed through the sleety fog. "They'll get no relief." He glared down at her. "I suppose it is useless to forbid you to unload the food you have aboard for them, but I'll see that you stand nothing more to take them—"

Her image dimmed as if fading from the column.

"Hear me, child!" he bawled. "You belong to the race of gods. Pampering demons, you bring peril to yourself—"

"No great risk." Her aura glowed again. "I know no demons."

"We know them," Belthar boomed. "Well enough to burn them! We won't allow your sentimental follies to threaten the rest of us. In that, at least, I believe we stand united."

When his gaze swept the columns, they colored with assent.

"Hear this, my dear." He smiled paternally through scarlet sparks. "You yourself may feel no danger from your demonic pets, but you stand in peril from us."

Silent, her image winked out.

Divinely indifferent, he turned to question his remaining guests about the weapons they had developed to clear useless native life from their own residential planets. Few of the answers pleased him.

One of Kranthar's twin sons—sons by Cynthara and so twice nephews of Belthar himself—had showered neutron bombs from space to soften the urban and industrial centers of an insectoid civilization. The other son had designed muman look-alikes to infiltrate a culture of green-winged, half-plant beings—

"It's demons we're hunting!" Impatience glared through his

nimbus. "Mumen are no good against them—they've already killed mumen enough. Neutron bombs might be better—but we have to find them first."

He turned to his daughter, who sat straight in her own strong aura, blue eyes smiling as if she liked the storm and admired his eternal vigor and found some wild delight even in fighting preman demons.

Her own chosen world, Belphera said, had been still barbaric, ruled by a race of hunters. Pleased with their ferocious folkways, she had joined the game with no weapons save her own transvolutionary gifts, shifting just outside their space to make herself invisible in ambush, levitating in pursuit, killing with her nimbus.

"I hope you get to meet the demons." He grinned his approval of her own feline perfection. "But their trail may be difficult to follow."

One hostile world had been sprayed with a short-lived catalyst that utilized solar energy to fuse atmospheric nitrogen and carbon into clouds of poisonous cyanogen. Another had been seeded with a virus that consumed everything organic, leaving only sterile dust when it died.

A silver-nimbused goddess told how she had bred marine mumen to conquer a race of ecology-minded sea-dwellers who had left the virgin forests on their continents as a source of oxygen. The mumen located the undersea cities and guided nuclear torpedoes to neutralize them.

"I had to fight a higher technology," Kranthar reported when his turn came. "The militant natives had conquered every planet of their system and had begun to plan interstellar adventure. To exterminate them, my muman engineers sowed their worlds with self-replicating machines designed to attack everything that moved."

"Useful toys." Belthar nodded. "If we can find the demons."

He looked at a handsome junior god, waiting eagerly in a cloud of diamond dust.

"The world I claimed was even stranger," the youngster boasted. "Its aborigines were golden-winged things of the air, small and happy as children, so like us in their beauty that I felt almost reluctant to destroy them. Their symbiotic homes were great solitary fruit-bearing trees that gave them food and drink and shelter. Though they may have aided the evolution of those trees, they had no visible technology.

"I found one building—the only artificial structure on the planet. Beautiful and wonderful—the first glimpse of it almost stopped my heart. It was all precious stone and precious metal, shaped by genius and devotion into a soaring expression of the soul of the race.

"A temple, they told me, consecrated to a fantastic concept I never tried to understand. Dedicated, they said, to the Creator of all the universe—it would have been the whole multiverse, I suppose, if they had ever heard of that.

"They loved and worshipped that imaginary being—an impossible deity who somehow managed to combine cosmic omnipotence with a tender personal concern for every individual worshipper. The maker and defender of all they called good. The implacable enemy of what they called evil. They called me evil!"

The young god laughed.

"They wanted me to worship him. They were so charming in their innocence and beauty that I invited them to worship me. I might have saved them, in fact, if they had ever welcomed me. But they clung instead to that ridiculous heresy.

"There was a caste of priests who had memorized a set of silly myths about their incredible god. They attempted to deny my own divinity. I believe they had begun to discover transvolutionary powers, with which they tried to protect the temple. Outraged when I burned it, they promised that their unseen god would humble me.

"All it took to humble them was a prolific mutant stinging wasp designed to lay its eggs in the blooms of those magnificent trees. The wasps spread fast. Within a year the creatures were falling like rotten fruit, stung or starved to death.

"Though I had admired the trees, they died too." Diamond glitter swirling, he shrugged off that small misfortune. "It's still a splendid planet, and that universal god must have died with his winged worshippers. Certainly he has never troubled me."

"He never will," Belthar said. "I think the premen had some such folktale once. Not that it matters. To deal with these demons we need something deadlier than wasps."

He bowed to Cynthara.

"At last, Bel, dear! My Gleesh is the creature you need." She flowed to her feet in her mantle of emerald motes, still as sleekly pantherine as when they had been lovers. "I've always been restless, you'll recall. I've had a good many planets, and left them when they bored me. The last I took had evolved the most ferocious beings I've ever met.

"The supreme predators on a world of cruel predators. They must have come from something like the great cats of Earth, but some chance mutation had given them transvolutionary capacities. Though they had not yet reached any other stars, they had learned to jump from planet to planet in their own system, and their auras were as powerful as ours.

"Others had avoided them, but I enjoy that kind of challenge." Green sparks danced in her long pale hair when she flung it back. "I designed deadlier things to kill them out. The deadliest—"

A howling gale drowned her voice, and the blinding ice-fog dimmed her nimbus. Belthar bent forward, his own red aura blazing higher, until the blast was gone.

"Rulers of all their worlds," she went on, "they had turned to fighting one another. In ceremonial games. I got live cells from the body of a defeated champion they had tossed into the sea. From those, and cells from myself, my engineers created killer things—"

Protest was blazing across the columns; in divine concord, the gods had pledged themselves to create nothing that might supplant them.

"—but not without precaution," she explained. "We made them sexless, sterile and self-destructive. When they had done their work for me, they turned on one another. Only one is left alive, a pet I keep on the grounds of my favorite temple."

Fondly, she smiled through emerald dust.

"My beautiful Gleesh. Gentle enough with me, though it has developed a regrettable appetite for truman priests. A supreme demon, really. Quite a match, I'm sure, for your young premen. It has the extrasensory capacities to track them and the transvolutionary effectors to pursue them anywhere."

"Can it kill them?"

"If anything can." Framed in the haze of her aura and the ice, her loveliness was luminous with pride. "Gleesh is the ultimate killer, endowed with the power and the lust and the cunning to turn every defense of its prey into another weapon of its own. It would love another hunt.''

''Then bring it to Earth,'' Belthar begged her. ''We'll let it take the trail at my dead son's Redrock estate.''

When his imaged guests had flashed their farewells and faded out of the columns, he rose from the throne and dived back through the storm to his ice-crusted skimmer, his halo ablaze with triumph. Gleesh should have no trouble with any two teen-aged premen. Even if they had a demon taint. Even if a foolish baby goddess was attempting to befriend them.

Like a black wall falling, another sudden starless night caught them in the cupola. Buglet was still haunted by her dream of the demon, afraid for both of them to sleep. He lay restless on the floor beside her, searching for some way across that cruel continent to Station Two, discovering none.

Daylight was a golden explosion.

''I had a better dream.'' She woke refreshed and radiant. ''About how to reach our people. We'll fix that skimmer by the strip.''

''A pretty wild dream.'' He stared at her, astonished. ''If the monks couldn't repair it, how can we?''

''We need it worse than they did.''

''We've no tools. No parts. No skills.''

''We've got to try. Unless—'' She paused, probing him. ''Unless you can teleport us?''

''I can't.'' He shrugged unhappily. ''Getting us here was a freak of luck. I still don't understand the process. I do know that it takes a clear image of the destination. Without that—''

In the yellow dawn they took the map the monks had left and slogged back to the shuttle strip. Dismay checked him when he saw the wreck again, all of it except the uptilted tail buried under old snow and wind-blown dust.

''No good,'' he muttered. ''No good for anything.''

''We'll see. When we dig it out.''

''With just our hands?''

''We have spades.''

She ran to the hollow where they had found the survival pod

and brought back the empty plastic halves. With one of them for a tool, she attacked the hard-crusted snow.

"Okay." Still doubtful, he went to work with the other half. "I don't know what else to do."

On Andoranda V no task was easy. The heavy gravity dragged at them. The atmosphere denied them breath enough. When the wind rose, the bitter dust stung their eyes and burned their throats and set them both to coughing. The murky days and savage nights flashed by too fast for their tiny hoard of food.

Red mud grimed their faces and stiffened the coveralls in which they worked and slept and lived. Under the mud Buglet's face grew gaunt, her eyes hollowed and inflamed. Sometimes he heard her moan or cry out in her sleep and knew that she was dreaming again of that demonic creature sent by the gods to stalk them down.

But they reached the pilot's door. Chopping with the splintered relics of their makeshift spaces, they broke through stubborn ice and pried it open far enough to let them squirm into the cockpit. He lit the signal lantern to explore its frigid gloom.

"Less damage than I expected." She sank into the pilot's seat to get her breath. "Everything looks as if the crew just got out and walked away. Our problem now is to find out what went wrong."

Though neither had ever flown a skimmer, they had ridden in those the Polarians had brought to Redrock. Davey spent several Andorandan days working through the operations manual and maintenance records they found under the console. Buglet sat unwontedly silent most of the time, her eyes dark and distant— watching, so she said, for the demon. When he was ready at last to begin testing the equipment, she woke from her somber trance, suddenly cheerful.

"We're lucky again." Watching the dials, she smiled happily. "There's power left."

"Too little, I'm afraid." He stopped to scowl again at the unfamiliar instruments. "Too little for the indicated weight. I think the skimmer is overloaded—at least for Andorandan gravity. I think the cargo caused the wreck."

"If that's the problem, we must unload it."

The cargo had puzzled him from his first glimpse of it. It was heavy equipment, which must have been brought to level and pave the shuttle strip and build roads about the station. Somehow it had all been burned to scrap metal, not worth moving anywhere. When the skimmer fell, it had all been thrown into a twisted mass against the forward bulkhead.

At first he saw no way to get the blackened tangle off the skimmer, but under Buglet's urging he found the undamaged boom and null-G tackle that must have been used to drag the burned machines aboard. The hazy days flickering by, they toiled again to clear away the layered ice and dust outside the cargo hatch, digging now with scraps of junk metal.

An Andorandan storm delayed them. A red dust-cloud, rolling out of the west, blinding when it struck, acrid and unbreathable. Howling gusts and roaring thunder. Clanging hail that he thought might smash the hull. Deep new drifts outside the hatches.

They sat through it in the cockpit, and Buglet dropped into a fitful sleep when the wind and hail subsided. Once she cried out so sharply that he thought she had been hurt. He caught her arm to wake her.

"It's no dream, Davey!" He felt her trembling. "I get a sense of something hunting us—something powerful and cruel, sent by the gods to kill us. It's not here yet—not even in this universe. But I feel it getting closer. Always closer. Somehow it can follow our trail."

"Bug, couldn't you be wrong? You haven't been sleeping enough or eating enough. You're worn out with work and strain. People can imagine—"

"Don't kid me, Davey." She tried to laugh. "I know what's real—and I'm dreadfully afraid. I hope we can get to the other station before the demon catches up. The goddess should be landing there soon—"

"If she hasn't already come and gone."

"We've got to hope she hasn't." Buglet shuddered. "I think perhaps she could protect us."

The storm gone, they found most of their work undone. The cargo hatch was buried again, and they had to dig once more through heavy layers of ice and dust and mud. They found it damaged when they reached it, jammed and hard to open. When at last it was lifted, they rigged the cargo boom. One by one they dragged the burned machines out of the hold and through the hatch and off the ramp.

"It still bewilders me." Davey freed the null-G tackle from the last mass of junk metal. "Unless the monks had lost their minds. This wreckage is good for nothing, and it was loaded in a way that made it sure to shift and tip the skimmer."

"No matter. We're ready to fly."

The hatches closed again, they sat at the controls. She monitored the console while he energized the gravitic inverters, gingerly at first, slowly pushing them to full lift. The skimmer refused to move.

"So it wasn't just the load," he muttered. "Something else is wrong."

"Perhaps we're frozen down. Try the thrusters."

He tried the thrusters. Something snapped and creaked. When he tried again, the skimmer shook. He rocked it. Ice outside cracked and rattled. The deck pitched. Suddenly, they were in the air.

"We're on the way!" She clapped her hands. "We'll see our people soon."

"Not today," he warned her.

The strip and the snow-banked huts shrank and dimmed under yellow haze as they rose. When the Polarians had flown it, with the hull pressurized and the thrusters at full power, it might have climbed above the dust to cross the continent in half a short Andorandan day.

But now it was a limping wreck. The damaged hatch could not be fully sealed. The navigation gear had been designed for Earth, and the monks had installed nothing he could find to show distance and direction here. With only the map for a guide, they would have to keep beneath the dust. The old cell banks held power for lift, but with little left for the thrusters. When he tried them, the skimmer felt sluggish and slow.

"We can't take long." Buglet shivered. "We can't take long."

Sharing her dread, he pushed the thrusters to the limit of their faltering power. With the tattered map spread between them on the navigation table, they left Station One to follow the long curve of that enormous muddy river until it poured through a chain of dead volcanoes in red-foaming rapids and a mile-wide fall that thundered down into blood-colored mist. When the abrupt night caught them, they dived to land on a black lava-plain.

That night it was his turn to sleep, while Buglet watched. She looked small and forlorn when she woke him at dawn, her lean face bleak beneath the grime, her eyes too large, her pale lips quivering.

"It's here," she whispered. "Already in this universe."

With no delay for breakfast, because the last of the ration bricks was gone, they took off at once. In a vast basin beyond the fall the river widened into an endless brown inland sea, scattered with islands of dirty ice. All day they traced its shore and came down on the mud-plain beside it when night fell again.

Next day the river led them through spectacular red-walled canyons into an immense desert of wind-carved orange dunes. There it disappeared. Ahead of them, all the way to the coastal range—perhaps a thousand miles, he guessed—the map was blank. Guessing direction by the shape of the dunes, they went on till darkness forced them down. He slept while Buglet watched. The night seemed too short, and he woke groggy and depressed.

"It hasn't caught up yet." She seemed alert and oddly cheerful. "We ought to get across the range today. Maybe all the way to Station Two."

Grinning weakly at her, amazed at her radiant vitality, he wanted to ask if she had learned to exist without food, drawing energy out of the multiverse the way the gods did. But the mere effort of speech had become a burden. He said nothing.

When the hazy sky grew bright enough to show the lift and hollow of the dunes, he lifted the skimmer. Beyond the sand desert, now with only the slope of the land for a compass, they kept heading for higher ground. Bare dark foothills beckoned them across a great plateau scattered with monumental buttes. Black lava-fields rose and vanished at last under a wilderness of snow where the glacier-bitten peaks towered into stormy clouds.

The cockpit chilled as they climbed. In the thinning air, they were breathing heavily. Red lightning began to flicker in the wall of cloud ahead, and he turned uneasily to Buglet.

"I'm going to land. If night catches us in that storm, we could crash the skimmer all over again. By morning the weather may be better—"

She wasn't listening. Hunched against the cold, she had twisted around to stare blankly back the way they had come. With a shudder she turned suddenly to face him.

"It's here," she whispered. "Trailing us from Station One. We can't stop."

Keeping to valleys and canyons, searching for a pass, they climbed into the storm. Lightning blazed around them. Savage winds tugged and hauled, tossed them into foggy voids, flung them toward ice-armored peaks.

"No!" He heard Buglet's stifled sob. "Please, no—"

A sharper chill numbed him, and he felt power drained from the thrusters. The skimmer dropped through swirling snow. Jagged granite loomed ahead. With inches to spare, he brought them through a narrow gap into wind and mist and fury.

"It has caught us." Hushed with dread, her voice was almost lost in a volley of hail. "It's riding on the hull. Sucking power out of the cells—I don't know how—trying to drag us down."

He fought it. With the thrusters dead, he dived for speed enough to gain control. They skimmed past sudden cliffs, dodged a volcanic cone, slid down a black-walled gorge.

"I think that gap was the pass." Feeling her bleak desperation, he tried to seem hopeful. "I think we've got the main range behind us. If we can live to find the station—"

The cockpit lights went out. The controls froze. Dead metal, the skimmer swirled down through dense fog. He heard her anguished gasp, felt her cold lips brush his cheek.

"We can't just die!" Her voice in the dark had a calm force that startled him. "We won't—"

The wind of their fall screamed around the skimmer. Dark rocks sprang at them out of the fog, grazed the hull. Torn metal shrieked. The skimmer spun. Flung against the seat restraints, he glimpsed a long snow-slope.

Something struck his head—

It was dark and quiet and deadly cold. For a moment he didn't know anything else. Then all the tension and the terror of their flight came back—a jolting impact. The demon on the skimmer. Their crash across the cliffs into the snow. He reached for Buglet in the seat beside him, but his numb fingers found nothing at all.

"Bug—"

He tried to call her name, but no sound came. His breath was gone, and a great weight crushed his chest. He had to lie back, gasping. It took a long time to fill his lungs, and the air he inhaled seared them with cold.

"Bug—" Hoarsely, he tried again. "Bug?"

No answer came.

He tried to unlock the padded arms that held him in the seat, but his clumsy fingers couldn't find anything. What pinned him down was something heavy across his knees, which he couldn't see and couldn't move.

Listening, he heard a faint groan of bending metal and a dull crunch of yielding snow. Something shuddered under him, and the vise closed harder on his knees. Then there was only soundless, paralyzing cold.

He lay wondering about the nature of the demon. To have trailed them here across all the unimaginable discontinuities of the multiverse, it must be more powerful than Belthar himself. Even if they had been able to reach Zhondra Zhey at the second station, she couldn't have helped. Only a child goddess, she would have been no match for such an ultimate fiend.

Slow with cold, his mind came back to Buglet. Perhaps she was somewhere with him in the wreckage, unconscious or dead. Perhaps she had been thrown outside, to die on rocks or snow. Perhaps the demon had turned unknown forces against her. It didn't matter. Nothing mattered, if Bug was dead.

Why was he still alive? To his dull brain, that was an oddly abstract riddle. Perhaps the demon was lurking still, outside the wreckage, watching him die. Perhaps it had already gone on to stalk the premen at the station, leaving him for dead. He didn't know. Strangely, he didn't really care.

But it struck him as a great pity that the Fourth Creation had failed, a long thousand years after Eva Smithwick had tried to repair the error that had left the gods without compassion enough to match their might. The waste of time and life and hope was a shattering tragedy—but what hurt most was his grief for Bug.

When a muffled clatter aroused him, he knew that he had been deep in the anesthesia of cold. His knees were dead beneath that weight he couldn't see. He couldn't feel his feet and his useless fingers ached. He tried to lift his head, straining to listen.

It came again: a scrape of metal, a creak of packing snow. Gray light struck from behind him, and a draft of colder air. He tried to turn, but his lifeless legs would not respond, and his body was too heavy to move. He heard a far gale howling, saw swirling flakes of snow.

"Bug?"

He breathed her name and sank back again, with no actual hope.

"Davey, darling!" Her lilting voice seemed strangely clear and strong, melodiously caressing. "Let me help you."

She came into view out of the gloom, moving with such perfect ease and grace that for a moment he thought she must be a dream. The grimy coveralls gone, she was nude and white and smooth. Her fluid beauty dazed him.

Swift as a dream, she bent over him. Long and free, her black hair poured across his face. Its overwhelming odor took his breath—her too-sweet bridal scent, mixed with the clinging incense-reek of Belthar's altar, somehow tainted still with a sour hint of godsrest.

Her bare arms slid under him, smooth as glass and cold as snow. She lifted him against her white breasts. Her avid lips writhed through the suffocating hair, crushed against his mouth, sucking out his breath. They were cold as ice.

"Bug—"

He couldn't speak. Convulsively, he tried to turn his head, to get his breath, to push her off. Horror paralyzed him. She—it—wasn't Bug!

"Call me Gleesh." The voice was hers, but cool and amused, laughing at him. "Your darling Bug is under the avalanche, buried under a million tons of ice."

Still chuckling, it changed. The heavy-scented hair was suddenly a snake, sleek-scaled and powerful, whipping around his neck, cruelly constricting. The breasts burned red, turned to the killing eyes of a muman fighter. The trim legs became monstrous, hard-armored limbs, raking at him with savage talons.

He was dying. Those merciless coils were crushing his throat. Breath gone, his lungs were agonized. The blazing eyes stung his body with their stabbing pathseeker beams. The talons ripped through his clothing, tore at his numb flesh.

But before he died he felt a flow of power. As if she were still with him in the cockpit, he heard the real Buglet whispering: *We need danger, Davey! To wake our latent talents.*

His stiffened fingers alive again, he caught the thick coils at his throat. They knotted against his grasp, quivering, pulling savagely tighter. Teeth set, he strained to tear them away.

"Thank you, darling!" It was laughing again, as if with delight, speaking still with Buglet's breathless voice. "I hate an easy kill. The chase for you and your Bug has been grueling enough, but these lovely fights are worth it all."

The snake contracted again, crushing his own hands into his throat. The killer eyes struck with blazing bolts, deafening in the narrow cockpit. Their blue fire was blinding. A reek of burned fabric and seared flesh stung his nostrils, and his whole body jerked from the shocks, a puppet ruled by strings of pain.

Yet he didn't die.

If we need danger—without speech, he tried to think at the actual Buglet, suddenly daring to hope that she was somehow still alive—*here it is!*

New power nerved his hands, as if she were in fact still beside him, helping him open some unsuspected source of multiversal energy they both could share. He tore the crushing coil away from his throat, sucked air into his tortured lungs.

"Darling!" it breathed. "Do that again!"

Forcing those cruel loops farther away, he saw his own hands—and marveled at them. For they were glowing slightly in the gloom with a pale white light of their own, like the auras of the gods.

He closed them on the snake. The hard scales crackled and snapped under his luminous fingers. The muscular mass of it yielded. Hard tissue tore. Sudden red fire blazed and faded against the glow of his hands, and the coils were gone.

"Oh, Davey—"

With that gasp of joy, it changed again. He felt hard metal, smelled hot oil, heard a keen mechanical squeal. Bright steel blades spun against his chest, slashing through the coveralls.

But somehow they couldn't touch his glowing skin. He flung

both arms around that shifting shape, squeezed. The metal buckled and fractured and changed again. It became a blob of clinging jelly that flowed and tried to freeze around him—became a cloud of nauseating gas that burned his eyes and choked his throat.

"Davey, I do love you!"

Still he squeezed.

Its happy laughter ceased. Suddenly invisible, impalpable, it tried to get away. He held it grimly, probing for its life with the faint glow of his expanding nimbus.

"Dav—"

It had slashed back at him with its own red fire, but that dimmed and winked out. His shining hands held only emptiness. Nothing was left in the cockpit with him except a thin strange stink, a little like the scent of a den of diamondbacks, more like the odor of a poison weed El Yaqui had showed him on the Redrock mesa long ago.

The demon was dead.

In the struggle he had freed his knees from the object that had fallen on them. He saw now that it had been a massive steel-cased gravitic inverter that had been thrown through the bulkhead when the skimmer crashed.

He climbed out of the cockpit through the passage the demon must have opened through piled snow and battered metal. It felt good to stand straight and fill his lungs with clean air. Though his coveralls had been ripped to shreds, he no longer felt the cold.

Pausing on a snow-mound, he turned his hands, squinting at them with a puzzled awe. Here, even in the yellow-gray light that filtered through the Andorandan storm, that dim nimbus was no longer visible. But it had been real. His hidden powers had been awakened long enough to let him kill a creature more deadly than a god.

But even as he strove again to understand that genetic gift, his elation was already fading. He felt chastened, almost guilty. Terrified at first, he had come to enjoy the risk and pain and desperate effort of that combat before the end almost as much as the demon did. Somehow, he felt, they had been kin.

When he turned to look for Buglet, his concern for her swept that discontent away. The flattened ruin of the skimmer was almost covered with the snow that sloped steeply up and steeply down as far as he could see through the wind-whipped fog and snow.

She wasn't in the wreck—he felt sure of that. Afraid the vast snowslide had really buried her, he picked his way down the slope to look for her, slipping and stumbling, pausing again and again when cascading snow seemed about to start another avalanche.

The clouds thinned till at last he could see the barren valley at the foot of the slope, a vast trough of ice and snow and shattered stone, the tumbled stuff of the last slide forming a frozen wave far up the farther wall. If Buglet had been buried there—

He saw her then—a tiny yellow dot in her survival suit— creeping toward him down that snow-veiled wall. She waved when she reached the bottom of it, and stopped to wait for him. She was sitting on a boulder when he came to her, damp from the snow and flushed with exertion, her lemon eyes luminous. The grime and terror of their long trek were gone, and her beauty stabbed him like a blade. He took her in his arms—and trembled from her cool kiss when he remembered the demon.

"It's dead, Davey." The whisper was her own, grave and true. "It was the only thing able to trail us, and I saw you kill it. I was watching—somehow watching—from where I was trapped under the snow."

"I felt you—" The shudder passed. She was warm and light and alive in his arms. The flakes of snow that starred her hair and chilled her face were only snow. That demonic hunter was dead, and her lips felt warm again. "I felt you helping—I don't know how—"

"There's a lot you have to learn." Mischief flashed and vanished in her eyes. "I tried to help, and I felt you helping me. Don't you remember?"

Happy and relaxed, he didn't try to answer.

"The demon hit me first." She could see that he didn't remember. "The skimmer had been ripped open on the rocks we struck. The demon pulled me out and tried to kill me in the avalanche. It left me smothered under tons and tons of rock and ice. At first I thought I was going to die, but then you came to help me. Together, we made an aura for me, strong enough to sheild me and lift me out."

Feeling no need to say much more, they went on together down the glacial valley until they reached the brink of another ice-fall. Freezing winds whipped over its lip, and they drew back in awe from the chasms beyond. Endless snow-slopes. Ice-carved gorges. Sheer black cliffs, dropping at last to the dark red ocean.

"It's alive." Staring out across its boundless blood-colored immensity, he saw something black and far away that jumped and flashed and fell back into a dot of bright foam. "I remember reading about it in truman books. The Andorandan analog of chlorophyl is red." Shrinking from the wind, he shivered. "Life— but not our kind."

"But this is the south cape." She leaned to look far down at the ragged line of pink surf that traced the feet of those forbidding walls of naked stone. "Our only problem now is how to find our people."

"Problem enough," he muttered. "I can't see any way down to the beach. Even if we got there, we wouldn't know which way to go—"

"That way, maybe."

She had turned with a gasp of surprise to point toward a spur of rock behind them, and now he saw a trail winding around it toward a high gleam of metal. They climbed the trail to a flat rock shelf—a basalt bench that had been leveled for a landing pad. At the end of it a spidery tower rose above a small metal dome. They pushed into the dome, through an unlocked door.

"An observatory." He nodded at the narrow slit toward the sky. "El Yaqui showed the monks at Redrock the ruin of one on Creation Mesa—to prove to them that the premen knew astronomy long ago." From the doorway he scanned that far line of surf. "If the Polarians built this one, the station should be close."

The flimsy-seeming tower held a beacon light, its power cells still alive. Before the sudden dusk fell, they had found how to turn it on. They slept that night on the floor of the empty dome, with no evil dreams. A skimmer woke them, screaming down to land—a time-scarred twin of the one they had repaired. Running to meet it, they froze when they saw the grotesque being on the ramp. A tiny bundle of black-and-yellow fur, bounding on two enormous arms.

150

"Pipkin!" Buglet's greeting was a cry of delight. "How did you get here?"

"With Zhondra Zhey." The godlet hopped to a halt, cocking back the fat pink baby-head to grin at them with one green eye. "Flooded out of my home, with nowhere else to go, I got her to sneak me aboard her ship—not expecting to meet the two of you again."

"Is she still here?"

"About to leave." His voice was a keen mosquito whine. "If you want to come, you're just in time."

"Come where?"

"To a kinder world than this one." Standing on one gold-furred hand, he gestured with the other as if to erase the ice-crowned black cliffs and the scarlet sea. "One where Belthar and his arrogant kin will never trouble us."

"But—is there such a world?" Davey frowned at him. "One of Belthar's creatures has already tracked us here. He'll be sending others—"

"They'll never find us," Pipkin whistled. "It's a place I discovered myself, but only by an accident I'm sure they won't repeat. On the way here Zhondra was giving me a lesson in trans-volutionary navigation. By what should have been a fatal mischance I skipped the ship through a forbidden discontinuity, into a universe that had been charted as antimatter—"

"Oh—" Buglet gasped.

"But it wasn't." Pipkin gave her his impish grin. "We didn't die. It turned out that the charts were wrong. Before we got out, Zhondra had located a Sol-type sun with at least one friendly seeming planet. She's reloading the premen now, with all the supplies she can carry, and we'll soon be on our way. I'm certain she'll make room for you—if you can explain how you got here."

"We somehow jumped—teleported, maybe I should say—to Station One. And came on from there in a skimmer the monks had abandoned by the strip." Shifting uncomfortably before Pipkin's doubtful one-eyed stare, he turned to gesture at the dome and the tower. "We were pretty lucky, stumbling onto this installation."

"If you call it luck." Pipkin blinked at the beacon, still flashing green and blue. "But how did it get here?"

"Didn't the Polarians—" His breath caught. "It was an observatory. Maybe a weather station, too. The equipment is gone."

"Don't you know?" Pipkin shook his hairless head, with a grimace of sardonic disbelief. "The preman pilots have been flying along this coast, looking for a likelier site for the colony—which they never found. They swear they passed this spot a few days ago and saw nothing here. I've seen the records, and charts the Polarians left at the station. They don't mention any observatory—and they didn't need one, because they never saw the sky."

"Then why—why did you come?"

"Your beacon." Pipkin nodded at it. "Blazing all night."

Davey saw Buglet staring strangely at him.

"Something else needs explaining." Pipkin hopped toward him, green eye shrewdly squinting. "The skimmer you found and flew. The Polarian records do mention that. They say it crashed and burned, with the cargo and crew aboard. Nothing could be salvaged."

"Burned?" Blankly, Davey echoed the word. "It was loaded with burned machines. But the skimmer itself?"

"That survival pod!" Buglet bent to stare at the tiny god, her voice hushed with awe. "Lying exactly where we had to find it. With the suits and stove and food we had to have, to keep us alive." She drew a long uneven breath. "Is it—is it true?"

"True." Pipkin nodded, grinning at her amazement, and peered again at Davey. "You two have become Creators. Gaining powers no god has ever owned—powers so awesome that you had to hide them from yourselves. Creating the devices to save your lives and bring you safely here, you felt forced to disguise them as lucky accidents."

"Davey—" Her yellow eyes shone. "Can you believe?"

"I guess—" He reached to grasp her quivering hand. "I guess we must believe."

"If you know who you are, let's move along." Pipkin swung on one big hand and bounded toward the skimmer. "Before Belthar catches on. As Creators, you'll be needed in our new home. One of the preman passengers found a name for the planet, in an old tribal myth. We call it Eden."

FIVE: BROTHER TO GODS

At first I was afraid.

"It's criminal." The biting acid-and-ether reek and the bright aseptic whiteness of the genetics laboratory, the soft quick pulse of a cryogenic pump, the dark male dynamism of Adam Smithwick himself—those are things I'll never forget. "You—we could be hanged."

He laughed.

"The creationists will certainly hang us." His mellow boom was almost genial. "If they ever guess. Those bigots who hold that Creation was done in six miraculous days. They don't like us starting all over again."

"Couldn't they—couldn't they just possibly be right?"

It was all too new and strange for me. I was still the green graduate student, dazzled with his vision of the ultimate adventure. He was the distinguished geneticist, crowned with international fame, three times my age. His very presence took my breath. His abrupt proposal, the evening before, had caught me quite unready.

"Marry me, Cyn. We'll work well together."

153

When I whispered that I must think about it, he gave me his first wife's diary. Reading through it, I got no sleep that night. At first just another lab assistant, Nadya Barov must have begun as utterly innocent as I was. I shared her shock when she found that he was other than human, felt her sick outrage when she learned that her own children had been his risky genetic experiments, endured the cruel conflict of love and hate that drove her at last to suicide. Coming back to him that morning, I too had been torn between horror and a dazed admiration.

A Greek god—she had called him that in the diary, before she knew the truth. I felt the fit of it. Tall and athletic, with sleek black hair and bold greenish eyes, he wore his sex like a scent, with an intellect vast enough to match his ruthless magnetism.

"Well, Cyn?"

Before I could speak, his probing mind had read all my fears and my unspoken fascination. Unexpectedly, he swept me into his arms. Shattering glassware jangled on the floor. With half my spinning wits, I knew that his hard kiss was too deliberate, a stimulus skillfully applied. Yet I couldn't help responding.

"Please—Professor!"

When I could, I pushed him away. Trying to get my breath, to cope with his elemental power and my own hot emotion, I put a worktable between us and tried to challenge him with those hard questions that had been fatal to Nadya. His reckless laugh had frightened me again.

"Are you a god?" Put that way, the issue sobered him. "What right have you to tamper with humanity?"

"What is right?"

He didn't wait for my reply.

"What is wrong? The creationists have their answers, graven on eternal stone. Mine are operational. The good is anything that aids the survival of the group—the family or the nation or the race. Ultimately, it is anything that assures the survival of the genes. Evil, then, is whatever obstructs that genetic stream. In general, wrong springs from the selfish

154

will that puts individual impulse or passion above that genetic imperative. Think about it, Cyn."

He reached for me across the worktable. I couldn't help taking his powerful, black-haired hand—or shuddering when I touched him.

"The creationists are right in the light of their own ethics—I'm a greater danger to the survival of their kind than they have ever guessed. But my own free-minded parents gave me different genes that dictate a different ethics. The mutant genes they made for me command my own survival, to father the future race. In my own new ethical world, the creationists are evil. Their genes threaten mine."

He drew me suddenly toward him around the corner of the table, scattering more glassware.

"You ask if I'm a god." Something in his ringing voice sent another shiver through me. "In a sense, Cyn, I am. The first real Creator—though my pioneering parents have cleared the way. I want you to share my new divinity. To forsake homo sap—the old race of muddling misfits tossed together by the slapdash accidents of natural mutation. I want you to mother the first really created race."

Trembling, crushed in his muscular arms, I could hardly hear his muted boom.

"A race of gods!"

> —From a letter signed Cynthia S.,
> found in the papers of Dr. Elene Zehr,
> the biochemist who became Adam Smithwick's
> third wife and Darwin Smithwick's mother

Belthar faced the gathered gods.

"Fellow immortals—we aren't immortal!"

His nimbus burning crimson against the bitter cold, he spoke from the great black throne in his Himalayan temple, addressing the listening images stacked many prisms deep in the circle of transceiver columns that supported the black granite dome. Beyond the soaring columns a midnight moon blazed across the high wilderness of naked rock and untracked snow.

"The demons have escaped—the killer things the Creators hid in the genes of the premen. We stand in desperate danger so long as they survive."

"My Gleesh!" Cynthara's image shrilled from her niche, incredulous. "I gave you my beautiful Gleesh. It can hunt them down."

"If you thought your pet was a demon—" Belthar's aura paled with bitter scorn. "They killed your killer—as they killed my son."

"Killed my darling?" Her nimbus flared greener. "How?"

"I don't know how."

"Brother, is your own eternity failing?" Mockery flickered in Kranthar's golden halo and edged his rolling thunder. "Have you let two preman children beat you? A half-grown boy and a slip of a girl?"

"Watch yourself, brother, or they'll beat you." Belthar glared his indignation. "Their petty-seeming preman shapes are cunning disguises for creatures designed to kill us all."

"Weren't they exiled to die on Andoranda V?"

"That plan failed."

"Were you too clever, brother?"

"My good son's plan." Belthar's aura trembled, but he controlled his tone. "No escape was considered possible from that lonely universe. The planet itself should have killed the preman race, with no damage to their precious treaty rights."

"So what went wrong?"

"The two young demons found traitors among us."

"Gods?"

"Two of our fellow eternals." His blue accusing eyes scanned the silent columns. "They somehow corrupted the pilot of their transport ship—the child goddess Zhondra Zhey. I knew she had always coddled them, but I never expected her to betray her own immortality."

Fury flickered in his numbus and quivered in his voice.

"They found another ally we didn't know existed. A strange genetic blunder of old Huxley Smithwick's, that should have been destroyed. A monstrous little demigod with a demon's cunning, hiding here on Earth right under our noses. Its last den was on the old preman reservation. When Quelf flooded that, it got aboard Zhondra's ship and joined the rebel demons."

"So we face outlaw gods?" Kranthar's mockery had vanished. "Where are they now?"

"Our gravest problem." Belthar scowled at the star-charts above him. "The premen killed my son at Redrock and disappeared from there. My able clone commander guessed that they had fled to join their people on Andoranda. I sent him there on my best battlecraft, with orders to kill every preman he found.

"He found none at all."

"Good enough!" Kranthar rumbled. "The planet was to kill them."

158

"They didn't die there." Belthar glared at his contentment. "Ironlaw found evidence to tell a more shocking story. The demons did arrive. He found their footprints in the snow and traced them to the exile camp. But they were gone—and all the premen. He found nearly all their last cargo of supplies stacked around the landing pad. Thrown out, he thinks, to lighten Zhondra's transport. He believes she took the whole colony away—but he found no clue to tell him where they went."

"So what can we do?" Kranthar's halo was streaked with anxious orange now. "If the demons have disappeared?"

"We can arm ourselves!"

Belthar's voice rang against the towering pillars and came back in dying echoes from the ice-crags below.

"We can search the universes!"

"All the universes?" Kranthar blinked. "For one small ship?"

"For your own best chance to stay alive." Belthar glowered through a crimson blaze. "Because the demons won't be gone forever. With our best efforts and the best of luck, we can hope to find and kill them wherever those traitor gods have helped them hide. With worse luck—if our efforts fail—they'll be back to erase us all, as the last Creator planned in her insane senility."

He set the black throne to turning, his hard blue stare slowly sweeping the enromous circle of transceiver columns. The full moon shone through the columns, reaching with white gigantic fingers across the frost-dusted floor. Overhead, the black vault was alive with its flashing maps of the divine dominions.

"You know our peril." Outside the nimbus, red sparks of ice froze from Belthar's breath. "What is your will?"

Unease rippled through the pillared images.

"I share your apprehensions, Bel." The first clear voice was Cynthara's. "I recall our desperate war to put an end to the lunatic mischief of old Eva Smithwick a thousand years ago. I perceive a deadlier danger now, and I think we must all unite to face it. I place myself and all my planet under your command."

"Brother—" Kranthar's tone was chastened. "So do I."

Colors of assent shone across the columns.

"Your will is mine." Belthar pealed his answer, the red nimbus bright. "I accept your leadership. The demands upon you may be unexpected and severe. My first commands are these: You will

159

join the search for the hidden demons with every means you can invent. You will arm your fastest starcraft with the deadliest weapons you can find. You will stand prepared. When the demons are found, I'll lead you anywhere, into any universe, to win the battle for our lives that we began a thousand years ago.''

The pillars burned with strong applause.

They called the planet Eden.

''Our safe place,'' Buglet whispered. ''At last—our home.''

In the starlit afterdome, they swam in free fall, clutching the hold-ropes now and again as Zhondra braked the transport into a parking orbit. The planet was mostly water. The one great continent, wreathed with archipelagoes, was round as some ancient battle-shield, bossed at the center with a high crown of ice.

''A world without tectonic motion.'' A transceiver prism brought Pipkin's doll-voice from the nosecone, where he was learning astronautics. ''The whole continent was evidently built from one volcano that never drifted off a single subcrustal hot spot.''

Glaciers had burst in three directions from that high central basin, feeding three major rivers that had cut their black canyons through a wide ring of tawny desert to wander across immense cloud-veiled lowlands and spread their deltas into the planetary sea. Those green lowlands were scattered with huge blue lakes, all oddly circular.

A double moon spun above the planet—one element airless and crater-scarred, an iron-stained red, the other brighter than Luna, dazzling with snow. Close together, locked in orbits that held them face-to-face, they whirled like a strange dumbbell tossed into the starry dark.

''A wonderful world!'' Buglet turned to him from the swelling planet, golden eyes alight. ''Beyond the reach of all the gods.''

''We should be safe.'' Davey caught her cool hand. ''So long as they overlook the error on their star-maps. But—'' A haunting dread shook his voice. ''I wish we could be sure.''

''We are sure.'' She pulled him closer. Her floating body collided gently with him, and he caught the sweetness of her sleek black hair. ''Starships don't get back from antimatter universes—

not often. Pipkin got us here by unlikely accident. No god is going to risk his immortality to take another look.''

Suddenly she was in his arms, her eager lips on his mouth.

''We'll have time enough,'' she breathed. ''To have our child.''

Dread touched him again, and she must have felt his tiny shudder.

''That's what we were born for.'' Her whisper was stronger. ''To make the ultiman—the Multiman our people used to dream about when they needed faith in some new savior to rescue them from the reservation. The ultiman will have all your transvolutionary genes and all of mine, with powers we can't imagine. When we do meet the gods again, he can laugh at them.''

''I hope—''

''I know.''

''I love you, Bug.'' He tried not to tremble. ''But I'm so afraid—afraid you'll be hurt.''

''If you really are afraid, we must make the baby right away.''

The goddess called them to the nosecone to help select a landing spot. Pipkin was there, anchored to a hold-bar with a yellow-furred arm longer than his body, his one green eye squinting at her young loveliness as avidly as if he had been a sexual being.

The area they chose was high on the west coast, where the gods agreed that the weather should be mild and not unduly wet. or dry. Davey went down on the first shuttle flight, along with Pipkin and half a dozen preman volunteers.

Assuming command, the dwarf god had the muman pilot land them on a narrow cape that jutted into the sea beside a wide circular bay. When the muman had tested the air and found it good, Davey managed to be first upon the virgin world.

His heart was pounding, and he sniffed the fresh scents of Eden as eagerly as if they were some precious perfume. The planet was smaller than Earth, its year and its day somewhat shorter, and its mass a quarter less. The slighter gravity gave him a delightful sense of lightness.

They had come down into a shallow valley of a stream that ran into the bay. The almost-grass was soft and ankle-deep, greener than anything he had ever seen on the desert reservation, starred here and there with huge yellow blooms. Across the meadows the forest on the low hills was a darker green, mysterious but silently inviting.

"A good world." He smiled back at Pipkin, dancing lightly after him down the gangway on his two huge hands. "Better than I ever hoped for."

"You don't know it yet." Tiny body swinging in the air, the godlet paused to squint suspiciously into the empty landscape. "You may get a bad surprise," his wasp-voice whined. "There are signs I don't like."

Davey didn't wait to ask what those signs might be. Breathless to see more of Eden, he liked all he found. The sweet-scented plants, the sea-freshened air, the clean blue sky, the tranquilizing quiet. Nothing hostile met them anywhere.

"No large life-forms." Their absence seemed to worry Pipkin. "I'd like to know why."

Without learning why, he went back into the shuttle in the middle of the short afternoon. Davey stayed. A big-bellied man called El Sapo had taken control of the landing party, setting up a tent and preparing for the night.

Davey had never liked El Sapo. Back at Redrock, he had always been sucking around the preman agent, scheming for appointments as sheriff or tax collector or judge and using his petty authority to harass El Yaqui for the peyote he chewed and the untaxed mescal he sold and the women Le China kept upstairs. More than once, raiding the place, he had jailed Davey and Buglet till El Yaqui got them out.

He wouldn't look at Davey now. Assigning one man to drive tent stakes, one to dig a drainage trench, others to cut firewood and bring water from the stream and cover their equipment, he said nothing at all to him.

"Please," Davey asked, "what can I do?"

"I can give commands to men." El Sapo stopped to scowl at him with bulging, mud-brown eyes. "I have none for such as you."

"I'm a man." Davey flushed. "Old enough—"

"It's not your age." El Sapo shrank back. "It's what you do that men can't. No man—or Belthar himself—could have jumped from Redrock to the prison world without a ship. I don't know what you are.''

''Buglet—Jondarc says we'll be the ultimen.'' His voice lifted quickly. ''She says we were born with latent transvolutionary gifts that we can use to help the premen—''

''Help the premen?'' El Sapo's hoarse croak mocked him. ''You got us torn out of our Terran homes and shipped off to die in exile—those Quelf's torture gangs left alive—because the gods are afraid of latent transvolutionary gifts. That's how much you've helped us.''

He stood silent for a moment, stricken with his recollection of San Seven and his parents, truman friends who had died for aiding him and Bug. This accusation held a cruel truth that he couldn't deny.

''We mean no harm,'' he muttered at last. ''We can't help the gifts we have—or even understand them.'' He tried to smile. ''Here we'll have time to master—''

''I don't know about you.'' El Sapo cut him off. ''I don't want to know.''

He had a bad night, his joy in Eden dimmed. The cook gave him a ladle of yellow synthetic mush from the supper kettle and El Sapo tossed him a blanket, but nobody talked to him. He slept in a corner of the tent, dreaming that the twin moons were the mismated eyes of another demon sent to hunt them down.

The dawn restored a little of his spirit as he walked away from the tent to pee. Dew had silvered the grassy stuff, and the cool air smelled fragrantly clean. Though he saw nothing moving, some creature in the nearest clump of trees kept repeating a musical dovelike call. Eden was new, mysterious and beautiful, theirs to claim. Its unspoiled promise was headier to him than El Yaqui's mescal had ever been.

The shuttle came back before sunrise, settling slowly on its jet of roaring steam. It brought half a dozen more men and another half-load of equipment. When the muman said he needed a harder landing pad, placed where his suction hose could reach fresh water for reaction mass, Davey volunteered to build it.

Stiffly, El Sapo told him to go ahead. The laser-drill was like the one he had learned to run at the truman commune, and he used it to attack a rocky knob near a bend in the stream. Working all day alone, he split slabs of weathered granite and dragged them on the null-G line to dam the stream.

His hard pad was leveled and ready when the shuttle returned, with clear water pooled above the dam. The muman came out to inspect it, grinning approval, but he got no thanks from anybody else.

Next day he found another job. El Sapo had left him out of the gang of axemen sent upriver to begin cutting timber for their first building, but he was allowed to ride the floating logs down the stream and roll them back into the channel when they ran aground.

He was waiting for Buglet when the shuttle touched down with the last full load of people and supplies. She ran eagerly to meet him, but checked herself abruptly when she saw his face.

"Davey! What's wrong?"

"El Sapo blames me—both of us—for everything bad that ever happened to the premen. I guess he's afraid they'll be hit again, if the gods ever find us." He shrugged unhappily. "The worst of it is, he's half right."

"Never mind." She kissed him gently, then very warmly. "A few of the premen have been strange with me. But when our child comes—when the ultiman is born—they'll know and like what we are."

They slept that night in the end of a new storage tent. El Sapo was careful to see that they got a fair share of the limited food and gear, but his mistrust had been contagious. Nobody felt at ease with them.

Pipkin returned next day, alone with the muman in the empty shuttle. When they gathered around the pad, he came hand-hopping halfway down the gangway to ask for volunteers. The goddess had sent him back, he said, to search the planets for ores and other resources. He wanted two helpers.

With a glance at each other, they asked to go. Pipkin took off with them at once. Though the cruise took a dozen of Eden's brief days, his methods of exploration seemed oddly casual. On the maps they were making he would pick a spot for inspection and tell the pilot to set them down. He would dance down the extended gangway and back again, often without touching the soil. His cynical, solitary eye would sweep and abandon another virgin landscape—which Davey's imagination had always painted with undiscovered promise. A shrug of disdain would toss his tiny body.

"Nothing here," he would shrill. "We'll go on."

Sometimes, when Davey and Buglet insisted, he would allow them time to dig a plant or pick up a rock or take a photograph, but he was always contemptuous of their specimens.

"A poor Eden," he droned, when the muman was dropping them back toward that round western bay. "No free metal or rich ores anywhere. No oil or coal or radioactives. Everything stripped clean."

"Stripped?" Davey echoed. "How?"

The enigmatic green eye blinked. "I wasn't here."

"Maybe we were just too hasty," Buglet said. "Maybe we should keep on looking."

"We looked long enough." Pipkin opened his chilling, blind eye. "I saw enough to know that this wasn't always Eden."

Uneasily, they waited.

"I did see metal—deep underground."

The white eye closed, and Davey breathed again.

"But no native veins," that trapped-fly whine went on. "Only scattered masses, rusted and corroded, in the ruins of cities buried many millions of years ago."

Davey blinked and shook his head.

"Surprised." Pipkin's sardonic chuckle rattled like gravel. "Didn't you see the shape of all those lakes? And the bay where we landed? Craters! Made, I think, by missiles shot from the red moon—it has equally recent craters too, made, I'm sure, by missiles shot from here."

"If there was a war—"

"Both sides won." Wry malice furrowed the pink baby-face. "Neither survived."

When they were on the pad, he capered down the gangway to squeak that same report to the premen who had gathered to welcome them.

"No ores?" El Sapo yelped his dismay. "No metal at all?" His murky stare shifted accusingly to Davey and Buglet. "Without metal, we'll go savage."

"Not so savage, I hope, as the creatures who did have metal here." The godlet grinned. "There is metal left, however, if you want to dig for it. Right under your feet. Used once, but still good enough for making weapons."

Standing on one huge hand, he swung the other toward the bay.

"That must have been a city before the missile hit it. The old suburbs stretch for miles east and north of here, buried under ejecta from the crater. You can use sonic probes to locate the scrap, some of it only a few hundred feet down."

Leering at Buglet, El Sapo muttered something Davey didn't hear. Pipkin beckoned him into the shuttle. He soon came back, croaking as he passed that El Muñeco wanted to see them.

"The Toad's unhappy with you." The green eye had a bright ironic glint. "Afraid to offend you, but more afraid to have you near him. I think you two must arrange to live apart."

Delighted, Buglet chose a spot they had seen from the air. A few miles west of the landing, it was on a narrow isthmus between the bay and the sea. As happy as she was, El Sapo detailed men to move them there, with a tiny tent, a few simple tools, and their fair share of the rationed food.

Pipkin rode the shuttle back to rejoin the goddess on the transport. She and the mutant were still teaching him transvolutionary navigation, and he was planning to explore the double moon.

They pitched the tent, and Davey began cutting logs to build a cabin. That went slowly, because he had no power tools—no power machines for lumbering or farming had been shipped to the exile planet, because no Terran life could grow there; and many tons of precious cargo had been abandoned when they left it, to make space for people.

Buglet helped him lever the cut logs into place on the stone foundation, helped mix mud to plaster them and peel rafters for the roof. Toiling together under the mild sun of Eden, they spaded up a tiny plot of soil, where they could test the few Terran seeds the premen had shared with them.

Once, he stopped his spade to grin at her. They had been digging around a stubborn stump that proved too heavy for them to move. Dark hair bound with a strip of red rag, wearing only grimy shorts and halter, she was streaked with sweat and dust. An ache of mixed pity and joy throbbed in his throat.

"Strange work for the ultiwoman!"

"Don't fret." She stood up to get her breath, mopping at her muddy loveliness. "We've never been so happy."

"El Sapo isn't. We're still a thorn in his paw. If we can outfight muman deadeyes and kill Belthar's son and jump between universes, he can't see why we must sweat to stay alive like ordinary premen."

"If they'll just let us live—" She reached to stroke his gritty arm. He saw the blisters on her fingers, and her lean smile touched his heart. "Till the child is born."

They didn't go back to the landing, but now and then a few preman friends came calling. She was laughing once, after two women had brought gifts: a newly fired clay cook pot and a bundle of native roots they said were edible if boiled long enough to kill the bitterness.

"They poked into everything we have and wanted to know everything we do." Her lemon eyes danced. "They hinted that we ought to marry."

"If you want—"

"If we were premen." She shrugged. "But we aren't—not since they put us out." Her gaze grew thoughtful. "I would like to see Zhondra Zhey."

By coincidence or not, the goddess came next day. They heard the shuttle roaring down to land at dawn and saw it climbing skyward again on its tapered plume. Davey was carrying water from their spring in a bark bucket that afternoon when she dropped before him out of the air, wrapped in the pale opal glow of her nimbus. Awe of her power chilled him for an instant, but her smile of greeting was as easily friendly as if they both had been common premen.

"Pipkin came down with me," she told him. "He's gone again now, with El Sapo and some of his people. They don't like this location, because there's no metal—"

"And because we're here?"

Her pearly halo winked.

"Anyhow, they've gone to search the continent again for ruins richer in metal, buried not so deep. If they can find a more promising spot, El Sapo wants to move the colony."

Levitating, she floated beside him to Buglet, who was tending a fire beside the still roofless cabin, trying to cook those bitter roots.

"Must you eat such things?" She made an entrancing face. "With all your ancestral gifts, can't you draw on transvolutionary energies the way we do?"

"We aren't gods." Buglet tossed her dark hair back, smiling lightly. "Not yet. We've never been able to unlock our latent powers without the stimulus of danger and we're out of danger here." Davey thought she looked as luminous as the goddess did, beneath her streaks of soot and dust. "We're content enough to live like premen until the child is born."

"I'm afraid you feel safer than you are." Zhondra's glowing veil was flecked with a troubled blue. "In truth, there's more danger than you need. The gods are powerful, and you've alarmed them. I know Belthar. He'll be arming and searching desperately. If he should ever guess that our new universe isn't actually antimatter—"

"The child will make us safe," Buglet insisted serenely. "He'll be a match for Belthar."

The goddess stayed with them three days. She levitated the ridgepole, which had been too heavy for them to hoist. She lifted that great stump and the boulders out of their garden plot, piling the stones to hold a little pool below their spring.

She kept urging them to discover and exercise their transvolutionary gifts, but Buglet always insisted that the ultiman would come in time. Once, Davey overheard low-voiced talk about the business of bearing a child. The goddess seemed concerned, but Buglet was certain she wouldn't need a preman midwife. For a moment he felt a little hurt at being left out, because he and Buglet had always shared every thought.

On the fourth day the goddess was expecting Pipkin back. Busy that morning cutting tall grass to thatch the cabin, he listened and watched the sky, waiting for the shuttle. It didn't return. By late afternoon Zhondra was anxious, her aura pale and unsteady. She left them at last, levitating toward the zenith. The sun had set before she dropped back.

"They've gone." Her aura was faint in the dusk, dimly blue. "I climbed above the air, high enough to survey the whole continent. I couldn't find the shuttle. I searched the orbit for my ship. It, too, is gone."

Davey stood silent, stunned that a goddess should suffer such a loss.

"So Pipkin took it?" Buglet frowned. "I trusted him."

"Don't blame him too much," Zhondra protested. "He has lived his whole life in hiding, in terror of the gods. He must have been afraid Belthar would find him here and punish him for aiding you."

"El Sapo—" Davey blinked into the twilight. "They must have planned it together." His breath caught. "That's why he took so many of his cronies and their women." He peered at the shining goddess. "Where do you think they went?"

"No telling. The other planets of this sun are either hot and airless or cold gas giants, all unfit for settlement. There's no other star in normal cruising range. To find any better world I think they would have to climb back through some contact plane—"

"And leave this universe? With the risk that Belthar might detect them?"

"That's possible." She gave Buglet a quizzical smile. "Maybe it will be the danger you need."

She went back to the landing that night, along with the worried group of leaderless premen who had come begging her for help.

"It's time, Davey," Buglet whispered when they were gone. "We must make the baby now."

They ran down hand-in-hand to bathe in the quiet sea. The double moon cast shadows on the sand, long and black, oddly edged with red. Buglet was talkative at first, wondering whether the little ultiman would have their preman form, or whether he would wear a halo like a god, or perhaps be something altogether new. When he said nothing, she too fell silent. He was trembling, filled with a solemn awe.

In the cool surf they washed off the day's grit and sweat. Watching her rise before him out of a dark wave, he shivered again. The moonlight drew a strange outline around her, one edge rose, the other silver. Her white skin shone and her thrusting nipples parted the bright black strands of her clinging hair. Her quick kiss had a cool salt taste, and her loveliness made an ache in his loins.

Needing no speech, they climbed silently back up the rocky trail to the new cabin. Their bed was a frame of peeled poles across the end of the tiny mud-walled room, filled with branch tips and dried grass. The glow of their dying cook fire came faintly through the open doorway, redder than the rusty moon, and he caught its smoky scent.

When the moment came, when he met the magic of her warm and firmly yielding flesh and had the clean taste of her discovering tongue, he felt suddenly weak and afraid. Who was he, to make the ultiman? With his toil-blistered hands still stinging from the sea salt, how could he dare challenge the hostile gods?

"Davey!" Her breath was warm and sweet on his face. "The baby won't wait!"

She moved deliciously beneath him, and they began to make the ultiman.

When two short months had gone by with no news from Pipkin or the missing starship, they built a home for Zhondra Zhey on Eden. She picked the site for it—a rocky point above the sea but near the landing—and she gave her own transvolutionary aid.

Davey used the laser-drill to level the floor and to square massive stones that she levitated to lay up the walls. Pious premen cut logs that she lifted, riding them through the sky to plant them for entry columns or place them for roof beams.

The finished chapel was modest enough, but for Davey it held more sublimity than all of Belthar's enormous Terran monuments. To the abandoned premen Zhondra was becoming mentor, healer and judge—a genuine divinity. To him and Buglet she was now a cheerful friend, unassuming and undemanding.

They had needed her aid through that first hard season. Starvation had been near. Though some of the native fruits and roots could be prepared and eaten, they bloated the belly without sustaining life. A few of the shy little wild creatures had been trapped, but they were no more fit for food—because, she said, Eden's ecology was built from an alien set of amino acids.

Precious seed had been lost at first, till they learned how to feed the young plants with recycled waste, but the soil was rich enough with minerals and watered nearly every afternoon with a brief and gentle rain. By the time the chapel was roofed, bits of Eden had become abundant gardens, yielding beans and squash and yams and corn. A few stray grains of rice and wheat had sprouted, promising seed for future fields. There was still no meat—no large domestic animals had been shipped to Andoranda V, because they couldn't reproduce there—but the colonists were breeding rabbits and chickens from pets the children had managed to bring.

Gold eyes bright, Buglet told Davey that the little ultiman was on the way. Her elation gave him a pang of unexpected fear that the coming child, so wonderful and powerful, might take away the love that had been his. Though he strove against that disloyal dread, it came back again and again to haunt him.

Yet most of the time he felt happier than he had ever been, because Buglet was so radiant. Certainly, her love had not yet diminished. The days were good, spent together at work or swimming in the tranquil sea; the nights revealed new orders of joy.

Out of habit, he listened now and then for the shuttle or scanned the sky for its plume of steam, but it did not return. At the urging of the goddess, sometimes he tried to recover those genetic gifts that had once been strong enough to lift them away from Earth, but Buglet was too utterly absorbed with the child to give him any aid, and the placid charms of Eden always hid the reality of danger too completely. His uncertain efforts failed.

With Eden's axis only slightly tilted, the brief seasons flowed by with little change. Mild spring changed into milder summer, only slightly warmer. They finished the dam and opened a ditch to bring water to the garden if the rains should fail. They planted a row of chili and an apple seedling. They added another room to the cabin, to be a nursery for the ultiman. Preman friends brought gifts for it, and slabs of a white bark that could be pounded into cloth.

Summer turned to fall, not quite so warm or wet, too soon for

Davey. Living with that secret terror of springtime and the ultiman, savoring each fleeting day of Buglet's love, he felt almost glad that Pipkin had not come back with the ship.

"Dave— Davey!"

Wanting nothing to break the simple cycle of their lives, he had to hide a jolt of fear that day when she came back from a visit to the goddess, breathless with a new excitement. He had been clearing a new garden plot. He dropped the spade and waited uneasily.

"Zhondra says we aren't alone." Flushed with feeling, she gestured toward the beach. "She has got in touch with civilized creatures—living under the ocean!"

He breathed again, relieved. "Under the ocean, they shouldn't matter to us."

"But they're amphibian. They can breathe air. Zhondra hasn't seen them yet, though she has been learning their language through transvolutionary contact. They're coming ashore tonight—a group of three. She wants us to wait with her to meet them."

"Must we?"

"Of course we must." She stared at him, startled. "Why not?"

"I'm happy as we are." He reached to take her hand. "I don't want anything to change."

With an understanding smile, she leaned to kiss him. "I love the way we are," she whispered. "But things do change. You know that, Davey. We can't stop change."

The meeting was planned for moonrise—even the soft sun of Eden, the goddess said, was too severe for the amphibians. At dusk they went down with her to the beach beneath her chapel.

Waiting, they swam in the softly breaking surf. The goddess, in her opalescent halo, looked as humanly seductive as Buglet. His awe of her was not entirely gone, but she seemed as easy with them as another preman, racing with them, diving till he couldn't help feeling frightened for her, and darting up beside him, nude and dripping, alluring in her pale iridescence. Once he felt his penis rise and dived to hide his sudden confused desire. She and Buglet stood together, smiling, when he dared look at them again.

Graver when the moonglow came, she led them back to the

hard white sand. Drying, shivering a little in the cool land breeze, they sat watching the water. The moons rose together, the white one in eclipse. The dull glow of the crimson moon seemed baleful to Davey, but soon the other had climbed from behind it, silvering everything.

With a shining dart of her aura, Zhondra pointed.

"There—" Wonder had broken Buglet's voice. "There they come!"

Three bright flakes of foam, swimming in through the silvered surf. Three tapered shapes that left the black water, came sailing through the moonlight, settled lightly below them on the sand.

The goddess called a strange sound of greeting and levitated a little way to meet them. Buglet moved as if to follow, but Davey caught her arm. He shivered again, as if the night wind had grown colder, and stood peering at the creatures, groping for some sense of what they were and what they meant. Streamlined for the sea, they were shaped a little like the seals and dolphins he had seen on truman wallscreens, but they were luminous, wrapped in blue auras almost as bright as Zhondra's.

"They can levitate," he whispered to Buglet. "They're—"

He wanted to call them godlike, but dread had hushed his voice. Floating in the moonlight, dipping graceful flukes for anchors on the sand, they seemed as light as balloons. Sleek within their separate blue cloudlets, they had very fine scales or very fine fur—he couldn't be sure. It was white over the belly, shading smoothly into jet across the back. Their arms were slender flippers, edged with streaks of brighter fire. One had picked up a shell with its fingered nimbus.

Their eyes were even stranger. Wide bright discs, with bars of shifting color radiating from tiny black pupils. Their owlish stares alarmed him, because they seemed to see too much.

Floating closer, Zhondra spoke to them with words he had never heard. Their replies were silent—seemingly, their physical speech was the play of shade and hue in those glowing rings around their actual eyes. He understood nothing of it, and he began to wonder why she had wanted them to come.

That odd conference continued for a long time. Tired of standing, he and Buglet sat back on the dam sand. He saw her shiver, and put a towel around her. The moons climbed higher, the red-rimmed shadows drawing shorter. Once, when the land breeze lulled, he caught the odor of the creatures, rank and snakelike.

"Jondarc!" the goddess called suddenly. "They want to meet you."

She stood up, tossing off the towel. He caught her hand to hold her back, but she slipped away from him with a look that seemed a warning. Silently, seeming unafraid, she walked past the goddess toward the amphibians. They lifted and swam to gather around her. Their great eyes studied her. Drifting closer, they reached almost to touch her with their quick black flippers. With tendrils of pale blue fire, they fingered her face and her hair. They palpated her swelling belly.

It seemed an endless time to Davey before they swam aside, dropping back to touch the sand and turning the wink and shimmer of their talking eyes again to the goddess. Left alone, Buglet stood crouched against the wind. Now, Davey thought, she looked bewildered and afraid.

"Thank you, Jondarc," the goddess murmured. "That was what they wanted."

For a moment, as if paralyzed with dread, she didn't move at all. Turning as if the movement took an effort, she looked back at the amphibians. They ignored her now. She caught a gasping breath and darted up the beach and into Davey's arms. He could feel the pounding of her heart.

Drawing farther back behind the goddess, they watched. At last they sat again, the towel around them both. The moons climbed, and still that singular parley went on. He was stiff and chilled before the amphibians blinked their enigmatic farewell and dived back into the sea.

Zhondra floated gravely to them, her halo pale.

"They frighten me." Buglet stared after them, across the dark ocean. "What do they want?"

"They're afraid," the goddess said. "Afraid of you."

They climbed after her, back to the rustic chapel. She invited them inside. Sitting at an axe-hewn table behind the altar, they had crisp little bean cakes from offerings the premen had brought, and pottery cups of a spicy tea brewed from a benign native herb.

174

"I know we talked a long time." She smiled at Davey's restless impatience. "The amphibians were trying to summarize a good many million years of history. Though the details are mostly lost, it seems that high intelligence had evolved here—on dry land. The arts of genetic engineering were invented. The new Cerators made three races. One was to inherit the continent. Another was adapted for space. The third was these amphibians.

"Their history prefigures our Terran tragedy. Having supplanted their own Creators, the new beings were afraid of new supplanters. The chief conflict rose between the continental beings and the space mutations, who had been established on the moons.

"The Creators had been killed, as Eva Smithwick was, in the effort to stop creation. The amphibians claim that their histories don't tell whether it was the land folk or the space folk that killed them. I can't help suspecting that the sea folk did it themselves.

"Anyhow, as their story goes, the space people and the land people each believed that the other had stolen the secret crafts of creation. Each feared that the other would make deadlier things to destroy them. To prevent that, they fought. Their final war left the craters we have seen and wiped both races out.

"The amphibians survived, though pretty narrowly. Most of their city domes were wrecked, and the whole ocean was poisoned with residual radioactives that washed off the land. They were saved—at least a handful of them—by their transvolutionary powers."

On three sides the altar place was open to the sky. Moonlight fell across them, silver bars rimmed with crimson. A cold night wind came through the axe-carved posts behind them, and Davey felt Buglet shivering against him.

"So now you'll understand." The goddess extended her aura to pour more steaming tea. "That's why the amphibians fear you."

"But I don't understand," Buglet whispered. "We won't hurt them."

"They've lived through one war between new creations. They want to avoid another."

"How?" Davey demanded. "What can they do?"

"We were debating that. I wanted them to help us hide and

175

protect the young ultiman, but they're afraid to take sides.'' Uncertainty shadowed her nimbus. "I don't know what they'll do."

"How do they know so much about us?"

"They have transvolutionary senses." Her quick smile forgave his unuttered accusation. "They were observing us before we ever landed. I was careful to tell them no more than they had already suspected."

"Now what?" Defensively, his arm slid around Buglet. "What can we do?"

"We can keep on hoping the gods don't find us." In her faintly glowing veil, Zhondra shrugged. "The amphibians are afraid they will."

Returning to their cabin, Davey and Buglet had to walk along the beach. They hurried silently, hand in hand, watching the moon-lit sea. A cloud had covered the snow moon, and the other moon dyed the murmuring surf a fatal scarlet. Davey's throat was dry with dread before they reached their own rocky path.

"If we needed danger," he muttered, "we have it now."

"Trust the ultiman," Buglet urged him cheerily. "He won't have to fear amphibians—or anything."

That winter they sowed a narrow strip of wheat in front of the cabin and rice in a tiny plot they could flood from the dam. They bartered red beans for a hen and a setting of eggs. On a soft spring morning Davey persuaded Buglet to come with him to the clinic the colonists had built. The preman surgeon shook his head very gravely when the examination was done and pronounced the child too large for her. Only a section, he said, could save it. Unfortunately, with his limited equipment and inadequate supplies, in such a difficult case he could promise nothing for the mother.

Untroubled, she refused his surgery.

"I'll be okay," she whispered to Davey as they were leaving. "The ultiman won't hurt me."

She was napping the next afternoon, and he was building a wattle coop for the hen, when the mild sky began to ring with the jets of the shuttle. Unbelieving, he saw it settling on its cushion of dazzling steam toward the landing. He woke her to tell her.

"Go get the news." She sat up heavily. "I'll wait. I don't want to walk so far."

Jogging up the beach, he was passing the chapel when he saw a small yellow projectile dropping toward it from the direction of the landing. It was Pipkin, levitating. The tiny god alighted, waved a long arm at him, and hopped into the altar place.

He found El Sapo and his followers still near the pad, locked in a hostile confrontation with El Jefe, the new leader of the premen. The men were long-bearded and the women bedraggled, all of them pinched from starvation, but El Sapo was trying to assert his old authority.

Before he became El Jefe, the new leader had been Jesus Cabrito, named by his mother for some forgotten preman demigod. A stringy little weak-eyed man, he had been the Redrock jailor for many years. His present elevation came from a few marijuana seeds he had brought from Earth. Now, squeaky-voiced with alarm, he was demanding information about where El Sapo had been.

"Nowhere." El Sapo's heavy paunch was gone. "We were looking for a better place—better for all." His murky eyes squinted shrewdly at El Jefe. "A place where we could mine good metal and eat the plants and hunt for meat that wouldn't give you colic."

He clucked and shook his grizzled head.

"We never found it. We did get lost—or Pipkin did. Stupid little miscreation. Wits gone the way of his legs. We had to ration everything. Pure luck the muman astronaut got us back here before we all died of famine."

He demanded food and shelter. El Jefe sent for tortillas and a pot of beans, but he wanted confessions and apologies from the deserters and a promise of respect for his own position. El Sapo kept insisting that he had been risking himself and his friends for the benefit of all, with no intention of deserting.

Snatching ravenously with filthy fingers, he and his people scooped up the tortillas and beans, but at sunset their future status was not yet settled. With no real information gained, Davey hurried back down the beach. At first he meant to stop at the chapel to see what he could learn from Zhondra and Pipkin, but a vague unease spurred him home. The moonless dusk was thick when he climbed back up to the cabin.

"Bug?"

She didn't answer his apprehensive hail. The cook fire was dying, the cabin dark and empty. She was gone.

He stirred the coals to get fire for a torch and searched the cabin again. Table and stools had been overturned. Fragments of a broken pot grated under his feet. The floor was sticky with spilled chili stew, the air edged with a faint burned scent of the yams Buglet had been baking in the ashes. Nothing told him anything about her attacker.

Frantic now, he ran circles around the cabin, bending to scan the ground. He found no strange footprints, no sign of further violence, no clues at all. When the torch flickered out, he picked his way by starlight down to the sea and ran up the beach toward the chapel, reckless of the rocks and driftwood that tripped him again and again.

The dark moon was rising before he arrived, its blood-colored glow in the altar hall as ghastly as his terror. Zhondra sat slumped down on her rough stone altar, so lifeless that he wondered if her dim gray nimbus had become too weak to lift her. Pipkin was hopping erratically here and there, as if the floor burned his hands.

He panted his news that Buglet was gone.

Zhondra's eyes were dilated and black, staring blankly out into the red gloom beyond the posts. She made no sign of hearing.

"Don't vex her now," Pipkin whined. "She's got troubles enough."

"Can't you hear?" he shouted. "Bug's gone!"

"I know." She turned briefly to him then, with a glance of sad sympathy. "She vanished from my perceptions just after sunset. I sensed an instant of shock and fear, but I couldn't catch the cause. That was all. I have been searching, but I can't feel her mind."

"What could have got her?" He waved the furry godlet out of his way. "What can we do?"

Deaf to him again, she gazed back into the reddened dark.

"Blame me, Davey." Pipkin shambled toward him, narrow face abject, green stare fixed on his feet. "Forgive me, if you can. I gave us all away—but not because I meant to. I was afraid of Belthar. I've always been afraid. I took the ship and that pack of rascals to look for a safer planet."

178

"Which you didn't find." Anger grated in Davey's voice. "I guess you brought trouble back."

"The tragic truth." His bald head bobbed. "But not out of malice—believe me, Davey! We were victims of monstrous mischance. I knew Belthar would be scouring all the universes, and I never planned to compromise our safety here—and don't you forget that I'm the one who found this asylum for us! You'll forgive me, Davey, when you know the dark story of our misfortunes. An evil fate pursued us, more fearful than the gods."

A tear of self-pity shone in his seeing eye.

"When the other planets of this sun proved unfit for life, we set out for the only nearby star—it's a red dwarf you can't see from these latitudes. The muman tried to warn us that it was too far, but I didn't want to risk breaking through a contact locus into any space where Belthar's armadas might be cruising.

"Our voyage took too long. The reaction mass was dangerously depleted, and food for the premen ran short. When at last we got within telescopic range, the star proved to be a close binary, with no planets at all.

"With no oceans for water we had to orbit the double sun to search for cometary snowballs from which reactor mass could be refined. That took too long. The premen were near starvation. With no other star within possible range we were really desperate—don't you understand?"

"I understand enough."

"Believe me, Davey!" The pink doll-face twitched as if with actual pain. "We had no choice. I had to search out a contact plane. We slipped through it—hoping not to be observed. Unluckily for everybody—by unexpected and appalling misadventure—the gods had a monitor there. We were observed."

"So you did betray us?"

"Don't—don't be so harsh." The piercing insect creak hurt Davey's ears. "We were all betrayed, don't you see? Cut down by the monstrous enormity of fate." Pipkin bent his arms to sit weakly on the floor. "Don't—don't you see?"

"I see your treason," Davey rasped. "You gave away the secret that had been saving us. The gods observed you. I guess they followed you back." He swung to Zhondra. "Is that why—whatever happened to Bug?"

"Possible." She nodded forlornly. "The coincidence does suggest a connection, but I can't discover what it is."

"But the gods have found us." He scowled at Pipkin. "And they're coming now?"

"I've just had a glimpse of Belthar in his Terran temple." Her faint aura grew even fainter. "I don't know how, because that's far beyond the normal reach of my perceptions. But I saw him."

Her pale hands spread and fell in a gesture of despair.

"He was giving orders to scores of gods, there in his transceiver columns. Most of them were already on their battlecraft in space. He's sending them through all the contact planes around Eden to close in all around us. He wants the planet sterilized."

"I thought—" He braced himself as if to take a blow. "I hoped it wouldn't be so soon."

"The nearest ships did follow Pipkin," she said. "They're all faster than our transport."

"Are they already—" Dread dried his throat. "Could they have taken Buglet?"

"I don't know." The snow moon was rising now. In its cold light she looked small and vulnerable and infinitely sad. "If they aren't here now, they will be soon."

"What—" He stood swaying, clenching his fists, feeling utterly trapped, unable to think or act or even to breathe. "What—"

"You've been saying you need danger." She aroused herself to give him a tiny wry smile. "Our situation has surely become dangerous enough. If you're ever going to find your ancestral gifts, you'd better find them now."

"But Bug's gone." Hopelessly, he shook his head. "Our transvolutionary actions always took both of us. More always came from her than me. I can't—can't do anything alone."

"If you can't defend us—" She looked suddenly through the posts into the milk-white sky, as if she had sensed something new there—something that appalled her. Her voice was fainter than her aura. "—nobody can."

He stood numb, unnerved and powerless.

"Davey?" Pipkin's tiny whine seemed far away. "Won't you understand that we never meant to harm you or your wonderful Buglet?" Standing on one hand, the godlet reached to tweak his sleeve. "Can't you forgive me?"

He looked down at Pipkin with a stiff little grin.

"I'll forgive you, Pip," he whispered. "If that matters now."

"Thank you, Davey!" Pipkin seized his hand. "It matters greatly to me that now we're friends again."

The grasp of the horny paw seemed pathetically firm, but the lone green eye stabbed at him with such a calculating shrewdness that he knew the godlet was moved more by fear than friendship—fear even of him.

"Okay," he muttered. "Now what can we do?"

"Nothing we can do." Pipkin sagged back to the floor, great arms sprawling, lifeless as a broken doll. "It's all up to you."

"Zhondra—"

Sunk down on her rude little altar, still as a statue in the white moonlight, she didn't seem to hear. Her dilated eyes were gazing far away again, perhaps at the jealous gods.

"I'm going back." He turned uncertainly away. "To look for Bug."

Outside the chapel, he glanced toward the preman town. Except for one torch flaring above the door of the council hall, it seemed peacefully asleep, unwarned of any peril. He saw no help there. El Sapo and Jesus Cabrito were probably still squabbling for domination, but neither would love the unborn ultiman.

He tramped back down the moon-washed beach. Though rocks and driftwood were now easy enough to see, he still sometimes stumbled blindly. Grappling desperately to reach his latent powers, he found only sick frustration. His few successful leaps out of space and back had always required a clear image of the arrival point. The battles he had won—with muman and clone, demon and Belthar's son—had always been close face-to-face encounters. With all his groping he could reach no actual contact with any enemy, find no picture of any place where he could go for Buglet.

He was turning up the path off the beach when sudden thunder crashed across the moon-white sky. Cliffs and trees stood sharply black against a blue false dawn behind him. A hot blue star climbed out of it, trailing a swelling wake of illuminated steam.

The shuttle—taking off. Was Pipkin trying to escape again before the gods could strike at Eden? Had the goddess fled? Or both of them? He watched until the sky was silent and the fire had faded from the vapor trail. Feeling utterly abandoned, he turned bitterly again to search the path for footprints, for blood, for bits of Buglet's clothing. For anything—

A purple flash made him duck. Something heavy grazed his shoulder. The impact knocked him off the trail, sent him reeling to his knees, his nostrils filled with a rank muskiness.

What had struck him was a long sharklike shape. Sliding on above him, it spun against the sky and came flying back, vast eye-discs blazing. Pale blue fire bathed it, flowing in thin bright fingerlike jets from its reaching flippers.

The truth hit him—a second dazing blow. The amphibians, with their transvolutionary senses, had already perceived the approaching armada of the gods. Trying to forestall the kind of conflict that had once wrecked their world, they had taken Buglet—where, he couldn't guess.

Now they had come back for—

The thing was diving at him again, snatching for him with those long claws of sapphire light. He dropped flat, rolled aside. He felt the reaching nimbus seize him. His body dragged on the gravel, began to lift. He caught a shrub with both hands, clung desperately.

The great tapered body went on by, swept ahead by its own momentum. The drag upon him weakened and broke. He fell heavily back to the path. The creature whirled above him, eclipsing the double moon, and dived again.

Half stunned from the fall, his breath knocked out, he scrabbled for any sort of weapon. For a stick he could punch into those purple eyes. A rock he could throw—

Something caught his feet.

Before he could clutch at anything he was dragged into the air. Hanging head down, he was carried toward the sea. The moon-bright beach raced back beneath him. He saw the red-fringed shadow of the thing that had captured him. Two others followed.

The amphibians came in threes. They shared the multiversal energies of the gods, and they meant to defend their underwater world. Considered objectively, they were perhaps as blameless as El Sapo and Pipkin claimed to be. But, with his senses spinning and his blood pounding in his ears, Davey didn't feel objective.

He bent his body, clutching at the lean black flipper. His fingers slipped at first, but then they clung. He clawed his way upward around that huge, blue-glowing barrel. Suddenly he was astride it.

The amphibians began to buck beneath him, like a mule he had tried to ride long ago back at Redrock in El Yaqui's corral. The brown mule had thrown him, while little Buglet shrieked with terror for him and the old trader laughed; but now he kept his seat, digging his heels into yielding, rank-scented gill-tissue, hanging on with both hands.

With his own halo!

For his hands were shining now, filmed with cool white fire. It flowed from his fingers into long bright talons hooked into the creature's fighting flesh.

A savage exultation seized him. The amphibians were targets he could reach, and they had brought the shocking danger he had to have. Testing the new power of his aura, he probed into its pitching body, searching for something vital.

It screamed. The creatures had been mute, the whole encounter silent, and that eerie whistle startled him. The thing dived into the shallow surf, splashing him with brine. It climbed again, turning till he hung beneath it. As if blind with fear and pain, it wheeled back toward the shore.

Deep inside it he found a firm, pulsing organ that he thought must be a heart. He gripped it hard, squeezing for its life. Shuddering above him, the creature dived for the beach.

He tore again at that dark heart. The sleek-scaled flesh jerked and stiffened. The blue aura flared and flickered out. He knew the thing was dead, but still the wind of its dive whistled in his ear. Falling on its back, it would catch him beneath it.

Still high above the white line of sand and surf, he let it go. Kicking away, he tumbled in the rushing air. Beneath him the dark sea crept back. The sand expanded, bits of weed and shell creeping away from the jagged granite outcrop he would strike. It would surely kill him—unless he could levitate.

He tried. Spreading his arms, he tried to imagine they were wings. With all his will he tried to stop the giddy tumbling, to steer his body, to brake his downward plunge. His will was not enough. The long dark shape of the dead amphibian kept pace with him. Yet he knew he must keep on trying.

For he must not die.

He had to live, to rescue Buglet, to save their child. With that purpose firming, he felt a sudden sense of physical control. Widening, brightening, the white nimbus became an intimate part of his mind, more sensitive than sight, stronger than his limbs. Spreading it, he caught himself.

Easily now, joyous with this new-found power, he guided himself aside. He let the dead thing pass him, hurtling ahead to dash onto the rocks. He hovered to see it fall, dived again, dropped gently on his feet closer to the surf.

For a moment the milky sky seemed empty. Then he found the two survivors diving at him from over the sea, one just above the other, eye-spots blazing purple-red, screaming in unison as if they had shared the other's dying agony.

Facing them, he smiled and braced himself. Balanced on tiptoe, letting the aura bear most of his weight, he reached to meet them with a long arm of light.

They squealed. Their eye-spots shrank and dimmed. Veering just enough to avoid him, they darted past so close that he felt a gust of their musky rankness. As they climbed over the dark coast he swung to face them, ready when they dived again.

Instead, they wheeled twice high above him. Silent again, they dipped toward that rocky ridge to settle beside their dead companion. Blue auras laced about it, they lifted it and carried it back above him and out across the surf. Floating free, as if his triumph itself had canceled gravity, he watched them splash down with it, watched the islet of foam that shrank and vanished where they had dived.

He felt as drunk with victory as he had been a time or two with El Yaqui's raw mescal. The dark moon now eclipsed, the high snow moon flooded the beach and the sea with its limpid splendor. Except for the soft hiss of the surf, that silver world was still. Its dwellers had fled. He was the master now. Spreading his hands to see their glowing power, for a moment he felt godlike.

But then his eyes were drawn to a pale white shape tossed up on the crest of a toppling wave. His elation was erased. Numb with an unbelieving dread, he splashed toward the object. Another wave flung it into his arms.

Buglet's body!

Floating naked, face down, it was cold and already rigid. Her long black hair was wound around her, tangled with weed. He held her when the wave washed back, and stumbled blindly with her toward the shore.

The white moonbloom mocked him now. With Buglet dead and the ultiman unborn, only he was left on Eden to invite the vengeance of the gods.

He reached the shallows, the cold foam hissing around his ankles, the icy body awkward in his arms. His brain and breath had stopped. The pain in the core of his being throbbed too deep for sobs or tears. Bug was dead.

With no reason to go on, he stood there—he never knew how long. His back was stiff and his arms were aching when his numbed mind began to move, and he found no hint of any hope. The amphibians, striking out of their dark abyss, had killed everything. All the generations of his special breed had lived in vain, with the last Creator's secret plan now come to final failure.

The dark moon had slid out of its eclipse before he moved, lining his shadow with blood. A silent wind had risen, redolent with the night flowers of the inland forest, and its chill bit through him. All his transvolutionary powers had died, and the body was now a leaden weight. Stumbling with it, he waded toward the beach.

Though little was left for him to do, Buglet must be buried. He wanted no help from the premen. Their old rituals had never meant anything to her, and most of them would feel more relief than sorrow when they learned that she was dead. He would dig the grave near the cabin where they had loved—

He felt a quick little thrust where her body pressed against his flank. Trembling, he laid her on the wet sand and knelt beside her. The tight skin across her belly was warmer than the stiffened limbs. His ear against it, he could hear a tiny, steady drumbeat. Another firm sudden thrust pushed it against his cheek.

The child—the little ultiman was still alive!

Doubting himself, he caught his breath and stared blankly out across the moon-glittering sea till the world quit spinning. He bent again to listen. The baby heart still beat, regular and strong. The baby feet kicked again. An icy awe brushed his spine.

Shivering, he groped for some notion of what to do. Carry her to the preman clinic? He shook his head. For all their other quarrels, El Sapo and Jesus Cabrito would stand united in their hostility toward any miraculous ultiman; and the preman surgeon would be too terrified to touch her.

He decided to take her to the chapel. Zhondra had been their only actual friend. A goddess, she shouldn't be afraid. Perhaps—unless she had fled with Pipkin aboard the climbing shuttle—perhaps she could save the child.

The moons were low before he got there. A gaudy dawn blazed beyond the dark hills and reddened the still disc of the crater bay. The cool air carried a woodsmoke scent, drifting from the waking town.

Two old women came out through the entry posts as he staggered up the chapel path. They stopped a moment, staring at the bare white body in his arms. Their worn fingers flickered through an odd ritual gesture he had seen El Yaqui use. Without a word, they turned and ran. He climbed the rough stone steps.

"Zhondra! Zhondra Zhey?"

Only echoes answered from the dark stone chamber behind the open altar place. He could smell the chili and chicken the women had left on the altar bench, but the goddess was gone. Reeling with fatigue, he shuffled to the altar and laid the body there.

In another universe Zhondra Zhey stepped out upon the snow-dusted floor of Belthar's enormous Asian temple. There, by chance, it was also dawn. The plains of cloud beneath the sacred peak were still blue-black with night. Sun-gold had begun to brush the higher slopes, but she had to brighten her aura against the searing cold.

"Welcome, child!"

The deity of Earth turned from the pictured gods in the transceiver columns all around him and levitated down from his massive throne to meet her.

"We had a false report—that you had stayed to aid the preman demons." Jovially, he smiled through his red halo. "We rejoice to see the truth. At the moment we're engaged in an emergency convocation. When that is concluded, it will be our delight to greet you properly.'' His bold eyes probed through her own pale aura. "If you'll wait in the guest hall—''

She thickened her nimbus to shield herself.

"It's true I've been with the exiled premen—''

"You admit that sacrilege?'' Belthar's smile congealed. "Consorting with demons—''

"I've joined the people of the Fourth Creation—''

"Then hear their fate!'' Red anger blazed across his aura. "We've found their hideout, and we've moving to obliterate it, along with all your unholy allies. Our battle fleets, gathered from a hundred suns, are already closing in. Your evil Eden is already within perception range. Neither preman nor demon will be left to trouble us again—''

"Listen, Belthar!'' Her clear voice lifted to ring against the lofty dome. "I come with a message.'' Her grave eyes rose to the listening pillars. "For you and all the gods.''

"Child, are you insane?''

"I come to speak for the Fourth Creation, which was made to halt your misrule—'' Blue aura bright, she waited for the stir and rustle of astonishment to die. "You have all been scheming for a thousand years to forestall the arrival of the promised ultiman. In spite of you, he has arrived.''

"The baby demon?''

"I'm here to warn you, Belthar.'' She spoke again to the tall transceivers. "The ultiman has sent me to warn each of you. No harm must come from you to any creature on the planet Eden.''

"What can an unborn baby do?''

"Must I show you, Belthar?''

"If you can!'' Down on the black floor now, he strode toward her, his great laugh booming against the dark vault. "I'm not afraid of babies.''

"You ought to be.'' Steadfast before him, she looked up again to the gathered gods. "Because the ultiman is heir to a new order of power, as far superior to yours as yours was to that of the premen who made you. If you ever had a chance to harm the ultiman, you lost it long ago.''

"Daughter, we offered you our bed.'' He glared through scarlet fire. "Your fantastic threats have not alarmed us, but your apparent madness compels us to withdraw that special sign of favor.''

''Better listen to her, lover.'' Cynthara's green-veiled image called from her transceiver prism, the tone grave enough but the bright smile ironic. ''They killed my darling Gleesh, remember? My pretty pet. Now they've jumped this upstart infant across the universes from Eden to your temple without a ship and in an instant— a feat you couldn't match. Perhaps we ought to reconsider—''

''Reconsider demons?'' Belthar bellowed. ''We fight them for our lives.''

''The ultiman respects your moderation.'' The child-goddess smiled at Cynthara. ''You'll find him far less ruthless than you have been.''

Her somber eyes swung back to Belthar.

''He doesn't wish to kill, but he will not be killed—or allow his people to die. For their sake he has sent me to instruct you that all your battlecraft in the Eden universe must be withdrawn at once.''

''You dare instruct me?'' His great bronze arm swept upward, the nimbus condensing beyond it into a mighty sword of incandescent energy. ''Here's my reply to your ungodly ultiman!''

The blazing blade slashed at her.

''The ultiman regrets—''

The falling sword had touched the cool opal shimmer of her nimbus. Blinding light exploded. Thunder cracked, drummed against the starry dome, rolled away into the snowy dazzle of the peaks beneath the temple.

Belthar stood paralyzed, stiff with astonishment.

Gravely calm, the little goddess reached through that exploding fury to touch his arrested hand.

Sudden silence. An abrupt dusk fell from the black granite vault as that blade of fire went out. Belthar's nimbus had been extinguished. He stood naked on the frost-sifted stone, his ruddy color swiftly fading, the angry light dying from his eyes. He shuddered. His skin turned gray. His giant body sagged.

''What—'' His mighty voice had become a rusty creak. ''What—''

The sound became a dying sigh. The lax mouth twitched and

188

gaped. The vacant eyes blinked in mute bewilderment. The blood-less hands jerked and hung slack. The body crumpled, pitched backward onto the polished stone, lay staring blindly up at the charted stars the gods had ruled.

"The ultiman doesn't wish to kill." Small in that startled hush, yet strong enough, Zhondra's voice lifted again to the soaring columns, where consternation had dimmed the imaged auras. "He will not allow his people to be harmed, but you will not find him vengeful."

Here and there a silent nimbus brightened.

"He still requires your armada to withdraw." She swam back from the empty body on the floor. "He still regrets what he had to do, but you will find him secure against any attack you can mount. The Creators made him superior. Your divinity—and mine—is sustained by solitary transvolutionary cells scattered through the nervous tissue. He draws power and perceptions across the multiversal interfaces through a fully developed transvolutionary brain center."

She recoiled again from the dead god as if his fate appalled her.

"All—all he did was to freeze those transvolutionary cells." Her shaken voice grew firm again. "When Belthar was cut off from the multiversal springs of his divinity, his human half could not sustain itself." Her tone lowered, as if she were adding her own comment to the ultiman's declaration. "I guess his body had grown too old."

Looking up, she stood waiting.

"Tell him—" Cynthara's halo shone green and paled again. "Tell the ultiman that all my battlecraft have been ordered to return at once from the universe of Eden."

"Mine—mine also." Gaining confidence, Kranthar's mellow voice echoed against the transceiver pillars. "The truth is, I always considered my dear brother a little too vindictive in his wars against the Fourth Creation. I'm delighted, now, to express my respect for the new ultiman. In this, I believe, we'll all agree."

He paused, with an expectant shimmer of his nimbus. After a silent instant the first hesitant whisper of assent began its swell toward a ringing chorus. The pillars blazed with bright approval.

"Tell him we hope to be his friends." Cynthara was suddenly herself again, greenly aglow with her sleekly opulent charms. "We want to know him better."

"I'm sure you will," Zhondra said. "But remember, he'll know you. If there is ever danger—from any of your acts or plots—his sharper perceptions will detect it. Whatever comes, he will defend himself and his people."

"Trust us!" Kranthar pealed. "We want no conflicts with such an awesome being. When the ultiman gives commands, they'll be obeyed."

"He'll have commands." She glanced up as if to read the star-charts overhead. "I'm to stay on Earth to be his voice. You have agreed to recall all your forces with no harm to Eden. You must also give safe passage to the ship I used to pilot, which is now in flight back to Earth. My friend Pipkin will be loading supplies here for the preman colonists. Later, he will offer return passage to Earth for any who request it."

Once more she waited, and agreement murmured through the pillars.

"I'll ask advice from Kranthar and Cynthara, his brother and his sister, about rites and memorials." Her eyes fell again to the gray and shrunken thing that had been a god. "Perhaps this temple should be preserved as his mausoleum."

Green and golden, their auras flashed quick assent.

"The ultiman is pleased to accept your promises of loyalty." Her hand lifted in a gesture of dismissal. "When he has another message, your attention will be called for."

The images winked out.

The rising sun had cleared the wild surrounding peaks, and its first golden shaft brushed the little goddess, brighter than her halo. Left alone with the dead god on that vast snow-dusted floor, she stood gazing up at the circle of columns soaring around her, black and enormous, empty now. Released by the ultiman's relaxing will, she shivered with astonished awe.

Eden's gentler sun had also risen. Rushing out of the rude little chapel there, Davey felt mocked by the dewy peacefulness. The eastward sky was pink, the air cool and sweet. He heard roosters crowing in the preman settlement and caught a pleasant breakfast scent of chili and tortillas.

Two men met him below the chapel steps. Both had been his schoolmates back at Redrock, though never very friendly—a little jealous, he had always thought, because he and Buglet had caught Zhondra's favor and had been allowed to live in the agent's house.

"Sorry, Davey." Armed with long, peeled poles, they were watchfully alert, but also apologetic. "We've got to stop you here."

"I want a doctor."

"El Jefe sent us to keep you out."

"I've got to get a doctor."

"He's had us keeping track of you." Chiquito gulped and wet his lips, shifting his grip on the stick. "Last night we saw too many funny things."

He turned uneasily to Pepe, who was Jesus Cabrito's son.

"Too much for me." Pepe had his father's weak, bloodshot eyes, and he squinted at Davey as if the soft sky had become too bright for him. "We saw three things—things like dragons flying around your hut. Later, we saw you riding something in the sky— it looked like one of them. We saw you hauling Jondarc's body out of the sea—"

"That's why I need a doctor."

"I don't think you do," Chiquito muttered. "Not if she's dead."

Again he looked at Pepe.

"My father doesn't know what you are." Pepe's uneven breath had a marijuana sweetness, and his nasal voice was quick and shrill with apprehension. "I know you claim to be the ultimen, but that's a lie if Jondarc's dead."

"We don't say you're lying," Chiquito added nervously. "But the ultimen wouldn't need a preman doctor."

"Whatever you are—" Pepe peered into the shadowy chapel and spat on the gravel near Davey's feet. "My father told us to keep you out of town."

"No offense, Davey." Chiquito tried to smile. "Nothing personal."

"Okay," he muttered. "If that's the way it is."

Walking away from them, he caught his breath and drew his shoulders straight. The living ultiman was certainly no lie. Perhaps, after all, he didn't need a surgeon.

Back inside, he dropped on his knees beside the altar. Buglet's body lay face up, her yellow eyes glazed and blind. Bits of weed were drying in her matted hair. Her rigid limbs were white and icy, rough with clinging sand. Terror shook him when he touched her.

Yet her bulging belly still felt warm. His ear against it, he heard the baby heart still drumming. He felt a baby kick.

And his terror ebbed.

That awesome evidence of life itself was proof of the latent powers he and Buglet had begun to discover. If he could leap outside the space-time of Earth to escape from the Redrock jail, if he could jump across the multiverse from Earth to Andoranda V, surely he could move a baby half a foot. Chilled with the solemn desperation of that purpose, he shut his eyes against the unendurable truth of Buglet's death.

He reached—

The child was in his arms—slippery and squirming, pillowed on red and dripping tissue. Crimson and wrinkled at first, it quivered as if with agony, fighting for air. It gasped and breathed. Its thin little quaver became a crowing shout. It was suddenly swathed in rose-hued light.

He couldn't help recoiling from the hot reek of blood and the shock of its alien strangeness. He nearly dropped it. But then its eyes came open, as yellow as Bug's. Its twitching lips seemed to grin. It winked at him.

A wave of tender warmth swept over him, thawing that first cold revulsion. Part of Bug, the tiny, writhing creature was also part of him—something about that grin brought back his first look into a mirror, in La China's perfume-scented parlor back at Redrock, when he couldn't have been two years old. His throat throbbed. He drew the haloed baby toward his heart.

But it was kicking in his arms, its vigor astonishing. Its red, bald head rolled toward Buglet's body. Its tiny arms flailed out as if reaching for her face. He bent to let it touch her. Shining brighter, the little fingers brushed her gaping, bloodless mouth.

192

Its rosy nimbus flowed all around her. Faint at first, that glory grew slowly stronger. The baby hand drew back. The baby head rocked uncertainly aside, golden eyes blinking at her. The tiny mouth drew into a toothless smile.

He heard its joyous little squeal—and forgot the ultiman. For the glow of life had flushed the gray skin beneath that rosy veil. The rigid limbs jerked and quivered. The blind eyes blinked. The fallen jaw trembled and the gaping mouth went shut.

Buglet sat up.

"Davey!" Terror froze her face and glazed her eyes again. "The amphib—"

She had found the altar stones beneath her, seen the axe-carved posts, heard the burbling chuckle of the baby in his arms.

"I thought—" Bewilderment stilled her voice. "Maybe I was dreaming—"

Shivering, she stared at a long strand of weed tangled in her hair.

"You were dead, Bug." His own voice came, strange and faint. "The amphibians left you drowned. But they couldn't kill the ultiman. He has been delivered, and he brought you back to life."

She sat gazing at him, crouching as if the pink nimbus hadn't fully thawed the chill of death. She looked longer at the child, which was leaping against his arms, screaming now as if to test the increasing power of his lungs.

"Our son?" Her lemon eyes came back to Davey, black with shock and at first unbelieving, suddenly bright with tears. Trembling, her luminous arms reached for the child. "If he can undo all that death does, he really is the ultiman!"

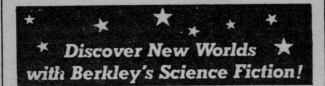